Wedding
BELLES

JANICE HANNA

Belles & Whistles

Wedding BELLES

summerside
PRESS™

Summerside Press™
Minneapolis 55337
www.summersidepress.com

Wedding Belles

© 2012 by Janice Hanna
ISBN 978-1-60936-632-2

Scripture references are from the following sources: The Holy Bible, King James Version (KJV).

The author is represented by MacGregor Literary Inc., Hillsboro, Oregon.

Cover design by Peter Gloege, Lookout Design, Inc.
www.lookoutdesign.com

Interior design by Mullerhaus Publishing Group
www.mullerhaus.net

Summerside Press™ is an inspirational publisher offering fresh, irresistible books to uplift the heart and engage the mind.

Printed in USA.

DEDICATION

To the wonderful folks at the Estes Park Museum. Thank
you for your kindness and your book recommendations. You
made my visit to Estes Park even more enjoyable! And to my
"Dream Team." You will never know what a blessing you've
been in my life. My heart and prayers are with you all.

HIGHER GROUND

I'm pressing on the upward way,
New heights I'm gaining ev'ry day,
Still praying as I'm onward bound,
"Lord, plant my feet on higher ground."

I want to scale the utmost height
And catch a gleam of glory bright;
But still I'll pray till heav'n I've found,
"Lord, lead me on to higher ground."

Lord, lift me up and let me stand
By faith on heaven's tableland;
A higher plane than I have found,
Lord, plant my feet on higher ground.

—Johnson Oatman Jr.

ONE

A Reckoning in the Rockies

Estes Park, prepare to be razzle-dazzled! Parker Lodge, located on the beautiful Fall River, continues to offer the best entertainment in town. This month's event is certainly no exception. Join us this coming Friday evening, April 26, for a rousing performance by local musician Jeb Otis, who will play several well-known ballads and folk tunes on his saw. Otis, who hails from the Estes Valley region, will be appearing at the lodge for one night only, performing before a packed house. C'mon out and share in an evening of fine food, rousing entertainment, and heartfelt fellowship. Front-row seating for the first ten guests to arrive. —Your friends at Parker Lodge

Estes Park, Colorado, 1912

"Jeb Otis says he's going to jump off Longs Peak and end it all."

"What?" Lottie Sanders looked up from the rippling waters of Fall River into her boss's worried eyes. "He's going to end it all? Whyever would he do that?"

"Oh, you know how he is." Gilbert Parker plopped down next

to her and sighed. "Melodramatic. Always wanting attention. Just like the other men in this town. He's frustrated because the Widow Baker won't give him the time of day, so I guess this is how he plans to remedy the problem."

"He's going to remedy the problem by taking his life?" Lottie swallowed hard. "Won't that defeat the purpose?"

"Who knows?" Gilbert offered a little shrug, and a hint of a smile turned up the edges of his lips. "But if it's any consolation, I reminded him that he's got a concert coming up this Friday evening, so maybe he'll wait till after that to do himself in."

"One can hope." Lottie thought about the many times Jeb and the other fellas who frequented the lodge had posed such ludicrous threats. How weary she'd grown of their antics. "What's it going to take to convince Jeb that he and Althea Baker are as different as night from day, anyway?" she asked. "They would make a terrible match. I'm surprised he can't see that for himself."

"True." Gilbert released a sigh. "But I guess it's true what they say—love is blind."

"Mm-hmm." *It's blind, all right.*

Lottie dipped her toes into the cool water and gazed up at the majestic Rockies still capped with snow, even this late into the spring. They provided just the right distraction from the handsome young man to her left, though she would much rather stare into Gilbert's beautiful blue eyes any day of the week. Not that she would ever come out and say so, of course.

"I know Jeb is just blowing off steam." Gilbert smirked. "Otherwise I'd be plenty worried. But we both know he's had his heart set on marrying for years now and is starting to feel…"

"Desperate?" Lottie turned her attention to Gilbert's handsome face, her heart rate skipping to double time. If anyone understood desperation, she did. Hadn't she waited a lifetime for Gilbert Parker to notice she was alive? Still, no one saw her jumping off a mountain peak, now, did they? No, sir. She would remain his faithful employee, calm and composed, no matter how badly her heart longed for more.

"Yep." He nodded. "Guess so. Seems like a lot of the fellas round here are losing heart."

They're not the only ones.

"Just sayin' we've got a lot of men bordering on grumpy because they haven't found wives. Wish I could think of some way to help 'em out. You know what I mean?"

"Wait…" Lottie startled to attention as she realized what he was getting at. "Are you talking about finding brides for them? Is that what this is all about?"

"It wouldn't hurt to see them happily matched," he responded. "And Estes Park could certainly use more women. How is the lodge ever going to sustain itself if we don't get more people coming through?"

"Well, yes, but…" Was he serious?

Worry lines appeared on Gil's forehead. "You know how concerned I've been about keeping the lodge open since Pa died. If we don't come up with a plan soon, I'll have to close up the place for good. Mama will be devastated if that happens, and she's already going through so much. This lodge is my pa's dream, and she wants to keep it alive." Gil raked his fingers through that thick blond hair of his, leaving it in a disheveled state. "I've got to admit, these days, the dream is looking more like a nightmare."

Lottie did her best not to sigh aloud as she pulled her feet from the water. In the three months since Gilbert's father had passed away, their spirits were lower than ever. She'd tried everything imaginable to bring in customers, hoping to turn things around, but so far to no avail. "I've given you all my best ideas—oyster suppers, Saturday night dances, pie-eating contests, horseback-riding expeditions, talent extravaganzas, flower shows.... We've tried everything to bring in visitors to the lodge."

She'd grown weary with it all, especially the dances, where more often than not she spent her evenings kicking up her heels with the wallflowers. Oh, how she wished that, just once, Gilbert would sweep her into his arms and waltz her across the room. Wouldn't that be lovely? Perhaps her thoughts would be freed up to think of other ideas to save the lodge, if only he would tease her with a dance.

A silence grew between them. Lottie squinted as ribbons of sunlight filtered through the trees, grateful for the distraction.

"I still say the problem is the lack of women," Gilbert said after a moment.

She gazed at his messy hair, wanting to reach out and fix it but not having the courage. "We've got plenty of women in town," she argued. "What about the Estes Park Women's League?"

"Most of those ladies are already married. I'm talking about new women. Fresh women." His cheeks turned red and he looked a bit flustered. "Well, not *fresh*, exactly. You know what I mean."

"I do." She bit back the laughter that threatened to erupt. "Just wait until the summer, Gil. We'll have quite a few new ladies come through. You'll see."

"Yes, the tourists stay for the season, but then they always leave again and go back to wherever they really live. They won't stay. We need women with staying power."

She felt her concern growing. If a passel of beautiful women came through, one of them would surely steal Gilbert away. Not that Lottie had any chance of winning his heart, regardless. He never seemed to think of her in that light.

Perhaps this would be the perfect time to drop a few hints. "*I've* stayed," she whispered.

"Yes, you have." Relief swept over his face. "And have I mentioned how grateful I am for that? When your sister moved away to Denver, I felt sure you would…" His words trailed off.

Ah. So *that's* what this was all about. He was still pining away for her older sister. Well, so be it. Let him mourn. At Mama's nudging, Winifred was happily courting a business tycoon from Denver now and couldn't be bothered with the likes of Gilbert Parker. Not that she'd ever paid him any mind. No, she'd been content to flirt and tease and then break his heart in the end.

"Anyway, I felt sure you would eventually go away too," Gilbert said, his eyes now riveting into hers. "Promise me you won't ever leave."

A wave of compassion swept over Lottie as she took in the sadness in his expression. "I can't imagine leaving Estes Park. I've spent my whole life here. I don't care where that silly sister of mine ventures off to or how much money her potential husbands might have. I love it here. Always have. I love every single thing about it, Gilbert. Every. Single. Thing."

There. Surely he would take the hint. She batted her eyelashes, just in case he missed the point.

Gilbert shrugged but didn't respond. Instead, he turned toward the river and sighed. Lottie forced her gaze back to the mountain, determined not to let him see the disappointment on her face. "Anyway," she managed, "I don't think Jeb and Althea are a good match, but who am I to talk of love and romance? I know nothing of such things. Maybe if Jeb would stop beatin' that devil around the stump and ask Althea to marry him, she might just say yes. Then he could lay his miseries to rest once and for all."

"He's tried a thousand different ways to propose, but she's not bitin'. You know that."

"So he's jumping off Longs Peak?" Lottie spoke the words matter-of-factly, as if men jumped off Longs Peak every day, just for the fun of it. "That's his answer to the problem?"

"Mm-hmm. Third time this month he's threatened to do so, but I think he just might do it this time."

"Nope. He ain't jumpin'." Lottie lay back on the grass, her gaze now on the brilliant blue sky above—what she could see of it through the overhanging trees, anyway.

"How do you know?" Gilbert's muscled arms flexed as he slipped his hands behind his head. Not that she was looking out of the corners of her eyes or anything. That would just be wrong. Or right, depending on which angle you looked at him.

"I heard Phineas Craven say that the fish out at Lake Estes are bitin' today. You know Jeb. He'll never take his life if there's a fish in the lake with his name on it."

Gilbert chuckled. "Guess I can relax then."

"Guess so." She laughed.

Lottie tried not to think about how much she would love for

him to sweep her into his arms but found that difficult, what with him being so close and all. She willed her racing heart to slow down.

Not that he would notice anyway. No, much like Jeb Otis, Lottie had tried seven ways from Sunday to draw the attention of the person she loved, but Gil wasn't biting. She'd stand a better chance of catching a shark in Fall River than snagging the likes of Gilbert Parker. Maybe if she laid aside her tomboyish ways, he might give her a second glance. And perhaps donning something other than her worn-out overalls and cowboy boots might up her chances as well. Then again, if she changed too much, what would folks say? Would they think she was putting on airs, like her sister?

Patience, Lottie. Slow and steady wins the race.

Gilbert rose and brushed the dirt from the back of his pants. "Guess I'd better head back inside. Mama's cooking up a feast tonight. Our three lodgers are going to have more than enough to eat." He rolled his eyes, and she got the point. How many months had they longed for an influx of lodgers? Still, only a few trickled in, and they rarely stayed long.

Lottie offered an encouraging smile. "I'll be in shortly. Can't take much time, though, because Pa wants me home for dinner. He and Mama are more finicky about that, now that Winnie's gone." She sighed. Sometimes it really presented a challenge, being the last remaining child at home. Not that she viewed herself as a child, of course. Certainly not. Especially when her thoughts drifted to Gilbert, which they seemed to do a lot these days.

He took off toward the lodge, and Lottie followed him with her lingering gaze. As he disappeared from view, she turned her attention back to the mountain, her thoughts now tumbling. If she could just figure out a way to save the lodge, she might win Gilbert's affection. What she needed was a plan, one that would pay off in dollars and cents.

No matter what it took, she would turn things around. And if she played her cards right, she might just come out of the deal with Gilbert Parker on her arm.

* * * * *

As Gilbert made his way through the clearing toward the lodge, he couldn't stop thinking about Jeb Otis and his threat to jump off Longs Peak.

"What a windbag."

'Course, Jeb was no different from any of the other locals who frequented the lodge's restaurant. The men of Estes Park kept Gilbert hopping with their grumbles and complaints about the lack of women in the area. He was reaching the end of his rope. After years of listening to their "I need a good woman" speeches, he'd had enough.

Sure, they could all use a good woman. No argument there. But did he have to hear about it day and night, month after month, year after year? Besides, they weren't the only ones pining away for a good woman. Didn't they realize he struggled with the same feelings? Clearly they didn't, or they wouldn't bother him with their drama.

Drama.

The word hit him again, this time nearly knocking the breath out of him as an idea rolled through his mind. He froze in his tracks and latched onto it then gave it a thorough chew.

Drama.

At once, a full plan of action came to his mind, one that must've tumbled from heaven above. Yes, for only a heavenly plan could be this inspired.

"That's it! Why didn't I think of this before?"

Gilbert turned on his heel and sprinted back toward the river, convinced that Lottie would love this idea. Didn't she always go along with his plans, after all? Hadn't she been his biggest supporter thus far?

Yes, and what a great partner she'd make on this venture. Perhaps, between the two of them, they could save the lodge.

TWO

Devilish Deeds in the Dining Hall

Folks, rumors are afloat here at the Parker Lodge, where we're cooking up more than our usual fare in the dining hall. A clever plan is under way to draw a new crowd of tourists and locals to the lodge, one sure to garner the attention of many across the nation, particularly those with a dramatic flair. Want more details? Just ask our manager, Gilbert Parker. He will gladly give you an earful if you ask for the particulars. I dare not say more, though I will leave you with a hint: What do you get when you merge a villain, a female in distress, and a handsome hero? According to Mr. Parker, the best entertainment this side of the Rockies. —Your friends at Parker Lodge

"Whatever gave you the idea I could pull off a theatrical?"

Lottie paced the dining hall at Parker Lodge, so flustered she could hardly think straight. She stopped long enough to cast a wary glance Gilbert's way as he took to stammering.

"Well, I, um, I…"

"I know nothing about stage plays. I don't sing. I don't act.

I don't dance." She paused to stare him down. "Well, other than the kind of dances we have on Saturday nights, but that's different. And even then I'm tripping over my two left feet."

"I'm not asking you to perform in the show." Gilbert cast her a fretful gaze. "Just to direct."

"*Just* to direct?" As if directing wasn't a huge undertaking. She tried to eke out a response, but nothing sensible came to mind. He must've lost his mind with this latest idea of his. She'd tried to tell him so yesterday when he'd first suggested it. What was the point of today's meeting with Jeb and the other fellas? To gang up against her, perhaps? To talk her into something she would soon regret?

"You've always been good at arranging things, Lottie." He offered her a boyish pout, one that almost melted her heart. Almost.

"Sure, Lottie," a couple of the fellas chimed in from their card table just a few yards away.

She busied herself clearing dirty dishes from one of the smaller tables in the lodge's dining hall. "Flowers, maybe," she said after a moment's thought. "Social dances, even. But…a stage production? A melodrama, no less? I wouldn't have a clue where to begin." The dirty plates clattered as she set them back down on the table.

Gilbert didn't look at all concerned. "It'll be great," he said with a wave of his hand. "Might just save the lodge too. Our three lodgers are gone now, so we're not bringing in any income at all."

Nothing like a little pressure to offer incentive.

"Have I mentioned that we don't even have a script?" She crossed her arms and stared at him. "You're asking me to create something out of nothing."

"Don't be silly. You've got enough fodder for a thousand

melodramas. You're surrounded by characters, after all." Gilbert pointed to the fellas—Phineas Craven, Jeb Otis, and the others, who'd stopped by the lodge for their usual Friday night card game. "Might as well take their drama to the stage, don't you think?"

No argument there. "But no one here has any acting experience." She wiped her hands on her dingy apron.

"Well, shore we do," Jeb drawled as he glanced up from his cards. "I'm always actin' up, ain't I?"

"You've gotta give it to him," Gilbert said. "He is, at that."

She released a slow breath. "What sort of story are you talking about, anyway? Something serious? A comedy? Musical numbers? What?"

"A comedic tale about a swashbuckling hero who rids his town of evil influence," he explained. "Something loaded with adventure and the spirit of the West. The hero would have to be genuinely good, of course. And handsome. Someone the ladies in the audience could swoon over." He squared his shoulders, and a couple of the fellas laughed.

"Our melodrama also has to have females in distress," Jeb threw in from his spot at the table. "Purty ones."

"And someone who wants to take over the town," Phineas added. "Them shows always have someone wantin' to take over the town. A real villainous sort a' fella to keep the audience on the edge of their seats. That'll do the trick."

"Better add a couple of gals with questionable reputations." Augie Miller raked his fingers through his thinning wisps of hair. "That'll up the ante. And there's nothing better than a show with its ante upped." He paused and then laughed. "Not sure that came out right."

Chauncy James glanced over the top of his cards, his whiskery mustache twitching. "While you're adding characters, you'd better throw in a saloon owner."

"True," Jeb said. "Wouldn't be much of a show without a saloon and purty dancin' gurls, least to my way of thinkin'."

Lottie plopped down in a chair. "Heroes? Damsels in distress? Saloons?" She paused to think through this proposition. "Fellas, you know how I feel about drinking and such. If we set part of the story in a saloon, we'll have to be very careful not to romanticize that way of living. Perhaps that could play into the plot. I do like the idea of a hero who saves the town."

"A handsome hero," Gilbert said.

"All right, handsome." She paused. "Let's say we actually come up with a story idea. And let's say some of you fellas agree to take on parts in this—this…melodrama. Where in the world are you gonna find women willing to play saloon girls and the like? I can guarantee you, the ladies in the Women's League won't be interested."

"Yes, but that's the best part." Gilbert beamed. "We're going to bring in ladies from all over the state." His eyes widened and his voice grew intense. "All over the country, even. Why, we could advertise all the way from Denver to Broadway. Actresses would come to audition for the best roles."

"W–what?" Surely he had lost his mind. "Why, pray tell, would they come at all?" Lottie asked. "There's nothing to draw them to Estes Park. Besides the scenery, that is. And the fresh mountain air. Certainly nothing to do with stage plays."

"That's the part we need you to figure out," Phineas said. "Don't figure you'll let us down, since you care so much about us and all."

His gray-blue eyes twinkled, and he flashed a crooked-toothed smile. "'Course, these belles from the East have to be in good health with a decent mouthful of teeth, 'cause we plan to marry 'em."

"W–what?" Lottie rose. "Is—is that what you all have in mind? I'm to bring these women here under the guise of acting in a stage play, when they're really coming as potential brides?" Suddenly it all made sense.

"Don't get your dander up, Lottie," Gilbert said. "No one's going to force them to marry anyone. Or to stay, for that matter."

"For more than six months, anyway," Jeb added as he rose from the card table to join them. "We'll get 'em to sign a contract to stay that long."

"A contract? For six months?" Maddening thoughts rushed through her head. "But in six months, winter will set in. They couldn't get down the mountain to Loveland if they wanted to."

"Exactly." The men spoke in unison.

She shook her head as realization set in. "Oh, no you don't. You're not pulling me into this ridiculous scheme of yours. I won't do it."

"You're not being reasonable, Lottie," Gilbert said. "What if they come and the show is a rousing success? Not only will they want to stay through the winter, they're liable to want to stay indefinitely. How can it be considered scheming when we're just looking to offer them new opportunities and a possible chance at happiness?"

"Let's go with another possibility." She fussed with her apron strings, frustration setting in. "What if the show is a dismal failure? What if we bring all these women from places unknown to put on the most ridiculous production folks have ever seen? What if we keep them here through the winter when they're snowed in and feeling blue?

What if we can't hold rehearsals because of the weather? What if we have the show and no one comes? These are the things we should be discussing, fellas. Why? Because we're talking about using real actresses here. They'll know the difference between a professional production and a thrown-together parlor show." She yanked off her apron and slung it over the back of a chair before taking a seat.

"That's why it's got to be spectacular." Gilbert rested his hand on Lottie's shoulder. "I know you can pull this off. You were always one for telling fancy stories when we were kids. Remember all the tall tales you used to come up with? Some were real spine tinglers. Others left me laughing so hard I could scarcely catch my breath. You have a God-given gift for storytelling and might as well use it to benefit the lodge." He gave her a little pout. "Please? For me?"

She paused to think through his words, realizing he hadn't strayed far from the truth. She had been quite a storyteller, back in her day. Still, he'd missed the point. Those stories didn't involve real people, especially not women coming from all over the country. But how could she turn him down when he looked at her with such pleading?

"It's one thing to make up children's stories and another thing altogether to write a play. I—I don't think I have it in me."

At this, all the fellas released a collective sigh.

"Well, shoot." Jeb reached for his worn Stetson and fingered the brim. "There goes my chance for happiness. Guess I'll have to head back up to Longs Peak, after all. If you'uns find my body after I jump, would you do me the favor of buryin' me in my brown shirt and Levis? No point in fancyin' up to meet my Maker. He probably wouldn't recognize me in a suit."

Lottie did her best not to groan aloud.

Gilbert sat in the chair next to her, leaning in so close she could scarcely breathe for wanting to slap him. Or kiss him. Right now, she couldn't decide which one made more sense.

Oh, but the sad expression on his face made her want to kiss him—yes, really, truly kiss him, right there in front of all the fellas. Now *that* would be a scene straight out of a drama, one sure to get the townspeople talking.

Heat rose to her cheeks and she shoved the idea away just as he leaned in to whisper, "Lottie, I need you."

She swallowed hard. "O-oh?"

"Yes. The lodge isn't going to make it if I don't do something. The competition is fierce, with the other lodges gaining ground every day."

"I know, but—"

"Did you hear about the Elkhorn?" Phineas interjected. "They're building a candy kitchen."

She shook her head. "I knew they were talking about it, but they're really going through with it?"

"Yes." Gilbert raked his hand through his gorgeous blond locks and sighed. "They've expanded their lunchroom too. They can seat almost two hundred people in there now. I heard all about it when I was in town today."

"I still don't see what that has to do with us," she argued.

"If they wanted to, they could put on a dinner show or concert for a large group. We can scarcely seat sixty—not that we've ever had that many at one time. So, what we lack in size, we'll have to make up for in quality."

"I see your point, but Gil, I just don't—"

"And this candy kitchen idea of theirs is just the icing on the cake. They're going to have taffy pulls for the children and home-made candies available all day long." He gave her an imploring look. "What's next? One of those one-armed bandits everyone's talking about? A full-out casino with a betting parlor and free whiskey for the winners? How can we ever compete with that?"

This time she didn't even try to hide the groan. She pushed the dishes aside and leaned on the table in an unladylike fashion.

He continued to torment her with the sadness in his eyes. "We will never resort to opening a casino at Parker Lodge. Not while I'm alive to tell about it. And you know where I stand on whiskey and the like. Goes against everything I believe. But how can we compete with the attention such places will draw?"

"I do understand, Gilbert. Clearly. And that's why I've been working so hard to—"

"We've done a lot," he said. "But we need something no one else is doing. Something original."

She released a slow breath and sat back in her chair. True, lodges like the Elkhorn were leading the way. With ballrooms, billiard rooms, parlors, and candy kitchens, they were winning over the tourists and locals alike.

"Don't you see, Lottie? These other lodges—great as they may be—are our competition. They're snagging all our business. That's why we've got to do something on a grand scale. Something memo-rable. Something folks will be talking about for years to come. That's why I think this Wild West melodrama idea is perfect. It'll get people talking, especially if we do it right."

She wanted to get people talking all right, but not about melodramas. Well, not the kind on the stage, anyway. Still, she couldn't seem to slow her racing heart, what with Gil being so close and all.

Lottie rose, determined to gather her thoughts. She tried to avoid the pleading eyes of the five men who now stared her down.

What should a girl do in a situation such as this? Coming up with ideas wasn't Lottie's strong suit. Hadn't she proven that with the dances, dinner shows, and other things she'd attempted? And putting things down on paper? Sure, she'd received high marks in school, but book smarts didn't make her a playwright.

Still, she had somehow managed to convince Gilbert Parker that she was quick on her feet because she tried so hard. Lottie gazed into his beautiful eyes. *Lord, help me. I've somehow bluffed him into thinking I'm clever. I certainly don't want to change his opinion now.*

"You can even have a part in the play, if you want." Gil wiggled his brows playfully. "I daresay you'll win folks over, whether you think so or not."

Lottie tried not to let the compliment go to her head. He was still on a fishing expedition, no doubt, trying to get her to play along with this crazy idea of his. Then again, Gil had always been pretty good at snagging fish.

"She'll have to play one of the fellas, with her hair so short 'n' all," Phineas muttered, looking up from his card hand. "Between the hair and the overalls, I don't think folks'd believe she's a lady."

"Well, *that* does it." Lottie felt her cheeks grow hot as her temper flared. How dare he say such a lowdown, underhanded thing?

"She ain't no boy," Jeb said. "If she'd put on a dress every now 'n' again, she'd probably look just like the other gals in town. If she'd comb those curls, anyhow."

A hint of a smile lit Chauncy's face. "Purtier, even, what with them green eyes."

Lottie felt steam coming out of her ears. Strangely, her anger was all mixed up with the oddest feelings of flattery at Chauncy's comment about her eyes.

"If you play the part of a girl, you'll hafta wear a purty dress, Lottie." Jeb narrowed his gaze. "Think you could do it fer a change?"

"Yes, do you think you could do yourself up like a girl for once in your life?" Augie threw in. He snapped his fingers. "That'll draw the men in, don't you think? Why, most of the fellas I know would pay money just to see you dolled up. I could do a big write-up in the paper about it. That would be a nice draw to get the locals in here."

"Ugh!" She stormed out of the room, too angry to respond. They'd crossed a line this time. Not only would she *not* direct their ridiculous melodrama, but she might just create a little drama of her own by leaving this place and never coming back.

* * * * *

GILBERT WATCHED LOTTIE as she shot out of the room. "We've done it this time, fellas," he said. "Gone and hurt her feelings, I guess."

Augie slugged Phineas in the arm. "You had to go and shoot your mouth off, didn't ya?"

"Didn't mean anything by it." Phineas shrugged. "It's just that I've never seen Lottie dressed up like a girl. You all know it's true.

And you've got to admit, putting an article in the paper to advertise her debut as a female might just draw in a crowd. I know a lot of folks—male and female alike—who would pay to see that."

"Still, now she's as jumpy as a toad after all those things we just said." Jeb plopped down in his chair and brushed his cards to the center of the table. "She'll never agree to play along now."

"It's not like she has to be in the show, anyway." Gilbert collected the cards and started to shuffle them. "I'd be happy if she would write and direct it."

"Aw, I think she'd be a natural fer one of the parts," Phineas said. "You gotta admit, she's got purty eyes."

"They're greener'n the pine trees in the springtime," Jeb added then sighed.

"And she's got a nice figure too," Chauncy said with a nod. "Leastways, what I can tell underneath them little-boy clothes."

"I suppose." Gilbert shrugged then began to deal the cards. He'd never really thought about it. Still, there might be some merit to Jeb's earlier comment. Folks from Estes would come out in droves to see Lottie dressed up like a lady.

"There's only one way she's gonna go along with this," Phineas said. "Someone's gotta convince her she can be a lady. Someone who can win her over with his masculine ways."

Every eye in the place turned to Gilbert. He swallowed hard and stopped dealing the cards. "M–me?"

"Well, shore," Phineas drawled. "The rest of us fellers is too old. She'd smack me silly if I sidled up next to her and starting payin' compliments. But you…" He gave Gilbert a scrutinizing look. "Yer about her age, give'r take a few years."

"Well, yeah, but she's like a kid sister to me. I've never thought of her in that way."

"Not sayin' you have to." Phineas rubbed his hands together, as if plotting Gilbert's fate. "Just sayin' you could show her a little interest. If she thinks yer interested, maybe she'll gussy up a bit."

"Yeah," Chauncy echoed. "Get her lookin' and actin' like a lady before the real ladies show up. I'll betcha they'd take her more seriously as a director if she looked the part."

Gilbert paused to chew on those words, finally responding, "You might be right." He resumed dealing, but his thoughts were now elsewhere. "I'll figure out a way to get her to play along. Pay her a little extra attention."

"Well, shore," Jeb said, giving Gilbert a slap on the back, nearly sending the cards flying. "This'll be easy fer you, Gilbert. Like lickin' butter off a knife."

"Maybe. Maybe not." He paused to think it through as the men settled down at the table to begin their game once again. Honestly, he'd rather lick butter off the sharpest knife in town than cross Lottie Sanders. He'd seen her riled up on more than one occasion, and it wasn't pretty.

Then again, *she* was pretty, overalls or not. Curly bobbed hair or not. And the fellas were right—those green eyes were something to behold, especially once they got to blazin'.

Maybe he could convince her to become a lady, one worthy of a part in their theatrical. Yes, with a little persuasive talk, she might just fit the bill. In the meantime, he had a lot of work to do.

THREE

FIASCO AT FALL RIVER

Friends, where do mystery, mayhem, and comedy converge? At beautiful Parker Lodge, located off Fall River at the entrance to the majestic Rockies. Even now drama abounds, and not just the sort folks pay to see. But what will come of it? Will Sadie Word go along with the twisted scheme Barry D. Hatchett has cooked up? Will she turn a blind eye to his financial woes or, like the heroines of yesteryear, rush in to save the day? Will she resort to using her feminine wiles to win the handsome hero, or will her boyish ways forever separate her from the man she secretly loves? To learn the answers to these and other intriguing questions, stay tuned for more information. —Your friends at Parker Lodge

THE MORNING AFTER STORMING OUT on the men, Lottie found herself more discombobulated than ever. How dare Phineas and the others poke fun at her appearance after all she'd done for them? And what was wrong with them, anyway? Did they think for one minute that she would actually go along with their crazy scheme to write and direct a stage play?

On the other hand, how could she not, with so many—Gil, in particular—counting on her?

With her thoughts in a whirlwind, she decided to take a break from her morning chores to head out to her favorite spot—the narrow inlet of Fall River on the south end of the lodge's property. There, she could pray. And think. Looked like she had a lot to think about.

Unfortunately, Gil followed on her heels. Ordinarily he would've been the perfect companion, but today she needed time to come up with a plan of action, something that made more sense than putting on a theatrical. He followed her to the water's edge, talking all the way. She found herself more unnerved than ever.

"Lottie." He paused, but she refused to look his way. "Lottie, can't we please talk about this? I hate it that you're not speaking to me."

She felt a lump grow in her throat but finally managed to speak above it. "Gil, you know I would do just about anything to help you. But there's got to be some other way. I can't abide the idea of putting on a play. I'm sorry, but I can't. The whole idea just seems so... overwhelming. We're talking about costumes and sets and ticket sales. I don't think you realize how much this would require of all of us. And who knows if we could pull it off or if people would come and see the show, even if we do somehow manage to accomplish it. You know?"

"I know there are probably a thousand things we could try, but I still say this will be the best idea yet."

Lottie pulled off her boots and socks and stretched her feet. "Even if I liked the idea—and I don't—I still don't see why you would choose me to direct. Whatever makes you think I can do this?" She folded up the bottoms of her overalls and waded out into the shallowest spot in the river. With the water rushing around her feet, she could think more clearly.

"You can do anything you put your mind to. I know you can. And I truly believe you're going to be the best director in town."

"Hmm." She pursed her lips.

Gil reached down to slip off his boots then rolled up his Levis. Taking a step in her direction, he slipped on a rock and almost fell. She reached out her hand to grab his. "See there?" he said with a wink. "Once again you're savin' my neck. It's a sign from above."

"It's a sign that you need to pay attention, that's all."

"Lottie." He gripped her hand and gazed into her eyes with greater intensity than before. "Those fellas last night were out of line with some of the things they said about, well...about the way you dress and all."

"Just the fellas?" She did her best to pierce him with her own gaze.

"Shoot, I'll admit I overstepped my bounds by putting you on the spot in the first place, but you have to know how much I've come to depend on you, Lottie. You're at the center of everything around here, so I can't imagine trying to pull off anything without your help."

Well, when you put it like that...

She glanced down at his fingers still intertwined through hers and bit back a smile. "Let's say I go along with this nutty idea of yours," she said at last. "What would I need to do?"

"Woo-hoo!" He grabbed her around the waist and lifted her into the air then turned in a circle in the shallow water. "I knew it. Knew you'd come to your senses."

"Gil, put me down! You're going to drop me!" She relaxed as her feet touched down in the water and didn't mind a bit that he stood so close. He seemed to be paying her more attention today. Trying to win her over with his charm, no doubt.

She caught her breath. "I—I haven't made up my mind yet. Just asked a simple question. What would I need to do? If you plan to pull this thing off by the fall, we'd have to move quick."

"I'd say it's critical to get the women here by the end of May so there's plenty of time to rehearse."

"It's not that easy," she argued. "I can't just have Augie put a notice in the paper and expect a bunch of single women to show up."

"Maybe you can." Gil reached with a fingertip to brush a loose hair off her face. "Maybe it is that easy."

"How so?"

Gilbert's fingers lingered on Lottie's cheek, bringing a tingling sensation. "He can send out the notice to other papers in Denver and New York, where people frequent the theater."

"But what's the draw? Will they be paid? We can't offer them money when there's none to be had. Sure, we'll make money if the show's a success, but what kind of professional actress would wait till then to get paid?"

"Right." He took a step back then began to walk along the bank of the river, kicking up water. After a moment, he looked her way. "I know what we have to offer them. You said it last night. We offer a free vacation in beautiful Estes Park—free lodging, food, every-thing—in exchange for being in the show. We bring them here for the fresh air and sunshine. Most of these theater folks live in the big city. They could use a getaway, no doubt."

"Still, real theater people are accustomed to being paid."

"We'll have to think on that. Maybe we could offer them room and board during the months we rehearse and then a share in the proceeds plus a small salary once the show debuts."

She paused to think that idea through. "Might work. Guess we could talk about it. What time frame are you thinking for all this?"

"If the ladies arrive at the end of May and stay six months, that'll put 'em here through the end of November. I'm guessing we can get the costumes and set pieces made in a couple of months, so maybe August first for a debut? The show could run from August through Thanksgiving when the weather gets bad."

"Not sure about all that. These women are going to be hoppin' mad when they realize we've figured out a way to keep them here through the winter."

"I don't see it that way. We might be doing them a favor, especially if a few of them actually fall for Phineas and Jeb and the other men."

"That's not the plan, Gil, and you know it."

"Still, you know how those poor fellas are, always hankerin' for a honeymoon. Maybe they'll finally get it if any of these women show an interest in them."

"Hankerin' for a honeymoon." She laughed. "Sounds like something Jeb would come up with."

Gilbert snapped his fingers. "That's it, Lottie! That's our new melodrama title: *Hankerin' fer a Honeymoon*. It's perfect!"

"I don't know, Gil." She paused to think about it. "Sounds a little hokey."

"Isn't that the idea? Most theatricals are over the top. Villains and vixens. Rescues and mayhem." He paused and slid his arm through hers. "Aw, c'mon, Lottie. It's gonna be great."

"If only we knew what we were doing. Then I'd feel a little better about things."

"Augie could help us. He's got a great head for business. Why don't we walk down to his office at the *Mountaineer* and see if he'll write up a piece for us to send out over the wire. We'll figure out how to word it to draw in single women. Watch and see."

"I suppose." In that moment, Lottie felt hope as she never had before. Maybe—just maybe—Gilbert and the other men were right. Maybe they could pull off a show and the lodge could be saved. And maybe the Lord would move heaven and earth to help her accomplish it. Not that the Almighty necessarily needed her help in saving anything, but she was always of a mind to help when she could. If the situation called for it. And if Gil kept looking at her with those beautiful puppy-dog eyes of his.

Before she could think twice about it, Gilbert slipped on his boots then took her by the hand and ran up the bank, tugging her along behind him. "C'mon. Let's get this show on the road." He laughed then added, "Literally."

She paused to grab her boots, but he didn't give her time to put them on. Instead, he kept on running toward the lodge, now sounding breathless as he called out instructions. "Better check in with my mother to make sure she's okay holding down the fort while we're gone."

Minutes later, Lottie found herself approaching the lodge carrying her boots and socks in her hands and leaving wet footprints on the freshly mopped floor.

Gil's mother met them just inside the door, looking more than a little concerned. "What are you two up to?" She glanced at the wet footprints. "Or should I ask?"

"Up to?" Gilbert flashed her a boyish smile and leaned in to give her a kiss on the cheek. "What makes you think we're up to something?"

"I'd know that look anywhere, son. Now what are you hiding from me? You two are on some sort of mission." Mrs. Parker looked back and forth between the two of them, which only proved to make Lottie feel more nervous than ever. Not that she found Mrs. Parker intimidating. On the contrary, the woman—in spite of her tall, sturdy build—was as soft as the filling in her chocolate pie. Still, Lottie decided she'd let Gilbert be the one to share the idea with his mother.

"We need an hour or so to go into town, Mama," he said.

"Into town? Why?" Mrs. Parker asked. Her gaze narrowed and crinkles appeared between her eyes. "And you might as well come clean, Gilbert. I'm going to figure this out, with or without your help. You were never very good at hiding things from me, you know. I'm very discerning."

Lottie couldn't help but laugh as Mrs. Parker turned her way. "We're on a mission, as you said. But it's one we can't divulge."

Mrs. Parker clasped her hands together. "Very intriguing. Well then, I'll just post the CLOSED sign and come with you."

So much for keeping the news from her. Minutes later the three of them were headed to town, deep in conversation about the melodrama. Lottie mostly listened while Gilbert explained. Or, rather, tried to explain. He didn't do the best job of sharing the plan of action. Of course, the plan hadn't yet been fully developed.

"Tell me one more time what made you think of this idea in the first place," Mrs. Parker said when he paused for breath. "Doesn't sound like something you would come up with, son."

Gil's eyes sparkled. "I'm telling you, Mama, it was just one word that made me think of it—*drama*. I was thinking about Jeb and the other fellas and all their drama, and the whole idea just sort of unfolded right there on the spot."

"That's how most heavenly ideas come," she said. "They just float down from a cloud and land on your shoulder, whispering softly into your ear."

"This one shouted." He kicked at a rock in his path and then chuckled.

"What do you think about all of this, Lottie?" Mrs. Parker asked. "You're a levelheaded girl. Surely this idea of his took you by surprise."

"It did." Lottie slowed her pace as she spoke. "And I must admit, I did a little shouting too. Didn't take to the idea at first."

"When did you come around, dear?" Mrs. Parker matched her pace to Lottie's.

Lottie chuckled. "Oh, about five minutes ago."

They had a good laugh at that one. Lottie began to share some ideas that might work for the play. "What do you think of this?" she asked. "We could have some funny character names—very melodramatic, of course. And I think we can piece together a set using things we already have. Same with the costumes, though we'll need a few extra pieces."

"Honey, you're the perfect person for this job," Mrs. Parker said.

"That's just what I told her." Gilbert captivated Lottie with the twinkle in his eye and an assuring nod. "She's perfect."

Emboldened by his words, Lottie shared more ideas about the play as they walked on. Where they came from, she couldn't say. Must be inspired.

Less than a mile up the road, they came across Phineas and Jeb standing at the edge of Phineas's property. The two men appeared to be in a heated argument. Their bickering ceased as Lottie, Gil, and his mother approached.

"What do we have here?" Mrs. Parker looked back and forth between the two men. "Feuding?"

Phineas pointed at his mangled fence and then glared at Jeb. "Katie Sue's been at it again. First she tore down my fence to get to my garden, then she ate all the dandelion greens. After that she went straight for my rutabagas. And it's not the first time. But it'll be the last, fer sure."

Lottie did her best to cheer him up with a smile. "Well, here's a bit of news that should cheer you up, fellas. We're headed into town to put an advertisement in the paper about the melodrama."

"And we're going to ask Augie to send the news out to other papers, all the way to New York," Gilbert added. "Won't that be fine? Just think of the ladies who will come. Pretty women. *Single* women."

Lottie groaned. "But remember, folks, this isn't about bringing in brides. It's about bringing in actresses for a play."

"Sure, sure." Gil raised an eyebrow and chuckled.

"Really?" Phineas's expression changed at once. "You've decided to play along with him, Lottie?" He paused and then let out a raucous laugh. "*Play* along with him. Ha!"

Jeb slapped Phineas on the back. "Good one!" He turned his attention to Lottie. "But how did Gilbert talk you into it? Last night, well, I just figgered you'd heard enough to keep you from wantin' to do anything with the likes of us."

Lottie slipped her arm through Jeb's. "Aw, Jeb, you know I can't resist you fellas for long. Besides, you know how convincing Gil can be." The fluttering eyelashes that followed couldn't be helped. "He showed me the error of my ways."

"Speaking of seeing the error of one's ways, why don't you fellas lay down your quarreling for a few minutes and join us? We're headed into town." Mrs. Parker crossed her arms, her brow wrinkling.

"Wonderful idea." Jeb nodded, turned to Phineas, and extended his hand. Phineas shook it, albeit hesitantly.

Before long, the five of them were headed into town together. Well, six if they counted Katie Sue, who followed beside Jeb, her tail swatting at flies as she lumbered along.

As they approached town, Lottie caught a glimpse of Chauncy sweeping the front porch of his woodworking shop. The happy-go-lucky fella paused to stare at their little group.

"What in the world are you folks up to?" He rested the broom against the side of the building.

"On a mission," Mrs. Parker said. "Why not close up shop for a few minutes and find out for yourself?"

He looked to the right and the left. "Been kind of a slow mornin'. Folks ain't in a shoppin' mood, I guess." His gaze settled on Katie Sue. "Besides, you got me curious."

He joined their merry little party, and they continued up Main Street toward the office of the *Mountaineer*. As they passed the Civic Center, the door swung open—and who should step out but Lottie's mother, dressed in her finest and sporting a new feather-happy hat. Lottie's heart sank. Truly, there was only one person in all the world who could put a damper on things—and that person was now standing directly in front of her with a mortified expression on her face.

* * * * *

GILBERT RELEASED A SLOW BREATH as he watched Lottie's mother approach.

"Stiff upper lip, son," his mother whispered in his ear. "How much damage can one woman do, after all?"

Plenty. But he didn't say the word aloud. Instead, he ushered up a silent prayer for the Lord to intervene in a miraculous way. This whole plan could come unraveled quickly if Mrs. Sanders got involved. He couldn't afford to take that risk right now.

Gilbert glanced at Jeb, Phineas, and Chauncy, who all looked nervous. No doubt. They knew the power behind the females in the Women's League. Those feisty gals could squelch a fella's dreams in a hurry, should they be of a mind to. And judging from the expression on Mrs. Sanders's face…she was of a mind to.

FOUR

HANKERIN' FER A HONEYMOON

Come one, come all, to the Fall River Theater at Parker Lodge, where the Wild, Wild West comes alive in our latest stage production. Filled with villains, vixens, and a host of other characters you'll love to hate, this action-packed drama is sure to please both locals and tourists alike. Enjoy catchy musical numbers and exceptional acting. What a show! Hankerin' fer a Honeymoon *will have you on the edge of your seat from start to finish. Will Jenna Rossity sweep in and save the town from impending doom? Will Justin Credible turn out to be the hero she's always longed for? To learn the answers to these and many other questions, purchase your tickets for the upcoming show! And while you're at it, why not bring along your sweetheart? This dazzling drama is sure to tickle the fancy of both the menfolk and the ladies.*
—Your friends at Parker Lodge

LOTTIE SWALLOWED HARD as she looked her mother's way. "Hello, Mama."

"Lottie." Her mother's eyes narrowed to slits. "What brings you into town in the middle of the day?"

"Oh, well, I…" She struggled to come up with an answer, one that might pacify her mother and cause her to forget that her daughter had—once again—shown up in town wearing overalls and an old, worn shirt.

From behind her, Katie Sue mooed, causing an unexpected distraction.

"Whoa now, girl." Jeb's quiet voice soothed the animal.

"What in heaven's name have we here?" Althea Baker appeared behind Lottie's mother, also dressed in her go-to-town attire and wearing a funny little hat with a silk bird perched atop it. If Lottie didn't know any better, she would swear the little yellow canary might take flight any moment.

Under the circumstances, it might be better if Althea took flight, judging from the disdain on her face when she saw Jeb and his cow. The poor fellow stared at the woman he'd spent so many weeks pining over and suddenly appeared quite forlorn.

"A–A–Althea," he stammered.

She looked down her nose at him and pursed her thin lips. "Jeb Otis. Do you mind if I ask why you're bringing your cow to town? Finally ready to slaughter the old girl?"

Jeb clamped his hands over Katie Sue's ears.

Phineas stepped into place beside Althea and spoke in a strained whisper, "Don't you ever let me hear you say that again, Althea Baker. You know perfectly well Katie Sue is the only family Jeb's got."

"And the only one he's likely to ever have," Althea mumbled before turning and walking the other way.

Those words got everyone in the group worked up, especially Phineas, who now came out swinging on Jeb's behalf, at least with his phraseology. "Old grouch," he said and then grunted. "Don't know what you ever saw in her anyway, Jeb."

The men took to gabbing about Althea, and not in a good way. Lottie found herself distracted by her mother. Still wearing a frown, Mama clucked her tongue, her face turning bright pink as she gestured to Lottie's overalls. "Lottie Sanders, if I've told you once, I've told you a thousand times, I don't like to see you dressed like this, especially in town where folks can see you in all your shameful glory."

Lottie bit back the "Dressed like what, Mama?" that threatened to erupt and simply clamped her mouth shut.

"And your hair." Her mother sighed. "Child, what am I going to do with you? Do you not own a hairbrush? Honestly, I thought you would have outgrown this childishness by now. Are you ever going to be a young lady, or will we forever have these ridiculous conversations?"

"Well, see, I..." *Ugh.* She wanted to say more but couldn't get past the fact that her mother had just called her a child in front of Gilbert.

Lottie had finally decided just how to respond when her mother interrupted. "You didn't answer my first question. What are you doing in town at this time of day? Aren't you supposed to be working at the lodge?" She reached inside her reticule and pulled out a fan, which she now took to fluttering at her neckline.

Thank goodness, Lottie didn't have to respond. Mrs. Parker took care of that for her. "Dorothy, it would seem that my son and your daughter have a secret plan, one they've been plotting. That's why I left the lodge and followed them into town. I had to get to the bottom of this or die trying."

This got the fan to stop midflutter. "What sort of secret?" She looked back and forth between Lottie and Gil, the feathers on her hat dancing to and fro as she moved.

Don't fret, Mama. It's not what you're thinking.

Not that her mama would necessarily disagree with the idea of Lottie pining away for Gilbert Parker. Sure, Gil didn't share the same social standing as Winifred's beau—that highfalutin banker, Mr. Collins—but even Mama couldn't argue the fact that Gilbert Parker would be a fine catch. If the situation at the lodge turned around, anyway.

Mama continued to fuss and fume, but Lottie found herself distracted by Gil and Mrs. Parker, who had turned and taken a few steps toward Augie's office. Lottie picked up the pace, determined to keep up. Oh, how she wished her mother would turn toward home. Unfortunately, that didn't happen.

"I don't know what you folks are up to." Lottie's mother huffed and puffed as she fought to keep up with them. "But I want to witness it firsthand. No doubt it's another of your foolish ideas brewing, Lottie. I need to protect you from yourself. Remember what happened the last time you came up with one of your oh-so-clever ideas?"

She shared an embarrassing story from the past, one where Lottie had tried to help Pa spread the word about Sanders' beef by wearing a placard around town for all to see. From there, Mama lit into another story about the time Lottie decided to help the local school raise funds for textbooks by selling home-baked goods. What a mess that had been. How was she to know the difference between the sugar jar and the salt canister? They looked alike to her.

Some of the other women from the Estes Park Women's League

came out of the general store and joined their group. By the time they reached the office of the *Mountaineer,* Lottie's nerves were a jumbled mess. She turned and took her mother by the hand.

"Mama, I know you don't understand me. And I know you disagree with my clothing choices. But if you will trust me—really, truly trust me—you'll see that my heart is good and my intentions are to make things better, not worse. I would like to ask you to trust me, just this once. Please, Mama?"

This appeared to stop her mother cold. Not that Lottie minded her mother's silence. No, she rather appreciated it, since most of the words that ushered from her mother's lips usually stung as they hit their intended target.

Oh, how she wished things with Mama could be different. Maybe someday they would be. In the meantime, she would stay the course. Yes, she would follow the Lord's lead, even if it meant writing and directing a theatrical for Parker Lodge. And she would do it all with a smile on her face.

* * * * *

GILBERT FELT HIS TENSION EASE a bit as they arrived at the front door of the *Mountaineer.* Once the advertisement was written, the heavy feeling in his stomach would lift. He prayed so, anyway.

The group was too large for everyone to fit inside the tiny one-man newspaper office, so most in the group agreed to wait outside.

"You ready, Lottie?" Gilbert asked.

She nodded. They would do this...together. He took a few tentative steps, his courage growing more with each step. Once inside, he caught wind of Augie at the typewriter, pecking away, the *click-click-click* of the keys providing a steady rhythm.

"I need a little favor, my friend," Gilbert called out.

Augie turned to face him, a smile lighting his face. "Well, hello there." He extended his ink-covered hand, but Gilbert didn't hesitate. He shook it with fervor.

"What did you do, bring the whole town?" Augie gestured out the window to the crowd outside then crossed the room to have a closer look. "And why the devil did Jeb bring Katie Sue?"

"It's kind of a long story," Gilbert said. "But we've come with some good news. Lottie has agreed to write and direct the melodrama, so we need to put together an advertisement for the women to come."

Augie's gaze shifted between them, finally resting on Gilbert. "You talked her into it?"

"He did." Lottie sighed.

Augie rushed back to his desk and put a piece of paper in the typewriter. "Perfect. But we'd better get this advertisement done quickly before she changes her mind. This week's paper is set to go to print soon. I'm assuming you'll want to make an announcement to the locals."

"That, and we need you to send out a wire to New York City," Gilbert explained, his words now rushed. "And Denver too, of course. And any other place you think we might find actresses."

"Hmm. I'll need to think on that one, won't I?" Augie stretched his ink-stained fingers then placed them on the keys. "Let's start with the basics. What's the name of the show?"

"You're gonna love this," Gil said, squaring his shoulders. "We're calling it *Hankerin' fer a Honeymoon.*"

"Hmm." Augie tapped his pencil on the desk, his brow wrinkled.

"Not sure folks in New York are going to be able to relate to something that…well, that…"

"Hokey?" Lottie asked. "I tried to tell him, Augie, but he liked it."

"Coming up with a great title is key," Augie said. "Think about it. Actresses from New York and Denver are accustomed to working with professionals. They'll want something with a melodramatic flair, naturally, but something professional too." He shifted his position in the chair. "I think we're better off with something simple that incorporates the name of the lodge and adds an element of suspense."

Gilbert paused to think it through, but nothing came to him.

"What about *Predicament at Parker Lodge*?" Lottie asked after a moment.

"That's it!" Gilbert looked at her, more amazed than ever at her quick wit. "You've done it again, Lottie. See how good you are at this?"

Her cheeks flushed pink, and for a moment he saw her as the beauty that she was—in spite of her boyish attire and her short, bobbed hair. He saw a young woman—lovely and fine—willing to share in both his victories and his woes. A woman with a smile so sweet it could melt butter. He didn't have time to think these things through, however, because Augie's words interrupted his thoughts.

"Yes. I like the fact that it incorporates the name of the lodge and the family into the show." He typed a few words onto the page. "Kills two birds with one stone, which is always nice."

"It's a great title," Gilbert said. "Though, I do have to wonder how Mama will feel about it. She won't be keen on everyone in the country knowing that the lodge is in trouble."

"Folks won't catch on to that," Augie said. "But it'll work for now, don't you think?"

"I guess." Gilbert shrugged, suddenly feeling a little unsure.

After a moment's pause, Lottie snapped her fingers. "Oh, I know! We could run a contest to decide on the final title."

"A contest?" Gilbert and Augie spoke in unison.

"Sure, why not?" Lottie's face lit up as she shared, her voice now quite enthusiastic. "We'll spread the word by putting up handbills around town. That way we can let folks know we're on the search for the perfect title to the new show. Everyone can participate. It will make folks feel like they're part of things, like we need them. We do, you know."

"Another great idea." Gilbert couldn't help the smile that followed. No one came up with ideas like Lottie did, after all.

"The winner will get…" She paused and squinted as she glanced out the window. "Hmm. Not sure what the winner should get."

"Well, free tickets to the show, of course," Augie said.

"Of course," Lottie chimed in. "But there has to be more to offer than that."

An idea struck Gilbert quite suddenly. "I know! The winner will get a week's free stay at the lodge in the honeymoon suite."

Lottie shook her head. "What if he—or she—isn't married?"

"Won't matter. The winner will still deserve our very best, and the honeymoon suite is the best we've got. So, what do you say?"

"I say we get crackin' on this." Augie grinned. "Now, how do you want the local advertisement to be worded? Let's start there."

Over the next twenty minutes they crafted two articles, one for locals and one for incoming auditioners. Come the thirtieth of May, actresses "unencumbered by the bonds of matrimony" would converge on Parker Lodge to audition for a show temporarily named

Predicament at Parker Lodge. Until then, well, Gilbert had a few predicaments of his own to iron out—like how they were going to pay for all this. And what they would do with all the women once they started arriving.

Oh well. One problem at a time. Besides, with a gal like Lottie Sanders at his side, a fella couldn't help but succeed, predicament or no predicament.

* * * * *

FEAR GRIPPED LOTTIE'S HEART as Augie read through the advertisement one last time. It all sounded good on paper—likely too good. But what would happen once the women showed up? Then what? Could they really see this thing through?

Suddenly she felt like hightailing it back to the lodge and burying herself in work. What had she done, promising to direct a theatrical production, one with real actresses, no less?

She swallowed hard and tried to work up the courage to tell Gilbert she couldn't possibly go through with this. Then she looked into his grateful eyes—those gorgeous baby-blue gems—and her heart melted at once. Her courage returned and confidence stiffened her backbone once again. Yes, with Gil at her side, the stage was set for mayhem and merriment.

FIVE

Predicament at Parker Lodge

Friends and neighbors, take note! The highly anticipated Parker Lodge
theatrical has just been renamed Predicament at Parker Lodge. *This*
new title exemplifies the spirit of the men of Estes Park and suits the
new, exciting story. The script is still a work in progress, but we can
share this juicy tidbit—the production will showcase the talents of a
cast of female actresses from across the country. Even now, the men
of Estes Park are anticipating the arrival of these fair maidens. So get
your tickets for Predicament at Parker Lodge *before the show sells*
out! Find out if Abel N. Willin will give his heart to Carmen Geddit,
or if Shirley Knott will succeed in pulling him away from the woman
he truly loves. Whatever you do, don't miss out on the best show
in town! —Your friends at Parker Lodge

THE NEXT FEW WEEKS flew by at a rapid pace. Every few days Gilbert
received word of another actress interested in coming to Estes Park.
From New York City to Atlantic City, interest had been stirred. And
a handful of the ladies would come from Denver, as well. He made

arrangements for the women to meet in Loveland at the base of the mountain. From there, they would caravan up the rocky road to Estes Park, where auditions would be held that same evening.

Figuring out what to do with the ladies once they arrived had been the biggest issue. Thank goodness, Mama was open to the idea of housing them all for the next six months until the show opened. With great zeal, the single men of Estes Park had pooled their funds to provide the necessary food to see the ladies through their stay. According to Jeb, it was the least they could do. Phineas had taken to calling it the dowry and even started calling the actresses "wedding belles." Gilbert hushed him up in a hurry every time he said it, though. No point in raising suspicions.

One problem remained: getting the women up the mountain. Traversing the steep incline from Loveland was tough, though not as bad as years past. Hopefully none of the women would turn back when they saw what they'd gotten themselves into.

The morning of the thirtieth dawned clear and warm. Gilbert silently praised the Lord for His favor. Truly, only one thing could've made this nerve-racking experience even rougher, and that would've been a rainstorm. He located Lottie walking alongside the river, likely praying. That's what he'd spent the morning doing too.

He paused to take in her appearance. She wore a simple green cotton dress, one he'd never seen before. Interesting how the wrapping on a package could make such a difference. In the simple, girlish attire, she seemed young, feminine, and carefree. Pretending to be interested in her would certainly be easier if she continued to dress like that. Instead of commenting on the change, he gave her a little smile and a nod.

"I know, I know…" She shrugged and tugged at the trim on her collar. "Figured if I had to meet the ladies for the first time, I'd better make a decent impression. But don't get too used to this." She pointed to the dress. "You won't be seeing a lot of it."

"Then I'll enjoy it while I have it." He extended his hand. "You look amazing, Lottie. That's a really pretty color. Shows off your green eyes."

Her cheeks turned the nicest shade of pink and she stammered a "Thank you," then took his offered hand. Together, they headed to the lodge to meet up with the men before heading to Loveland.

* * * * *

LOTTIE COULD HARDLY THINK straight after hearing Gil's compliment. Had he called the dress pretty, or was he referring to her? Perhaps she would never know. Still, she could bask in the possibility that he'd been referring to more than the dress, which she knew to be anything but lovely. When they reached the lodge, Lottie went in search of Mrs. Parker. She found her in the dining hall, frantically scrubbing at a stain on the floor.

"Mrs. Parker, are you going down the mountain with us to fetch the ladies?"

The older woman glanced up, a frazzled look on her face. "No, I think I'd better stay here and work on getting their rooms ready. I've got fresh sheets on the beds and have mopped the floors. I've been hard at work in the kitchen too. The chocolate pies are cooling and the venison stew is cooking."

Lottie swallowed hard. She would never say so out loud, but Mrs.

Parker's cooking—particularly her venison stew—left something to be desired. It certainly wouldn't have been Lottie's first choice to welcome the women to town. Instead of commenting, she simply smiled. "How can we ever thank you for all you've done?"

Mrs. Parker's eyes filled with tears as she stood. "Thank me? Oh, honey, the thank-yous need to be reversed. You're doing all of this to save the lodge. I'm the one who should be thanking you."

Lottie gave her a warm hug. "Happy to do it. And I'm sure the show is going to be a huge success."

"I'm only the tiniest bit nervous about all of these big-city women seeing our little lodge." Mrs. Parker's nose wrinkled. "Hope they're not put off by the rustic feel."

"We made all the details as clear as we could in the correspondence. They have some idea of what they're getting into," Lottie said. "Besides, plenty of folks pay good money to come to Estes for the rustic feel. There's no need to apologize for it. It's likely just what the doctor ordered for these gals. Most are probably ready to get out of the big city and relax for a spell."

"True." Mrs. Parker released a slow breath. "Guess I'm not showing much faith, now am I? I could be celebrating the fact that this is happening. If I can keep myself calm, I'll do that."

"They're going to love you, Mrs. Parker." Lottie gave her another tight squeeze.

"Just in case you have any doubt in your mind, I really am looking forward to the girls staying with us."

"I'm so glad."

Mrs. Parker took a seat and smoothed out the wrinkles in her skirt. "I've always read that verse about going into all the world to share the gospel message, but I never knew how to get there. I'm not really what one would call a world traveler, after all." She grinned. "So, how good of the Lord to bring the world to me."

"Never thought about it like that," Lottie said. "But you're right. He's bringing the world to our doorstep."

Gilbert appeared at her side, a crooked smile on his face. "And the world is waiting to be picked up in three hours, so we'd better get a move on."

Minutes later, Augie, Jeb, Phineas, and Chauncy showed up in three Stanley motorcars, which they'd rented from Freelan Stanley, their inventor. Lottie couldn't help but wonder if Mr. Stanley knew what they were up to. Not that he would try to stop them. Oh, no. The local entrepreneur certainly found Parker Lodge no real competition for his big, beautiful Stanley Hotel, which was filled with well-to-do guests year-around.

Lottie followed Gilbert outside and smiled as Phineas tooted the horn on his large black Stanley Steamer. He let out a whistle when he noticed Lottie in her green dress.

Gilbert opened the passenger side door for her. "Your carriage awaits, my lady." He offered a sweeping bow, and she giggled.

"Thank you, Gil." She batted her eyelashes. "My goodness, it's large."

"That's why they call it the 'Pullman of the Road,' my dear," he said. "Large enough to easily seat half a dozen or more, with room left over for luggage."

"Perfect for a day like today, kind sir." She gave a little curtsy.

"Stop flirting and climb in, Lottie," Phineas said. "Let's go fetch some brides."

She did her best to shush him as she took her seat. "Phineas, remember, these are actresses, not brides. Don't you dare hint at such a thing."

"Well, a man can hope, can't he?"

"To himself, maybe, but not aloud." She draped a scarf over her hair and secured it in place.

Gil hopped into the seat behind Lottie's. "You'll scare the women away if you start talking marriage on the very first day, Phineas. Remember what we discussed."

"I know, I know." Phineas reached for the gearshift.

"We brought them here to perform in a show," Lottie added. "And if they happen to fall in love, well, so be it. But if they don't, then you have to be all right with that as well. Understand?"

He put the car in gear and sighed. "I guess."

"Besides…" She narrowed her gaze. "You don't even know if you'll like any of these women yet. How do you know you'll take a fancy to one when you haven't even met them?"

"They're female, ain't they?" He quirked a brow then touched down on the accelerator, jarring the vehicle forward.

Lottie clutched the door. "Yes Phineas. They're female. And you've got ten chances to find the needle in the haystack. That's how many women are waiting for us down in Loveland."

His eyes bugged. "What are we waitin' fer? Let's get crackin'!"

Minutes later they caravanned down the mountain toward Loveland. The motorcar bounced and bobbled as the road jutted this way and that. Chauncy and Jeb followed in the car behind them, and Augie brought up the rear. Lottie sensed Phineas's excitement in the way he drove—carefree and a little too fast.

"Where did you say we're supposed to meet them again?" she raised her voice to be heard above the noise of the engine.

"The Aspen Hotel at noon," Gil called out from the backseat. "From what I've gathered, we'll have ten women waiting there, some from Denver, some from New York, and two—sisters, if I understood their letter correctly—from a theater company in Atlantic City. A handful have been there a day or so, but some just arrived on this morning's train from Denver."

Lottie turned her attention back to the scenery and spent the remainder of the trip offering up silent but frantic prayers that these women—whoever they were—would find themselves at ease.

By the time they arrived at the Aspen, Lottie had almost convinced herself they could pull this off. Surely, with the Lord's help, all would be well. After all, these women knew what they were getting into. Mostly.

Gilbert helped her out of the motorcar, and seconds later the other men clustered around them. Jeb looked as if he might be sick at any moment, but the other three appeared to be faring well.

"Everyone ready?" Gilbert asked.

She offered a lame nod, and they all took a few tentative steps toward the hotel. Once inside the spacious lobby, it took a moment for Lottie's eyes to adjust. When they did, she saw an older woman, tall and thin, who sat ramrod-straight in a lobby chair, fussing with her sensible straw hat. Thin wisps of salt-and-pepper hair peeked out from underneath the brim. The woman wasn't much to look at, to be sure, but had a certain presence about her. She narrowed her eyes, the wrinkles on her face now more exaggerated. They provided a stark contrast to the sturdy physique.

"You think she's one of 'em?" Jeb whispered.

"Likely." Phineas looked a bit panicked. "How old would you say she is?"

Jeb squinted and leaned forward as if to examine her closer. "A hundred and three?"

Phineas snorted. "Nah. I'm guessin' in her late fifties. But she's got some wear, that's fer sure. And I sure wouldn't want to meet up with her in a dark alley. She could take me down in a hurry."

"Either she's had a rough life or..." Jeb shook his head. "She's had a rough life."

"That, fellas, is what is commonly known as a tough old broad." Chauncy laughed.

"No kidding. And she ain't much to look at, is she?" Jeb whispered. "I seen women twice that purty get run outta town with an ugly stick."

"Jeb, hold your tongue." Lottie spoke in a strained whisper. "I'm sure she's a lovely woman."

"Lovely. Humph." Jeb snorted. "If that's lovely, then I'm a scholar." He leaned over and whispered, "And we all know I ain't no scholar."

The woman gazed to her right and then her left, an irritated expression on her face. She stared Lottie's way.

"You the gal we're looking for? Lottie Sanders?"

"I'm Lottie. I, well, welcome to Colorado, Miss..."

"Flossie McAlister. Stood outside in that heat for nigh on to twenty minutes. I thought your telegram said noon."

"Yes, you're so right. See, we left the lodge in plenty of time but encountered a bit of trouble on the bend just outside of Loveland. An overturned hay wagon. You understand."

"I understand that it's hot out there and we've been waiting. In my line of work, we don't like to be kept waiting. If you say an event is going to begin at noon, it needs to begin at noon."

Lottie bit back the urge to respond with "Yes, ma'am." No point in letting this bossy old soul know she held the upper hand.

"We're here now." Gilbert's voice exuded confidence. "Where are your bags? I'll be happy to collect them for you and get you loaded into the Stanley Steamer."

"Ooh, the Stanley Steamer?" A happy-go-lucky voice rang out from behind them. "I've heard about the Steamer for years, of course, but never ridden in one."

Lottie turned as the woman with the jovial voice joined them. Her chins—all three of them—jiggled with delight when she laughed, which she did with abandon.

The woman grabbed Flossie by the arm. "Oh, sister, why ever did you come inside? Those mountains out there are magnificent. I've never seen such beauty. And the fresh air. Why, I could breathe it all day!"

"Which is exactly what you will be doing for the next six months," Flossie said with a smirk.

"Oh! I guess I will, at that." The happy woman giggled again.

"Fanny, how you do go on." Flossie rolled her eyes. "Folks, this is my twin sister, Fanny."

Twin? Lottie could hardly believe such a thing possible, for the women were nothing alike, in size or expression. She extended her hand. "I'm Lottie Sanders, director of *Predicament at Parker Lodge*. So glad you could join us."

"Oh, you sweet girl." Fanny giggled. "Happy to be here."

"Well, what are we waiting on?" Flossie asked. "I say we gather the troops and head on out." She called for several other women to join them and then took off across the lobby, leaving everyone in her dust.

"Please slow down a bit, sister." Fanny started to follow her and then glanced Lottie's way. "I'm lugging around a bit more poundage than my sister, so I don't move as fast." She stopped walking and panted. "There now. Just had to catch my breath. I struggle with heart palpitations." She glanced over at Jeb and her eyes widened. "Well now, if *that* doesn't set a woman's heart to skipping double time, I don't know what will." She extended a hand. "Fanny McAlister."

"Fanny, eh?" Phineas whispered in Lottie's ear. "Ironic."

True, the woman was rounder in some parts than others— and the name definitely suited her in more than one way—but she had a smile that would light up any room, one that Jeb seemed to take a liking to.

The thought had barely passed through Lottie's mind when a woman—probably in her early forties—took a few steps in their direction. She wore her red hair in an upswept fashion, bits of it loose around the neck, but most piled atop her head in a clever array. Her perfectly powdered nose didn't quite cover up the hint of freckles showing through. Oh, but those beautiful almond-shaped eyes! Who had eyes like that? And that lovely dress! Why she'd chosen to travel in a white dress, Lottie couldn't even guess. Had she no common sense?

Next to her, Augie straightened his necktie and squared his shoulders. "Well, now," he muttered, "*that's* a fine specimen of a woman." He turned his attention to helping her. "Can I help you with your luggage, Miss...?"

"Margaret." She paused with dramatic effect. "Margaret Linden of the Manhattan Lindens."

"She has an air about her, don't she?" Jeb whispered.

"It's an air all right." Chauncy fanned himself and laughed. "Stinkin' highfalutin woman. I can smell her perfume all the way over here."

"I hope she can act," Gilbert said. "She looks the actress type."

Lottie continued to stare at the exquisite woman, who was poised and composed. "Oh, she can act, all right. She's giving an award-winning performance right now." Indeed. The woman had a captive audience in the men, to be sure.

"Ooh, I like that one." Chauncy let out a whistle as he pointed to a beautiful blond with curls around her face and tiny flowers in her hair. The lithe beauty carried herself with great fluidity as she moved across the lobby of the hotel. Her elegant movements put one in mind of a swan floating across a lake. Not that Lottie had seen a lot of swans, but she rather envisioned them to look like this woman, who introduced herself as Grace.

The young beauty wore a soft, flowing gown, which seemed to fit her personality—light and graceful. She wore her hair up in a loose chignon, and the neckline of her dress scooped low, though not in a revealing way. More carefree and soft.

"Too petite for me," Jeb whispered. "She's so lightweight I might break her."

That got a laugh from the other men.

"What about that one?" Phineas pointed to a middle-aged woman. Her hair was raven black, curled in tendrils around her face. Her yellow dress was perfectly pressed. Her dark brown eyes didn't offer much in the way of invitation. In fact, they made Lottie rather ill at ease. The woman extended a white-gloved hand but looked as though she'd rather not have any of them shake it. Lottie stood, unsure of what to do. Finally she shook the woman's fingertips, though only for a second.

The woman introduced herself as Hannah and then added, "This town is rather dirty. If there's one thing I believe in, it's good hygiene." She gave Phineas a glance, her eyes narrowing to slits. "Yes, well, I will have my work cut out for me, won't I?"

He stammered some sort of response then reached for her bag. She slapped his hand and insisted she would get it herself.

To Lottie's right, Gil released a slow breath. She followed his gaze to see a young woman—truly a beauty—headed their way. The woman had a perfect face, with the prettiest green eyes. Her flowing brown curls draped her shoulders, spilling down onto the beautiful green-and-blue gown with white puffed sleeves. Store-bought. No doubt about it. The woman's flawless alabaster skin put one in mind of a porcelain doll, and her pink cheeks glowed with excitement.

"She's quite beautiful, isn't she?" Gil whispered.

"She is," Lottie agreed. "And she knows it. Look at the way she holds herself."

"Is that a bad thing?" Gilbert continued to stare.

Lottie elbowed him. "Stop drooling, Gilbert Parker. Your mama taught you better than that."

"I'm not drooling. I'm just—" He didn't say anything else but took a few steps in the woman's direction. "Can I help you with your bags, Miss…Miss…?"

"Cornelia Witherspoon," the young woman responded and then

flashed a lovely smile, one filled with innocence and wide-eyed won-der. "If this isn't the prettiest place I've ever seen, I certainly don't know what is."

Three other women approached, all dressed in what the fellas liked to call "slim pickin's" attire—low-cut gowns, in bright colors. They introduced themselves as Sharla, Patricia, and Cherry.

Lottie collected her thoughts and jumped into action, guiding the women, who now numbered nine, outside to the automobiles. Moments later, they and their belongings were piled inside, ready to begin the journey up the mountain. Still, one person appeared to be missing: a Miss Prudence Stillwater. What could have happened to her?

Lottie glanced across the street and noticed a young woman, one who appeared to be in her midthirties, seated on a bench in front of the general store, her gaze on the needlepoint in her hands. "I won-der if that's her." She started in the woman's direction. "Pardon me."

The woman looked up, fear in her eyes. "Y–yes?"

"Your name wouldn't happen to be Prudence Stillwater, would it?"

"I–I'm Prudy Stillwater." Her voice lowered. "Are you Miss Lottie Sanders of the Parker Lodge Theatrical Society?"

"I am. Happy to make your acquaintance." Lottie extended her hand and Prudy took it, her touch light and fearful.

The poor woman looked scared to death. Still, they didn't have any time to waste. Lottie led the way to the automobiles and watched as Prudence climbed into the car driven by Augie. Not that he seemed to notice. No, his gaze was still permanently affixed to Miss Margaret Linden, who had taken the seat next to him.

"I've never seen so many Levi's in my life." Margaret fanned her-self. "It's quite…rustic."

"I've never seen so many men in need of shaving," Hannah added from the backseat. "Is there no barber in Estes Park?"

"Sure, there's a barber," Augie piped up. "But the men don't get over to see him much. Most are too busy working the land, taking care of their cattle and such."

"Well, now, a woman could forgive a man a great many things if he took care of things like that." Cherry giggled, but Hannah didn't look amused.

Thank goodness Lottie didn't have time to think about it. Gil's voice rang out with a happy, "All aboard for Estes Park!" and Lottie sprinted toward her car.

Minutes later they pulled out of the Loveland depot in the three larger-than-life Steamers. They traveled in a row up the steep mountain road, pausing for deer and elk along the way.

"The view is simply breathtaking," Fanny said from the seat behind Lottie. "We don't get this kind of wildlife in the big city." She leaned out the open window and drew in a deep breath. "Oh, but it's worth whatever agonies we've suffered in making such a long journey to land in a place like this. That air! It's so—so fresh!"

"Nearly as fresh as some of the fellas I've worked with in the theater," Grace said and then giggled. The other ladies found her comment to be delightful, as was evidenced by their girlish laughter.

The happy caravan continued on through the foothills, pausing to look at the river portion of their drive. They met another vehicle on its way down the mountain from Estes. "Hold on, ladies," Gilbert called out. "We've got to back into this turnaround to allow the truck safe passage. He has the right of way because he's in the larger vehicle."

Grace's eyes grew wide. "This is rather frightening," she said.

"Oh, you should see it in the wintertime," Gilbert said with the wave of a hand. "You can't even get through. And when it rains, watch out. These roads are so slick, you're liable to go sliding off the edge."

Lottie glared at him, but he didn't appear to catch on. Hopefully he would stop sharing such frightening information before he scared the women.

"I just can't get over how steep this road is." Grace paled. "I had no idea what to expect, but now I know. It's very…very hilly."

Minutes later, several of the ladies were feeling poorly. The shy one—what was her name, again? Prudy?—had asked Augie to stop his car so she could calm her stomach. Lottie tended to her as best she could, but the woman looked terrified. By the time they reached Estes Park, most of the ladies were grumbling and complaining.

All but Fanny. She alone emerged from the Stanley with a broad smile on her face, one that gave Lottie a glimmer of hope that everything might turn out all right after all. Now, if only they could get through tonight's auditions.

SIX

CHAOS AT CANYON ROAD

We at Parker Lodge are looking forward to the upcoming theatrical, and all the more now that the cast has arrived and auditions are set to begin. After witnessing the arrival of the famed actresses from the East, local resident Jeb Otis has suggested a new title for the Parker Lodge melodrama: Chaos on Canyon Road. *According to Jeb, the sudden influx of nearly a dozen beautiful women, coupled with a somewhat precarious journey up the mountain, left him feeling somewhat discombobulated. So what about you, friends and neighbors? Ready for a show filled with more twists and turns than Canyon Road? Then get your advance tickets for the upcoming melodrama today!*
—Your friends at Parker Lodge

GILBERT LEANED BACK against a tree and sighed. "I can't believe we still have to hold auditions tonight. What were we thinking?"

"I don't know." Lottie sat beside him and tugged at the collar on her dress for the umpteenth time. "I mean, have you ever—and I mean ever—heard or seen so many complaints? I thought my sister was difficult, but some of those ladies this afternoon were—were…" She paused, her eyes widening. "Well, anyway, they were."

"They were, indeed. And I think the word you were looking for is *impossible*."

"Yes, and that Flossie McAlister was the worst of them. Did you hear what she said to me when I told her the story idea for *Predicament at Parker Lodge*?"

"No." But this certainly piqued his interest.

"She said it would never work, that there aren't enough twists and turns." Lottie sighed and straightened the portion of the skirt she was sitting on. "Do you think she's right, Gil? I mean, honestly, I don't know the first thing about putting together a real story. Not one folks pay to see, anyway."

"Twists and turns are good." He shrugged and leaned forward to place his hand on Lottie's arm in an attempt to summon up the courage to speak his mind. "Lottie, listen…I don't want you to take this the wrong way, but if she's willing to offer advice, maybe you'd better listen to her. She's been in the theater for over thirty years, from what she told us today. She's done dozens of shows, and many of them have been huge successes."

"We don't know that for sure. Could be she's making the whole thing up."

He shook his head, more determined than ever. "You and I both know that's not the case. You can tell by looking at her, she's been hardened by her life in the theater. But maybe God will round out those rough edges if we take the time to include her in the development of the show."

"And what if I come across looking like a fool?" Horror crossed Lottie's face. "Is that what you want? I'm already humbled enough, setting myself up as a director when I've never directed a show before."

"I know, I know. But I still think it's better to look a little foolish in front of one cranky woman than in front of a roomful of paying customers."

"Humph." Lottie leaned back against the tree and closed her eyes. "This discussion is over, Gil. I've had enough drama for one day. Well, until auditions this evening. Then the on-stage drama begins."

He gave her a moment to calm down before sharing his thoughts on that matter. "I still don't see why we couldn't just assign the parts," he said at last. "I mean, you know the script better than anyone. Why not just give each lady a part without going through the rigmarole of auditions?"

Her eyes popped open and she glared at him in her usual Lottie-like way. "Because they're real actresses, Gil. They'll think this is some sort of sham if we don't hold auditions. I'm already completely unnerved. No point in making things worse."

"Well, for now, I'm glad the women are safely tucked in their rooms, with Mama looking out for them. She'll have them all happy and well-fed in no time."

"Well-fed?" Lottie groaned. "You know what she's made for supper, right? Venison stew."

"Ack." Well, that was concerning. "Maybe they'll overlook her poor cooking in favor of her personality."

"One can hope." Lottie's eyes fluttered closed again and Gilbert spent a moment examining her face as she rested. The cute way her nose tipped up. The high cheekbones. The delicate lips. Yes, Lottie

Sanders was all girl. And she looked mighty fine in that dress too. Maybe he could talk her into going along with the fellas on this idea of dolling up for the show. Folks would come from all over the county to see her dressed as a true lady.

He knew he would, anyway.

"What are you staring at?" Her voice rang out, but her eyes never opened.

"Staring at?" He played innocent but wondered why his heart skipped a beat.

"I can feel you looking at me." Her eyes opened and she squinted as she turned his way. "What? Do I have dirt on my face or something?"

"Oh, I, um…" Gilbert reached to run his index finger along her cheek, feeling its softness. "There." He pretended to brush something away. "All clean now."

"Hmm." She closed her eyes again and grew silent.

He was determined to stay focused on the matter at hand. No point in wondering what Lottie would be like as a full-fledged woman.

* * * * *

LOTTIE AND GILBERT HEADED BACK up to the lodge to speak with his mother. They found her in the dining hall, sweeping the large area that had been converted into a stage.

"Well, hello you two." She rested her broom against the wall. "Wondered where you'd gotten off to. At the river, no doubt."

"Needed a few minutes to clear my head," Lottie said. A yawn followed.

"Can't say I blame you there. Those women are a piece of work, aren't they? But you can rest easy, Lottie. They're all settled into their rooms now."

"Wonderful news," Lottie said. "How did that process go?"

"Well, Flossie and Fanny are staying in the Knotty Pines room," Mrs. Parker reported. "Ironic, since that cranky Flossie has about the naughtiest disposition I've ever seen." She laughed. "Several of the younger women—Grace and a handful of others—are in the Cedar Lodge room. Margaret…" She snapped her fingers. "Linden. Yes, Margaret Linden of the Manhattan Lindens did not care for Cedar Lodge, so I've shifted her to the Chalet Suite, along with Hygiene Hannah."

"Hygiene Hannah?" Gilbert quirked a brow.

Lottie gave Mrs. Parker a funny look. "Why do you call her that?"

"She's scared of dirt, and that scares me. Never met a woman so afraid of her surroundings."

"Ah. She did seem a bit particular in that way," Lottie said.

"Particular?" Mrs. Parker let out an unladylike snort. "She had plenty to say about the condition of the Chalet Suite, and none of it good. I spent hours getting that room ready, but apparently it's not clean enough to suit her."

"Hmm." Lottie found herself at a loss. "What can we do?"

"She'll just have to get used to it. I daresay all of the women will acclimate in time." Mrs. Parker put her hand to her heart. "Well, maybe not the trio with the low-cut gowns. What were their names again?"

"Sharla, Patricia, and Cherry." Lottie sighed. "I have a feeling they're going to be a handful."

"More like an eyeful, if you ask me." Gil laughed. "The fellas are already taking dibs on who will end up marrying them."

"Can't say as they seem like the marrying sort," Mrs. Parker said. "Though it's not my place to judge."

"What about Cornelia…that really pretty girl with the gorgeous eyes?" Gilbert asked, appearing a little too interested. "Where did you put her?"

Lottie did her best not to groan aloud.

Mrs. Parker quirked a brow. "I put her in the River's Edge room with that really timid gal. What's her name again?"

"Prudy," Lottie said. "Actually, Prudence, but she goes by Prudy."

"Well, I think she and Cornelia will get along well, though they are opposites in most every respect. And I have a feeling Prudy will find the sound of the rushing water soothing as she tries to sleep."

"Good," Lottie said. "That poor girl doesn't look like she's slept well in ages."

"She'll sleep like a baby here. No doubt about it. And if the ladies really do stay on through the fall and winter, they can use the fireplaces to stay warm." Mrs. Parker reached for her broom and began to sweep once again.

Before long Lottie headed to Gilbert's office to gather the scripts for the night's auditions. When she entered the dining hall just before dinner, she found Fanny and Flossie talking to Mrs. Parker and Gilbert.

"Oh, you precious, precious girl!" Fanny squeezed Lottie's hand. "This place you've brought us to is spectacular in every way. I've never seen such lovely views. Simply breathtaking."

Flossie grunted. "One would think you'd never been outdoors, Fanny."

"I've never been outdoors...like this. Why, already I've seen deer and a moose."

"Elk," Gilbert said.

"Elk." Fanny clutched her hands to her chest. "With giant tusks."

"Antlers."

"And the birds! Oh, they're lovely. I've never seen such variety. I would like to close my eyes and capture it all. Commit it to memory."

Flossie clucked her tongue. "Keep your eyes open and you'll stand a better chance of not falling in the creek."

"Actually, it's a river," Gilbert said. "Fall River."

"Not very deep." Flossie's nose wrinkled. "Or wide."

"At least if we fall in Fall River, we won't drown!" Fanny giggled. "Oh, that's priceless. Fall in Fall River."

Flossie rolled her eyes. "Sister, how you do go on."

From across the room, Mrs. Parker rang the dinner bell. All the women gathered around and were soon joined by Augie, Jeb, Chauncy, and Phineas.

"Do they work here too?" Grace asked, her gaze on Chauncy.

"Nah," Lottie said. "But they usually show up around suppertime."

"No wives to cook for them?" Fanny asked. When Lottie shook her head, Fanny whispered, "Well, the food must be good, then. Keeps 'em coming back for more."

Hardly. But this probably wouldn't be the time to mention it.

The ladies gathered in a line at the front of the room, and Mrs. Parker dished up heaping bowls of the steaming venison stew. Once all the ladies were seated, Gilbert rose and removed his hat then offered up the blessing.

Cornelia appeared startled. "Can't remember the last time I heard a man pray," she said. "'Less you count the reverend at the church I visited as a youngster." She gave Gilbert an admiring smile, one he returned straightaway with his boyish dimples now prominent.

"That young fella has a nice speaking voice." Fanny pointed at Gil. "I could tell by the way he prayed. Nice projection. Good tone." She squinted and gave him an inquisitive look. "I daresay he would do just fine on the stage. And this show's gonna need a hero, is it not?"

"Oh, well, I…" To be honest, Lottie had been so preoccupied with the female roles that she hadn't really thought about the men's parts. "I think some of the other fellas are hoping they'll get to play a role." She gestured to Augie and the others.

"Those men?" Hannah shook her head. "Can't imagine a one of them as hero material, to be quite honest."

"Looks can often be deceiving." This time it was Prudy who chimed in, though her words were so quiet Lottie had to strain to make them out.

The women dove into their food—eagerly at first, but then with what appeared to be some trepidation after they'd had a few bites.

"What did you call this again?" Hannah pushed her bowl back as if it held poison.

"Venison stew." Lottie pretended to take another bite.

"Ah." Hannah stared at it. "Can't say as I've ever had anything like it."

The other ladies agreed, and none of them ate much.

Thank goodness the chocolate pie that followed dinner proved quite tasty. The women ate it like they might never eat again.

As soon as dinner ended, several locals—mostly men and

children—showed up to audition. Lottie rose and addressed the crowd, ready to get the auditions under way.

"Folks, thank you all for coming. Please take the time to fill out the audition forms and to prepare yourselves. I've got a handful of audition scripts here." She pointed to the table, her nerves suddenly kicking in.

The ladies grabbed the forms and went to work, filling them out. Cornelia approached, a concerned expression on her face. "Looking at this form, I can see that signing on the dotted line means I'll be committing to stay through late November. Six months."

"Well, there's nothing legally binding," Lottie assured her. "And if for some reason, you feel you simply can't stay, we'll certainly understand. I'll be disappointed, but I'll understand."

"Just one question…" Fanny next took a few steps in Lottie's direction, her brow wrinkled. "The woman who prepared the meal tonight—Mrs. Parker—is she, well, is she going to be doing all the cooking? This might affect my decision, I'm afraid to say."

Lottie lowered her voice. "Gilbert and I have already spoken about this and will come up with a plan. Trust me when I say that you won't starve. In the meantime…" She glanced Mrs. Parker's way. "Please spread the word to the women that they can meet in the kitchen at midnight for a snack. I'll make sure there's something available every night, starting tomorrow night." She lowered her voice another notch. "But this has to be between us, all right?"

"A woman never divulges her food sources, honey." Fanny slapped herself on the rump and laughed. "Now, if you'll excuse me, I need to warm up my voice before auditioning. It's something

Flossie and I always do, you see." She gestured at several of the other women. "Looks like we're not the only ones."

Off to the side of the room Grace did some dance warm-ups, stretching and bending in elegant style. A couple of the women sang "*la-la-la*," in an attempt to warm up their voices, no doubt. Sharla, Patricia, and Cherry did a funny little dance that involved kicking their legs up in the air. Cornelia stood off in the corner rehearsing some sort of speech. Fanny joined her sister and they began to rehearse a fascinating scene about a mother and daughter. Lottie couldn't make heads or tails out of what they were doing but found it all intriguing.

"I can't tell if those two sisters are fighting for real or acting out some sort of a scene," Mrs. Parker whispered as she dropped into the empty seat next to Lottie.

"Surely they're acting. Flossie looks worked up."

"That's what makes me think it might be real." Jeb took the seat to Lottie's left. "Bossy Flossie. That's what I'm calling her. That woman has an attitude, to be sure."

Hannah closed her eyes and paced, her lips moving but with no sound coming out.

"Do you suppose she's praying?" Mrs. Parker's brow wrinkled.

"I haven't got a clue. I've never seen anything like it." Lottie clapped her hands to get the group's attention once more. "Time to begin, everyone. Grab your scripts and let's get going."

Mrs. Parker disappeared into the kitchen and Gilbert took her seat next to Lottie. "Ready for this?" he whispered.

"As ready as I'll ever be."

Cornelia went first. She did a fine job of reading for Miss

Information, the heroine in the show. Unfortunately, Gil couldn't seem to take his eyes off her. That might be problematic, particularly if she ended up playing the lead role.

Next came Margaret, who rose and approached the stage with the same air of superiority she'd exuded back in Loveland. "I'll need a fellow to read the hero's lines."

Augie rose and took a few steps toward the stage, but Jeb beat him to it. "Allow me, miss." He pulled off his hat, revealing messy hair underneath. From a few seats away, Hannah cringed.

Margaret did a fine job of reading too. In fact, so did Hannah. And Flossie. And Fanny. And all the others, even the low-cut trio, though they thrived on acting flirtatious and silly. Prudy struggled a bit with her audition. Her voice trembled as she read through the lines. Still, she wasn't half bad.

Lottie breathed a sigh of relief when the ladies completed their auditions. Could it be that the Lord had provided just the right woman for every female role?

And the men! Though she had long accused them of being dramatic, Lottie had never guessed they might perform tolerably well on a real stage. Phineas surprised her with his somewhat convincing rendition of the evil villain. Chauncy, though bumbling at times, seemed the great comedic sidekick. And Jeb and Augie did a decent job too. So did the children and the other men from town. As the audition process drew to a close, Lottie felt hope as she never had before.

"Thank you all for coming." She rose to face the group. "I can tell this is going to be a remarkable show. We'll be posting a list of the cast members on Sunday at noon on the front door of the community church. That way everyone in town can see it."

Sharla raised her hand. "Does that mean we'll have to go to church if we want to find out what part we got?"

Hmm. Lottie thought through her response. She'd never considered the fact that the women might not be churchgoers. "If you don't want to attend the service, you can just stop by and look at the list at noon. Will that work?"

Sharla nodded.

"Rehearsals will be four evenings a week and on Saturdays. We'll have more information available at the first rehearsal. Thank you again for auditioning."

As folks headed out the door, Lottie sorted through the audition forms with Gilbert looking over her shoulder. "I think that went pretty well," he said. "Don't you?"

"A little too well," she said. "Makes me wonder when the ax is going to fall."

"Ax?" He looked perplexed.

"Yes." A shiver ran down her spine. "You know how you sometimes get that feeling just about the time you think all is going well?"

He nodded. "Yes, but you have nothing to worry about, Lottie." His gaze shifted across the room to Cornelia and he rose and walked her way.

Lottie watched him leave, the heaviness in her heart returning. Flossie slipped into the empty seat next to her. "I realize you have a lot to think about right now," the older woman said, "but I feel compelled to share something with you."

"Oh?" Lottie braced herself.

"Yes." Flossie released a breath. "I don't mean to hurt your feelings, Lottie, but this is one of the weakest audition scripts I have ever read." She held up her copy of *Predicament at Parker Lodge.* "The dialogue is stilted, the plot is contrived, and not one thing about it rings true."

"W—what?"

Flossie clutched the script. "You promised the people an action-packed drama."

"Yes." Lottie's thoughts felt scrambled as she fought for a response, and tears stung her eyes. "I—I know."

Flossie waved the script in the air. "You call this action-packed? It's filled with clichés, loaded with exaggerated stereotypes, and riddled with grammatical errors."

"Oh, I, well…"

Thank goodness Fanny arrived at that moment, just as a lone tear dribbled out of Lottie's eye.

"Now, Flossie…" Fanny clucked her tongue. "It's not that bad. We've certainly seen worse. Remember that show we did back in '03? Terrible! We felt sure it would close before it opened to the public, remember?"

Flossie paled. "Well, yes, but…"

"Who turned things around?" Fanny looked her sister in the eyes. "*You* did, Flossie. You turned things around. You took the time to help that young director with his script and his directing, did you not?"

Flossie's gaze shifted to the ground and then up to Lottie before she whispered, "Yes, I did."

"And what did the reviewers say?" Fanny asked.

"They said it was the best show Atlantic City had seen to date." Flossie's hardened expression softened into something that almost resembled a smile. "Guess they liked it."

"They loved it, and you know it." Fanny took hold of Flossie's arms. "There has never once been a show without flaws. Most of them need someone to step in and save the day. This poor girl just needs someone on her side."

"It's true." Lottie hung her head in shame. "I need your expertise, to be sure."

"Every theater person throughout time has needed a boost at some point." Fanny stared at Flossie. "Sister, we were young once, remember?"

"Of course I remember," Flossie said. "What a ridiculous question."

"You're missing my point," Fanny said. "We were once green around the gills just like this young woman standing before us. Remember our very first show back in '91? You were a silly chorus girl, and I couldn't carry a tune in a bucket. I shudder to think where we would be today if Mr. Jamison from the Poughkeepsie Theater Company hadn't taken the time to take us on in spite of our inexperience."

Flossie sighed.

"That's all she needs, Flossie," Fanny spoke with great passion as she slipped an arm around Lottie's shoulder. "She needs a shot."

Flossie mumbled something about how they were all going to need a shot of whiskey if someone didn't step in and save the day... to which Fanny responded, "You *are* that someone."

After that, well, Flossie fell silent. So silent, in fact, that Lottie wondered if she would ever speak again.

* * * * *

AFTER A BRIEF CONVERSATION with Cornelia, Gilbert noticed Flossie and Fanny talking to Lottie, who appeared teary-eyed. He headed their way and caught the tail end of their conversation. He sensed Lottie's frustration, of course, and felt bad that Flossie had stirred her to tears, but if what he'd heard was right, the older woman spoke the truth. The script did need work. Not that he had anything to worry about now. No, from the looks of things, God had brought just the right people and at just the right time. With Bossy Flossie taking the reins, the details would practically iron themselves out.

If tonight's auditions were any indicator, the melodrama would come together with little effort and the very real predicament at Parker Lodge would soon be a thing of the past. Guests would come out to see the show and leave content. They would spread the word, and before long others would come. Over time things would turn themselves around. He would keep his father's dream alive by filling the lodge with paying customers. And all because of Lottie's willingness to humble herself.

He would have to remind himself to thank her later. Right now he was simply content to breathe a huge sigh of relief.

SEVEN

HOMESTEADERS GO A-COURTIN'

Recent auditions for the Parker Lodge theatrical came off without a hitch. Locals and out-of-towners alike showed up to read for parts. What a night! What talent! What flair! What enthusiasm! Truly, a memorable evening for all involved. So, who will play the various roles? Stay tuned for more information. Our cast list will be posted on Sunday at noon on the door of the Estes Park Community Church. We can share this little tidbit—we will have a very fine-looking female ensemble, thanks to the addition of ten professional actresses. Add to that our local talent and we've got the makings of a wonderful show. So hang onto your hat, Estes Park friends! You're about to witness drama as you've never seen it before. —Your friends at Parker Lodge

THE MORNING AFTER the auditions, Gilbert put together a plan to take the ladies on an excursion up into the mountains. He called on Jeb to bring his hay wagon, and Phineas agreed to bring several of his strongest horses. At nine thirty the women gathered in the dining hall, anxious to be on their way. Lottie appeared in her overalls, and many of the women gave her curious looks.

Sharla—dressed in another low-cut gown—wrinkled her nose at Lottie. She turned to Gilbert. "I'm not quite sure I understand that girl. She dresses like a boy...on purpose?"

Gilbert fought to keep his gaze on Sharla's face and not the low-cut dress. "Well, I don't think she's trying to look like a boy. Mostly she just likes to be comfortable. And around here the women work really hard, so frilly dresses and such aren't as practical. You'll see what I mean when you've been here awhile. People don't pay as much attention to dressing up, at least not the working people. Some of the ladies in town, maybe, but not those who work for a living."

"Still, none of the other women dress like that." Sharla gestured in Lottie's direction. "Your mother, for instance. And some of the women from town who showed up for auditions. They wore plain dresses, but at least they were dresses, not pants."

"I think she's cute," Cornelia chimed in. "Sort of kid-brother-like."

"Right." Gilbert shrugged. "I know some of the fellas have been trying to talk her into taking one of the roles in the play and dressing up in lace and frills. They seem to think the locals will come out just to see that." He chuckled. "They might be on to something. I know a lot of folks would pay to see Lottie dressed like a girl."

Cornelia's brow wrinkled. "Might not be a bad way to get people to the show, but I do wonder if her feelings would be hurt in the process. She's such a sweet girl, so kind to everyone. Putting her on display might wound her. I would hate to see her hurt in any way."

Gilbert felt a twinge of guilt as he thought through her words. "I suppose you're right. Sometimes we just think about how something will benefit us and not the other person. Thank you for the reminder to be careful of her feelings." He gave Cornelia an admiring look, grateful for her thoughtfulness.

"Of course." Cornelia's eyelashes fluttered. "I enjoy helping."

At this point, Sharla took off across the dining hall, waving at Patricia and Cherry. Left alone with Cornelia, Gilbert decided to broach a delicate topic. He turned to face her, more than a little distracted by her sweet smile and beautiful eyes.

"How do you feel the auditions went?" he asked.

She frowned. "I see a few possibilities, though I do have to wonder about the local talent. Some of the men are rather…" She lowered her voice. "Well, rather unskilled in the art of acting."

"Really?" This perplexed Gilbert. "I thought they did a fine job. Just goes to show you that I know very little about the acting craft."

"It would seem a lot of people around here know very little about acting." Her eyes narrowed, and he could read the concern on her face.

"I can't speak for everyone in town, but trust me when I say that the drama skills of the men are fully intact. In fact, I've never met a more dramatic bunch." Gilbert gave her a playful wink.

She returned his wink with the most delightful smile he'd ever seen. It sent his heart fluttering in a way he hadn't experienced since…well, since Winifred left for Denver.

He didn't have long to bask in the feeling, however. Several of the ladies approached, led by Sharla, Patricia, and Cherry.

"Are the fellas coming along for our trip to the mountains?" Cherry asked with a twinkle in her eye. "I had my eye on a couple of 'em last night."

Gilbert cleared his throat. "Well, Jeb is coming, for sure. We're using his hay wagon. And I heard Augie say he's coming. Chauncy too."

"Mmm. That Chauncy is something to look at." Sharla sighed. "A little rough around the edges, but handsome as all get-out."

"Yes, he is quite handsome." Grace's delicate cheeks flushed and her gaze shifted to the ground.

"Much nicer than that older fella." Patricia wrinkled her nose. "What was his name again? You know the one I'm talking about, don't you?"

"Phineas." Cherry crossed her arms. "Not the most likable man, now, is he? A little pushy."

"He's what I commonly refer to as an 'old coot.'" Patricia laughed. "Reminds me of my uncle Henry, only with a surlier expression on his face."

Gilbert paused to think through their words. He'd never considered Phineas pushy. Strong and determined, maybe…but pushy?

"Phineas is supposed to come and bring his team of horses," Gilbert said. "Otherwise we might be walking to the mountains, not riding."

"I somehow doubt he'll show." Lottie's voice rang out from Gilbert's left.

He turned to face her. "Why not?"

"Well, as you know, Phineas hasn't had a drink in years, but I have to wonder if he headed straight to the saloon after the earful Flossie gave him last night at the auditions. She pretty much took his head off during that scene I asked them to run together. You didn't see that?"

"No. Are you serious?"

Lottie laughed. "I'm just teasing about the drinking part, but I have a feeling that woman could drive a man to drink in no time. They had some serious words both during and after the scene. At first I thought it was part of the act, but I was sadly mistaken."

"They're two peas in a pod," Cornelia observed. "And I daresay they will both win us over in the end."

Gilbert smiled at her. *There she goes again, seeing the good in everyone.*

Minutes later, Augie arrived wearing his Sunday-go-to-meeting clothes. *Rather odd for a trip up the mountain. Must be gearing up for his mayoral campaign.* Chauncy, in a stunning move, showed up with his hair combed. He'd really and truly combed it. And Jeb, for once, had shaved. Strange, how different he looked without the whiskers. He arrived with the large hay wagon, pulled by his old mare, Sadie. Gilbert ushered the women outside still wondering if Phineas would show. One lone mule could hardly pull a wagon filled with women.

Hannah wrinkled her nose and sneezed three times as she got close to the hay. "We're riding in a hay wagon?"

"It's the best choice for getting such a large group where they need to go," Gilbert explained. "And Phineas's horses"—*if he shows*—"are strong. They're accustomed to pulling a lot of weight."

"Well, that's a relief." Fanny swatted herself on the backside. "I'd hate to think we'd only make it halfway up the mountain and then roll back down again."

At this, all the women laughed. Well, all the women but Prudy, who looked terrified at the proposition of rolling backward down a mountain.

Hannah sneezed—once, twice, then a third time. She reached inside her pocket for a white handkerchief, which she used to dab her nose. "Is there something we could put on the hay before sitting on it? I'd hate to get my dress dirty."

"Like what?" Jeb asked.

"Maybe a quilt?" She folded her hankie and eased it into her pocket. "Something like that?"

He shrugged. "The only quilt I've got is the one Sadie—my mule— uses. But I think she would be happy to share. She's very generous."

Hannah sighed and muttered something about how there wasn't enough money in the gold mines of Colorado to entice her to sit on a mule's quilt.

Jeb took a couple of steps in Gilbert's direction. "Watch out for Hygiene Hannah there," he said. "She's worried about germs and such. Never met anyone quite like her."

"Poor thing," Lottie chimed in. "She's definitely stumbled into the wrong part of the country for that."

"Well, she'll get accustomed to things in time. I hope."

"Let me help you into the wagon, ladies," Jeb said. He extended his hand and, one by one, the ladies climbed aboard. Gilbert couldn't help but chuckle at the sight of them in their fancy dresses, boarding the hay-covered wagon. He kept a watchful eye on them to make sure no one got hurt but occasionally turned back toward the road, hoping Phineas would show up with his horses. If he didn't, all bets were off. Jeb's mule couldn't possibly lug this many people up a mountain.

Fanny was the last to climb aboard. Unfortunately, she required a bit of assistance, and not just from one of the fellas, but two. With a bit of pushing and pulling, she made it onto the wagon, though the huffing and puffing from the effort left Gilbert feeling winded.

"I've never been accused of being the smartest gal in the group, but even I know we're not going anywhere with that mule pulling us." Fanny turned to Jeb with a bright smile. "Now don't take that personally, Jeb. I'm sure Sadie is a fine animal. Just not strong enough for the task."

Lottie chuckled as she scratched Sadie's ears. "If you think Sadie's great, you should meet Katie Sue."

"Ah, yes." Jeb began to sing Katie Sue's praises, talking about her beautiful hair color, her terrific views on hard work, and her ability to make him smile even on the toughest day.

Fanny remained silent, her brow wrinkled all the while. When he finished his dissertation, she finally spoke up. "So, Katie Sue… is that your wife, Jeb?"

Jeb's face turned all shades of red. "Um, well, no. Katie Sue's my cow."

A couple of the ladies chuckled, and one—Cherry—actually snorted.

Fanny gave him a compassionate look. "You spoke of her so fondly, I felt sure she was a woman."

"Nah. It's just that Katie Sue and I go way back. I've had her since she was a little bitty thing. Lately, though…" He paused and shrugged. "Well, I've been giving thought to selling her. Several of the others too."

This piqued Gilbert's interest, to be sure.

"You can't do that, Jeb," Lottie said. "It just wouldn't be right. I can't imagine you without Katie Sue."

"You're really thinking of letting her go?" Gilbert asked.

Jeb nodded but didn't say anything for a moment. He finally came closer to Gilbert and whispered, "Look…I'm not really a man of means. I barely get by. But I want to contribute in some way now that the ladies are here. I've agreed to chip in to cover expenses each month, but that money's got to come from somewhere."

"You're saying you'd sell Katie Sue to cover the cost of the women?" Gilbert could hardly swallow this idea.

"Yeah." Jeb reached over to adjust Sadie's harness. "Guess that's what I'm sayin'. Guess it's a fair trade—my favorite cow for a passel of females."

"Still…" The very thought just seemed wrong. And from the look on Lottie's face, she didn't care much for the idea, either.

Not that he had time to think about it. Just as Gilbert started to offer Jeb some alternatives, Phineas showed up with his team of horses. The older fella wore a scowl on his face, one that deepened as he glanced Flossie's way. Still, he'd apparently spent some time grooming this morning. The whiskery chin was shaved clean and his matted hair combed nicely.

Phineas mumbled to himself as he prepared the team then took the only free spot on the hay wagon, next to Flossie. They ended up back-to-back, neither willing to look at the other. Gilbert had a bad feeling that one of them—or maybe both—would cause a scene before the day was up.

Minutes later the wagon was headed up into the mountains. Though Prudy and Hannah looked a bit uncomfortable, most of the other women appeared to have the time of their lives. Cornelia and Margaret chatted and laughed. Fanny told story after story about her years in the theater. Sharla batted her eyelashes every time Chauncy glanced her way, which seemed to bother Grace. Could it be the delicate beauty had her eye on Chauncy?

What an interesting dilemma, to have so many men and women about. Talk about the perfect setup for chaos and disaster. And speaking of disaster, Cherry—*heavens, that dress!*—leaned forward every chance she could get, revealing far more than Gilbert cared to see. He did his best to keep his gaze on the road.

Around eleven o'clock they arrived at the base of Longs Peak, settling on a beautiful green field filled with sunflowers and Indian paintbrushes. Jeb pulled the team next to the creek with a gentle "Whoa, Nellie!" and hopped down to assist the ladies.

One by one they made their way out of the wagon. Of course, Phineas and Chauncy were happy to help. Augie might've been too, had he not been so preoccupied, tending to Margaret's needs and bragging about his upcoming mayoral campaign. He did offer Prudy a hand after she tripped and almost fell out of the wagon.

Poor Prudy. Gilbert couldn't help but feel a little sorry for her. She didn't seem to fit in with the rest of the ladies. She'd no sooner stepped down from the wagon than her dress got caught in a bramble bush. Seconds later she stepped into a mud puddle and soaked her stockings up to her ankles. Not that he was looking, of course. But with everyone talking about it, how could he avoid the subject?

Phineas did just fine in assisting the ladies until it came to Flossie. He offered her a hand, but she slipped and tumbled right into his arms. Not that she stayed there long. Oh no. He lost his grip and she slid to the ground, landing on her backside with a *thud*.

"Oops." Phineas offered her a hand up then muttered a red-faced apology before walking away.

Minutes later Lottie and Jeb set up a picnic area, creating an appetizing display of the many foods that Jeb pulled from a basket he'd brought from home. Gilbert offered a prayer and they dove right in.

"Jeb, you made this potato salad?" Fanny gave him an admiring look then took another bite.

He nodded, his cheeks turning red. "Yep. I like to dabble in the kitchen."

"And you made the beans as well?" She took a big bite of them.

"Sure. I got bags and bags of beans, so I cook 'em whenever I can. I've learned how to make them a dozen different ways."

"Can't imagine you could make them any better than this." Fanny took another big bite and then offered up a contented sigh. "I've truly never had anything so tasty. In fact, I think I'll have seconds." She reached for the bowl and scooped out another helping. "Hope no one minds, but I'm still a little hungry after last night." She shook her head. "And that oatmeal this morning...gracious! Never tasted anything quite like it." She clamped a hand over her mouth. "Oops, there I go again, saying too much. Still, a body could wilt away with no more food than I've put in it over the past day or so."

"I daresay you won't wilt away, Fanny." Flossie rolled her eyes. "Little fear of that."

This got a chuckle out of some of the others.

"You never know, Flossie. This clean mountain air might just inspire me to diet and lose a few pounds." Fanny swallowed more potato salad. "Or it might just inspire me to make more room for the good stuff." She rubbed her belly, and the women laughed.

"I'm just happy to have good food," Flossie said. "After last night, I was ready to pack my bags and head back to Atlantic City."

That certainly got Gilbert's attention. Looked like he'd better come up with a solid plan to get Mama out of the kitchen. But how could he go about it without hurting her feelings? Just one more thing to pray about.

Fanny took a bite of corn bread and a blissful expression crossed her face. "I've died and gone to heaven," she said. The other ladies followed suit, nibbling on pieces of corn bread.

Gilbert watched as the women relaxed and had a good time. Perhaps—with Jeb's good home cooking in their bellies—they would consider staying.

To his left, a sweet voice interrupted his thoughts. "Gil, this whole place is a little slice of heaven, isn't it?"

He turned to face Cornelia, taking note of the look of wonder in her eyes. He nodded, overwhelmed by the fact that heaven appeared to be staring him straight in the face at this very moment.

She gestured to the mountains and sighed. "I've never been a terribly religious person, but I must admit, there's something rather spiritual about these mountains."

"'I will lift up mine eyes to the hills, from whence cometh my help,'" Gil quoted his favorite Scripture aloud. "'My help cometh from the Lord, which made heaven and earth.'"

Cornelia sighed. "Well, aren't you just the poet. I've never heard anything so beautiful."

As he gazed into her eyes, Gil had to admit, he'd never seen anything so beautiful. And how wonderful of the Lord, to draw her heart to the very mountains that he had always loved.

"I, um, well, I didn't write that, exactly. It's from the Bible."

"One of my favorite psalms," Fanny chimed in. "The one hundred twentieth."

"One hundred twenty-first, sister," Flossie corrected.

"One hundred twenty-first," Fanny echoed then smiled.

With the skies overhead a brilliant blue, the mountains nearby capped in white, and the fields alive with colors of every sort, the whole excursion felt like something out of a painting, not a real-life adventure.

Gilbert took a bite of potato salad and leaned back, drinking it all in. Out of the corners of his eyes he caught a glimpse of Lottie and gave her a smile. Without her hard work, none of this would have been possible. He would have to remember to thank her later. Right now…well, right now he'd rather keep his eyes on Cornelia.

* * * * *

LOTTIE TRIED TO FOCUS on the women and enjoy the picnic but found herself distracted, watching the interaction between Gil and Cornelia. No one could deny the young woman's beauty. And her clothing! Lottie had rarely seen such exquisitely fitted dresses. Unlike Cherry and a couple of the others, Cornelia presented herself as a true lady in every sense of the word, one Lottie might be tempted to emulate, should she think it necessary.

Was it necessary?

Watching the smile on Gil's face, seeing the way his eyes lit up when Cornelia leaned in to speak to him, Lottie could only conclude one thing: *he's looking for a woman like that, not a girl who dresses in overalls and keeps her hair bobbed short.*

She made up her mind right then and there to let her hair grow out and invest in some new fabrics for dresses. Even if she hated the thought of dolling herself up, she'd do most anything to win Gilbert Parker's heart.

Fanny tapped Lottie on the arm. "I can tell you're lost in your daydreams. Everything all right?"

"Oh…yes. Thank you." Lottie took another bite of corn bread and leaned back to gaze at the beautiful blue sky overhead. It was beautiful…and *almost* successful in distracting her from Cornelia's giggles.

"I had an idea," Fanny said from the spot next to her. "Actually, I've spoken to several of the ladies and we're all in agreement, so I hope you'll play along."

This got Lottie's attention. She sat up. "What is it?"

"Well, I told you that I've been a bit concerned about the food. If that venison stew was any indicator, we've got several terrible meals on the horizon." Fanny put her hand up. "Now, before you go telling me about the midnight-snack idea once again, let me share a thought. You're worried about hurting Mrs. Parker's feelings. Is that right?"

"Right."

"What if I told you that we've come up with a way for someone else to do the cooking—say, someone like Jeb." She pointed at him and smiled. "And what if I told you that Mrs. Parker was going to be so busy that she would look upon this idea as a blessing?"

"I would say you were a miracle worker." Lottie grinned. "So, what's this idea?"

"I've been hearing from some of the fellas that the lodges

nearby have a lot more to offer than Parker Lodge. For instance, the Stanley has great design and character. And the Elkhorn has a candy kitchen."

"Right."

"What you need is something to compete, something to bring in families."

"That's why we're doing this melodrama, to draw in families."

"Yes, but you need revenue between now and then. So, here's my idea. I think Mrs. Parker should start a pie parlor."

"A pie parlor?"

"Yes," Fanny said. "You know, a bakery where a chef—in this case, Mrs. Parker—bakes up delicious pies all day long. You could sell it by the slice, even become known for your pies. For all the woman lacks in the cooking department, she more than makes up for it in baking. If all her pies are half as good as the one she served last night, this pie-parlor idea will take off in no time."

"What a terrific idea." Lottie thought it through and then snapped her fingers. "Parker's Pie Parlor! What do you think of that for a name?"

"Sounds yummy. I can hardly wait for a big, thick slice of chocolate pie."

"And coconut cream," Margaret chimed in. "That's my favorite."

"And lemon meringue." Sharla licked her lips.

Cherry's eyes sparkled as she exclaimed, "And cherry! Don't leave me out!"

"Apple!" Prudy's animated voice rang out.

"Persimmon!"

"Persimmon?" The women turned to Hannah.

"It's my absolute favorite." For the first time since arriving in Estes Park, the young woman giggled. "Oh, I do love persimmon pie loaded with cream and cinnamon. In fact, I love baking just about any kind of pie. And cake. And cookies."

"You...love baking?" Lottie could hardly imagine such a thing possible, what with baking being such a messy affair and all.

"I throw away all my inhibitions when I get into the kitchen." Hannah's face radiated joy. "There's something so freeing about baking. Eases my troubles."

"Well, that's the answer then!" Fanny clapped her hands. "You'll help Mrs. Parker by day and perform on the stage by night. Do you think you can handle the work?"

Hannah's eyes sparkled. "Oh, I'm a hard worker. I love having something to do. Idle hands are the devil's workshop, you know."

"Then I must work for the devil." Sharla fidgeted with the bow at her waist. "My idea of the perfect day is lying in bed till noon then taking a leisurely nap after that."

"I love this pie-parlor idea." Lottie felt herself more energized than ever. "And I think the folks around here will like it too. In fact, I know they will."

"Well, if you really want to keep the locals coming in, offer to use their recipes," Fanny said.

"What do you mean?"

"Gilbert told us about your contest to name the play. Why not do something similar with the pies? Involve the people. Win them over again by running a contest to see whose pie recipes are good enough to show up on the menu at Parker's Pie Parlor. Why, folks'll be standing in line to get their family recipes to you. Just watch and see."

Lottie smiled. "Has anyone ever told you that you're brilliant?"

"Rarely." Fanny laughed until her midsection took to jiggling. "But I'll hang onto those kind words for years to come, Lottie. Thank you very much."

"You're welcome. I meant it. The fact that you and Flossie have been so kind and so willing to help...well, it means a lot to me."

"Oh, trust me, honey, this pie-parlor idea was completely self-serving. For one thing, I happen to love pie. For another, I happen to know that Jeb Otis is a skilled cook. If we can just talk him into showing up at the lodge to do the cooking—both now and during the shows—I'll probably put on ten pounds." Fanny turned to give Jeb a little wave. He gestured for her to join him in a game of horseshoes.

"Looks like someone wants you." Lottie giggled.

"Mm-hmm. And this is one woman who wants to be wanted." Fanny rose—with a little help from a couple of the other ladies— and headed off to talk to Jeb.

Lottie thought about how funny it was, the two of them getting along so well, what with him being so tall and thin and Fanny being just the opposite. Still, opposites did attract. Wasn't that what Winifred always said? Perhaps that's why Winnie always took such a liking to Gilbert, him being so down-to-earth and her being so highfalutin and all.

Gil. In her lengthy conversation about pies she'd forgotten all about him. She looked around and saw that he'd taken off across the meadow with Cornelia at his side.

Off the ladies went on an excursion to pick flowers. Well, most of the ladies, anyway. Just about the time Lottie decided to join them, Flossie appeared with a script in hand. "Ready to get to work?"

"Out here?"

"Sure. No better time or place to look at the revisions my sister and I have made to your script. If I can pull her away from that horseshoe game, anyway. What do you say?"

Lottie stared longingly after Gilbert, who tagged along on Cornelia's heels across the meadow. Turning back to Flossie, she shrugged. "I say let's get to it. No time like the present."

EIGHT

Twists and Turns on Trail Ridge Road

Like the beautiful mountains and valleys found in the Estes Park region, the upcoming theatrical at Parker Lodge is filled with high highs and low lows. We promise, your emotions will soar to new heights as you watch our hero and heroine fight their way to the top. During the low moments, you can boo and hiss at our evil villain and even toss a rotten tomato or two his way. Best of all, you can enjoy that special moment when true love wins out—when love's true kiss is shared and hearts are forever melded together. Yes, the theatrical at Parker Lodge is sure to give mountain-lovers plenty of peaks to climb and valleys to wade through. So grab your sturdiest mountain shoes and let's get going! —Your friends at Parker Lodge

LOTTIE GAZED WITH GREAT LONGING at Gil as he took Cornelia by the hand and led her across the flower-covered field. When she turned back to face the twins, Fanny gave her a sympathetic smile.

"I know it's a sacrifice to stay here and work on this, but it will be worth it if we come up with a script worthy of a paying audience. And trust me, if you're looking to catch a certain fella's attention, nothing will stand a better chance than giving him what he wants."

"O–oh?" Lottie could hardly imagine what she meant. "And what would that be?"

"Why, a show that will bring in money for his family's lodge, of course." Fanny giggled. "What did you think I meant?"

"With you, it's hard to tell."

Flossie opened her script, and right away Lottie could see that she'd covered it in scribbles and scratches.

"Oh my." She was determined to get this over with as quickly—and as painlessly—as possible.

"It's not as bad as it looks," Flossie said as she took a seat on the quilt next to Lottie. "Though, we did stay up late into the night coming up with ideas and new characters to fit all of the folks who auditioned last night. I hope you're pleased and not overwhelmed or wounded in some way."

The strangest twisting took place in Lottie's chest. For, while she was pleased that the ladies would take the time to fancy-up her script, she couldn't help but feel a little let down that so much work needed to be done. Was it really that bad to begin with?

"Help me down, sister." Fanny extended her hands and Lottie and Flossie worked to ease her down onto the quilt beside them. "There now. All set. Of course, getting back up again might be a challenge, but we'll cross that bridge when we come to it."

"Looks like we have a lot of work to do." Lottie gestured to the script. "What are your thoughts?"

"They are many." Flossie thumbed through the pages.

"Ah." Lottie's heart sank.

"Now, let's start with the characters." Flossie's businesslike voice kicked in. "One thing you simply must know right off the bat is this: when you create a villainous character—male or female—that character can't be all bad."

"What do you mean?"

"Think about it, Lottie. Think of the most villainous person you know."

Visions of Althea Baker came to mind. Lottie didn't speak her name aloud, of course. Not that Fanny and Flossie would recognize the name, anyway.

"Your villain has to have some redeeming qualities." Fanny reached for the plate of chicken and grabbed a drumstick.

"Redeeming qualities?" Lottie echoed.

"Yes." Fanny took a bite of the chicken then spoke around it. "Don't you see? Your good guys can't be all good and your bad guys can't be all bad. Even the worst person in the world has some redeeming qualities." She swallowed and gave Lottie a smile.

"Hmm."

Flossie turned the page and pointed to a section of text. "And another thing—you don't want to give your villain away right off the bat. Make the audience suspicious. Plant clues. Lead them astray, even."

"True," Fanny said. "And as for your hero, the more flawed you can make him, the better."

"Flawed? But doesn't that defeat the purpose?"

"Not at all. For, as we said, good guys aren't all good and bad guys aren't all bad. Think of the very best person you know."

Lottie thought at once of Gilbert, of course.

"Surely that person has at least one flaw, does he not?"

"Y–yes." Gilbert's flaw, at least the most apparent one, came rushing to mind right away. He liked pretty girls. Girls who looked nothing like Lottie.

"The goal here is to make the audience work a bit to unravel the details in their minds." Fanny wiped her greasy hands on her skirt. "Nothing can be easy. We call it upping the ante. Things can't be easy for the hero, either. He needs to struggle."

"I see." Lottie gazed in the direction Gilbert and Cornelia had walked and did her best not to sigh aloud.

"There's got to come that inevitable point in the show where the audience is convinced that the hero will fail at his task," Flossie said.

"Really?" Lottie found this difficult to believe. "I always thought heroes were heroes from start to finish. The whole purpose of adding a hero is so that he can rescue the damsel in distress and end up falling in love with her, right?"

"In stage plays, not necessarily in real life." Fanny sighed. "At least that's been my personal experience. I've known many a so-called hero who got it wrong in the end." She took another bite of the chicken and grew silent.

"But for the sake of the play, our hero will get it right," Flossie said. "Only, at some inevitable point, the audience has to be led astray. They must believe he will fail at his task to rescue the heroine and give her the happily-ever-after she deserves."

Lottie sighed. "What else?"

"Since we're talking about the heroine now, it's important to add a scene where she's in some sort of distress."

"I thought I did. The scene at the train depot. Did you read that?"

"Yes, dear, but you didn't go deep enough into her emotions. It has to be believable. Think back to the last time you felt like no one cared enough to come to your rescue."

Lottie tried not to let her frustration show. How many times had Gil looked past her needs to tend to Winifred's? And hadn't he extended a hand to help Cornelia out of the wagon today, completely overlooking Lottie? Had he thanked her, even once, for all her hard work on his behalf?

Suddenly she felt a bit ill.

Oblivious to her ponderings, Flossie forged ahead. "When that happened, what were you thinking? The key is to take those emotions, all of that very real angst, and transfer it to the page."

Fanny reached to take Lottie's hand, gazing into her eyes with great intensity. "Then, when your character speaks those lines, they sound real because they are real. They're birthed from real-life experience. And your audience members will respond to them because they've felt the same way."

"I—I see." She did. Perhaps a little too clearly.

"Since we're talking about the female-in-distress scene," Flossie said, "I want to challenge your thinking a bit."

"Oh?"

"You've made your heroine too soft. She's counting too much on being rescued."

"What do you mean?"

"She's lily-livered. Comes across as weak."

"Isn't that the idea? Our heroine—Miss Information—needs a man to sweep in and save the day. That's what people will expect. And Justin Credible is the man for the job. He's handsome, strong, and knows just what she needs when she needs it. Won't the audience be expecting as much in a melodrama?"

Fanny clucked her tongue. "Lottie, this is 1912. Do I need to remind you that women across this country are fighting for the right to vote? Suffragettes are marching with banners and placards so that we can have a fair shake in the political arena. So, while we want to show a strong hero, we have to stay in touch with the times. Understand?"

"Your audience members won't care much for your heroine if she's weak or if she counts too much on a man to rescue her," Flossie said.

"I guess I see your point, but I don't know how to balance that against the traditional melodrama format. So how do we remedy the problem?"

"We've remedied it for you," Fanny said. "Now, I hope it won't hurt your feelings, but we've taken the liberty of doing a complete rewrite of your play."

Lottie swallowed hard and said nothing.

"The answer to your dilemma was in front of you all along," Flossie added. "This place—Estes Park—is loaded with enough real-life drama to transfer to the stage."

Over the next twenty minutes or so, the twins unfolded their plan for the show. Not only had they completely changed the script, they'd added a host of characters, both male and female. Lottie listened as they described—with great animation—just how the story would unfold. At first the sting of having her original story overlooked was almost too much to take. But as the women shared their vision, reality stared her in the face. These women were a gift from God. She could either accept that gift or reject it. To accept it meant a beautifully plotted show and a happy audience. To reject it meant she would get her way and the show would move forward as currently written—with no depth.

When they finished speaking, Lottie rose and tugged at her overalls. "Ladies, you have misjudged me."

"We—we have?" Confusion registered on Fanny's face.

"Yes." She looked down at them and grinned. "You were worried about hurting my feelings, and I need you to know that my feelings have been spared. This story idea you've come up with is brilliant. Better than brilliant, really. I love every single thing about it and can't wait to see it come alive on the stage."

"Oh, I'm so glad!" Fanny extended her hand and Lottie reached down to help the robust woman rise. Turned out to be more of a task than she'd imagined. Before all was said and done, Flossie sprang up to help.

"Well, I'm glad we're all in agreement." Flossie looked relieved. "Thought we might end up having words."

"No, the idea is wonderful. And I'm assuming you've got cast members in mind?"

"Do we ever!" Fanny grinned. "Wait till you see."

She pulled out the cast list and the ladies talked through it as they walked along the edge of the creek. Lottie fought the temptation to kick off her boots and wade in the water.

"The show will be a rousing success." Excitement washed over Lottie as she spoke. "And I do hope it's enough to save the lodge."

"Save the lodge?" Flossie stopped walking.

Lottie clamped a hand over her mouth. "Oh, I can't believe I said that out loud. You ladies weren't supposed to know."

"Know what?" Flossie's gaze narrowed.

Lottie paused and tried to decide how much to share. Oh well. She'd already put her foot in her mouth. Might as well give them the full story. They were bound to find out anyway.

"The Parkers are in trouble." Lottie tried to quiet the tremor in her voice as she spoke. "They've had trouble drawing folks to their lodge since Gil's father died. He always kept the place up so nice, but Mrs. Parker and Gil are struggling."

"Oh my." Fanny appeared stunned by this news.

"With other, grander places to stay in town, visitors are fickle," Lottie explained. "They want newer and nicer places like the Stanley Hotel. And who can blame them? That's why we came up with the idea for the melodrama, to raise funds to keep the lodge open. We've tried so many things in the past—talent shows, Saturday night dances, game night…all sorts of things. But nothing has really brought in customers, at least not as many as we'd like to see."

"Well, why didn't you say so?" Fanny slapped her thigh. "I'm loaded with ideas for raising money. Do you know how many benefits we've done over the years? Dozens! There was last month's operetta to raise funds for the families of those who lost loved ones on the Titanic. That was quite spectacular and brought in a lot of money for those poor, devastated folks." Her eyes misted over.

"Don't forget the one-act play we did years and years ago for the victims of that awful Galveston storm," Flossie added, "and the outdoor musical extravaganza for the families affected by those wildfires a couple of years ago."

"And the benefit for Bellevue Hospital last summer," Fanny added. "We can't forget that one. We raised enough money to help them open the new children's wing."

Lottie felt hope as never before. Her eyes flooded with tears. "Ladies, I don't know if you believe in the power of prayer, but I must say, you are the answer to mine."

"Believe in prayer?" Fanny laughed. "I never make a move without praying first. How do you think we ended up in Estes Park, Colorado?"

"I knew it." Lottie reached to squeeze Fanny's hand. "I just knew you had to be prayer warriors. It shows."

"I believe in prayer," Flossie said. "But I believe in hard work too. So let's get busy talking about ideas to raise money." She gave Lottie a pensive look. "Let's go back to what you said earlier about the things you've already tried. You mentioned talent shows. How did those turn out?"

"Oh, we had a handful of folks sign up."

"Did you sell food?"

"A bit. Not much, though. You've tasted Mrs. Parker's cooking. As you're already aware, she's not the best cook in town."

"Right, but with Jeb onboard, I do believe we stand a real shot at bringing in money from the food. A dinner theater is the way to go."

"Perfect!" Lottie clasped her hands together, thrilled with the idea. "And just so you know, he's got the best garden in the county and has cooked up all sorts of tasty things. You should taste his white bean chili. He makes it for poker night sometimes. The fellas all swear it's the best they've ever eaten."

"Well, then, we can coordinate the names of his food to correspond with the theme of the show."

"Same with the pies," Fanny said. "We can have Justin Credible Apple Pie, Hugh Dunnit Pecan Pie, and so forth. What do you think? We can sell it by the slice for our dessert theater productions. Folks can choose their option—dinner theater or dessert theater." She began to talk about the role good food played in a theatergoer's experience. By the time she wrapped up her little speech, she'd won Lottie over. In fact, with a new script, a new chef, and the temptation of delicious pies looming, the whole experience suddenly seemed quite…tasty.

* * * * *

GIL REACHED OUT TO HELP Cornelia walk across the rough-hewn bridge over the creek. She accepted his hand with a smile. The feel of her soft fingers against his palm sent a shiver through him. Still, he'd better stay focused. Though he'd love to spend the day with her, there was still plenty of work to be done back at the lodge. He also needed to talk with Lottie about the cast list, which they planned to post tomorrow.

Minutes later he and Cornelia joined the others. He took a few steps in Lottie's direction, his curiosity piqued by the excitement in her expression.

"Everything all right?" he asked.

"More than all right. Oh, Gil, these women are such an answer to prayer."

"Yes, they are." His gaze drifted back to Cornelia, who gave him a shy smile.

"You just won't believe what a blessing Flossie and Fanny have been. They want to help us, Gil—really, truly help us."

He was struck by the expression of pure joy on her face. How long had it been since he'd seen her this carefree?

She shared the plan the twins had come up with. He especially loved the idea of the pie parlor. And the dinner-theater idea was perfect.

"Do you think Jeb will be our chef?" she asked.

"Oh, I think so." He chuckled. "I think he'll take any excuse he can get to be around the women. So spending more hours at the lodge won't be a problem, I'm sure."

Gilbert had just opened his mouth to say something else when a shrill voice rang out: "S–s–snake!" He turned to see Prudy standing behind him, her face ashen.

All the women began to squeal at once. Well, all but Lottie, who took a couple of steps in the direction of the snake for a closer look.

"That's no snake." She chuckled as she reached to pick it up. "It's just a stick."

"O–oh." Prudy still looked as if she might faint.

Gilbert chuckled. Thank goodness for Lottie. She might not dress like the other ladies, but she certainly knew how to get the job done. And right now? Well, right now he needed a gal who knew how to get the job done.

* * * * *

LOTTIE COULD HARDLY wipe the smile off her face as the wagon headed back down the mountain toward the lodge. Even watching

Cornelia squeeze into the spot between her and Gil didn't upset the apple cart. No, with so many new ideas buzzing in her head, who had time to be upset?

"Can I ask you a question?" Cornelia leaned over to whisper in Lottie's ear.

"Sure."

"I overheard Flossie talking about the new script a few minutes ago. Does it hurt your feelings a little that she and her sister have changed it so much?"

Lottie brushed some hay off her pants. "Oh, I'll admit it stung at first. But I don't know anything about putting together stories like they do. Not really."

"Gil and I had a long talk about you just this morning," Cornelia said.

"O–oh?" This certainly got Lottie's attention. "You did?"

"Yes." Cornelia giggled. "He's just the sweetest fella, isn't he? And so kindhearted. But anyway, he thinks you hung the moon. And he went on and on about the stories you used to tell when you were a kid. He says you were quite the storyteller."

Joy flooded over Lottie when she heard that Gilbert had been bragging on her. Still, his compliments were exaggerated. "I guess some would say that. I never really thought about those stories as anything special, though. They were just a way to pass the time. They gave me something to do, and a way to escape the…" She paused to think of the word. "The everydayness of my life." A sigh followed.

"Why the sigh?" Cornelia seemed genuinely concerned.

"If I could pretend to be something—or someone—I wasn't,

then the pressures of the real world went away. In my mind, the pretend stories were more fun. More real, even." She gestured to the mountains. "And look at the backdrop God gave me. Isn't it perfect for a made-up story?"

"It's pretty perfect for a real-life one too." Cornelia kept her face turned toward the mountains. "Where I come from, we don't see mountains. Or scenery, for that matter."

"You're from New York?"

"Yes. Born and raised in the city. My parents sent me off to finishing school, but I got the acting bug. I don't think they've ever quite forgiven me for choosing a life on the stage. They had something else planned for me."

"Like what?"

She laughed. "Marriage to the perfect young man—respectable and from a good home."

"Sounds like we have more in common than you know." Lottie bit back a laugh.

"They would've had me married with babies by now." Cornelia sighed. "And I must admit, there are times when I wonder how different my life might've been, had I chosen to go that route." She glanced over her shoulder at Gil. "Maybe it's not too late."

"O–oh?"

Cornelia grabbed Lottie's hand and gave it a squeeze. "Maybe that's why I traveled all the way to Colorado, to meet the man I'm supposed to marry. Do you think such a thing is really possible?"

If it had been any of the other women asking, Lottie would've said yes in a heartbeat. But Cornelia? The very girl Gil had his eye on?

Choose your words carefully, Lottie.

She released a slow breath. "Cornelia, I do believe God could bring a person from one side of the country to the other to meet someone special. It's possible. When you follow His lead"—she swallowed hard—"anything's possible."

"I feel the same way," Cornelia whispered. "In my heart of hearts, I do."

Lottie fell silent, unable—and unwilling—to add more to this conversation. She'd lost Gil once to Winifred. Would she now lose him to the beautiful young woman seated to her left? The one with the lovely clothes and refined big-city manners?

Fortunately, Cherry interrupted her thoughts. "What happens around here on Sunday?" she asked. "If we're not going to start rehearsals until Monday, do we have a free day to do as we please?"

Lottie shrugged. "Most everyone goes to church. Would...well, would you like to join us?"

"I haven't been to church in a month of Sundays." Cherry laughed. "If I went, it might just be too much for the Lord to take."

"He can handle it." Lottie grinned. "I daresay He'll meet you there. At least, that's where I always feel the closest to Him."

"Ooh, I don't know how you could top this experience." Cornelia gestured to the mountains. "This is the very spot where heaven and earth meet, and I'm standing here so close to God I can almost touch Him."

Lottie looked around at the ladies, remembering Mrs. Parker's words: *How good of the Lord to bring the world to me.*

"Being here is blissful, isn't it?" Lottie said. "But I'll make you all a promise...if you go to church with me and don't feel this same, exhilarating feeling that you had on this mountain today, I won't expect you to come again. Deal?"

Cornelia shrugged. "If you say so. But I still say I'd rather worship right here." She turned her gaze back to the mountain.

Lottie's thoughts shifted to the days ahead. With so much to do, so much to accomplish, someone needed to stay focused. And she could tell, judging from the way Gil stared at Cornelia, it certainly wasn't going to be him.

NINE

MENACE IN THE MOUNTAINS

Residents who auditioned for the upcoming melodrama at Parker Lodge are abuzz with excitement over the posting of the cast list, which will happen today at noon, just after morning service, at our local community church. Mum's the word until then. We can share that the play has been completely revamped and the new script will be available at the first rehearsal on Monday evening. Our contest to rename the show is still in full swing. Phineas Craven has suggested Menace in the Mountains. *Perhaps you have other thoughts. One thing is for sure—a full cast of quirky characters will cause the audience to laugh...and cry. Until then, what joy to share in a Sunday morning with our out-of-town guests. They are sure to love the welcome at Estes Park Community Church, where God's love abounds and His grace extends to folks from all walks of life.* —Your friends at Parker Lodge

LOTTIE AWOKE EARLY on Sunday morning, so excited she could hardly stand it. She put on a dark blue dress and did her best to fuss with her unruly curls. For a moment she toyed with the idea of trimming them back a couple of inches but then remembered the way Gil gazed at Cornelia's lovely long hair. With a sigh, she pulled her hair back with a green ribbon, one she carefully chose to match the color of her eyes.

She arrived at the church at nine fifteen and entered the little chapel, her heart aflutter. Several of the women—Flossie, Fanny, Cornelia, Grace, Hannah, Margaret, and Prudy—arrived minutes later, followed by the low-cut trio, who all appeared in brightly colored dresses that left little to the imagination. Sharla slipped into a pew and said something about feeling faint. No doubt because of the tight corset under her bright green gown, one with a particularly snug waistline. Patricia's garish red dress was embellished with ruffles and bows. And Cherry had been a bit heavy-handed with the rouge, perhaps. Sharla too, for that matter.

By the expressions on their faces, some of the local women were a bit put off by their new guests. Maybe they would still provide a warm welcome in spite of first impressions. One could hope, anyway.

Instead of sitting with her parents, Lottie planted herself in the middle of the ladies. Might as well let folks know where she stood regarding their new guests. She received a few curious glances from the regulars, and Mama gave her a "What do you think you're up to, Lottie-Lou?" look, but she focused on the hymnal.

The preacher's sermon on turning from a life of sin had Sharla squirming in her seat. She actually muttered a few words when he reached the part about the woman caught in the act of adultery. Lottie's mother, who was seated in the pew in front of them, turned and glared at her with narrowed eyes.

"What did I say?" Sharla whispered into Lottie's ear. "That old bat glared at me like I was a sinner headed straight for the pit of hell."

Lottie sighed and then whispered her response. "That old bat was—is—my mother."

"Oops. Sorry." Sharla let out a nervous giggle then faced front once more. Several times over the next few minutes she giggled again, her face turning red.

The service moved forward as usual, though several of the locals—mostly the men—seemed intent on the new women. Not that Sharla and Cherry seemed to mind. They even winked at a couple of the fellas. Unfortunately, one of them happened to be Mr. Herridge, the local butcher, whose wife looked as if she might take off the ladies' heads at any moment.

By the time the final hymn was sung, Lottie felt as if they were all on display. And that feeling continued as the women convened in front of the church after service. Sharla and Cherry continued to giggle and say inappropriate things. Lottie squeezed her eyes shut and offered up a silent prayer that the local women would hold their peace.

Unfortunately, they did not. Mama pulled her aside for an earful.

Lottie listened for a few minutes but finally put her hand up. "Mama, wait. What are you saying? You think we were wrong to bring in actresses for the show? Is that it?"

"I never said that." Mama's lips pursed. "Though many have said far worse than that." She clucked her tongue. "Trust me when I say that tongues are wagging, and not in a good way. People are unhappy with the idea of so many single, unattached women roaming about."

"You make them sound like elk, Mama."

"You know what I mean. Everywhere you turn, there's another one. They've interrupted our quiet little town."

"But that was the idea. Estes Park has always been open to folks coming in from the outside. That's how most of our people make their living, catering to tourists and such."

"These ladies aren't tourists, Lottie." The pitch of her mother's voice elevated. "They're not here to contribute to the welfare of our community. That, I can assure you."

"Well, of course they are. They've come all this way just to make our little melodrama successful. That has to say something. And the ones I've taken the time to get to know are really great women, Mama. I think you would like them—especially some of the gals like Cornelia and Margaret—if you spent time talking to them."

"I don't believe I'll be getting to know the sort of women you've brought here this morning," her mother said. "And none of the other ladies in town are keen on the idea, either."

"But Mama…" Lottie felt a lump rise in her throat, which made conversation difficult. "That's—that's just silly."

"Not as silly as you think, Lottie. Folks are riled up."

"Why?" Now she managed to speak in spite of the lump. "What reason do they give for making such a fuss? What in the world have these new ladies done to create such a stir, after all?"

Her mother gestured to Shayla. "For one thing, it's how some of them dress. I'm all for finery, but the dress that one is wearing is entirely too revealing."

"I did notice that, of course." Lottie felt her face turn hot. "But, Mama, she knows no other way. She needs guidance."

"Guidance, my eye. She needs a good swift kick in the backside."

Before Lottie could respond, Althea Baker joined them, her face red.

"Did you see that one in the gray dress?" she whispered. She had the nerve to show her legs just now."

"Prudy?" Lottie could hardly believe this. Truly, there could only be one logical explanation. "She stepped into a mud puddle during our excursion up the mountain yesterday," she explained. "I'm sure she was just trying to share the story of how she got soaked in mud. That's all. Trust me, she would be the last person to deliberately try to entice men." Why, the very idea was preposterous.

Lottie's mother fanned herself. "Say what you will, a proper woman doesn't show her ankles in public, particularly in front of men. And I shudder to think of what went on up on the mountain yesterday, what with all those men and women traveling together unchaperoned."

"Unchaperoned?" Lottie bit back a laugh. "Mama, there were sixteen of us altogether. We traveled in a group."

"Humph."

"Mama..." Lottie's temper flared and she felt the heat set her ears aflame. "I have a difficult time understanding your treatment of these women. Aren't you the one who's always saying we should treat others the way we want to be treated?"

"Well, of course, but—"

"And as for the lipstick and such, plenty of women in Estes Park—you included—wear a bit of lipstick or rouge. I've never heard you complain about it before."

"All things in moderation, Lottie." Her mother continued to fan herself. "You can't tell me that you believe the amount of rouge on that one woman's face is acceptable. She's—she's painted herself so that the men will take notice. And they're taking notice, all right."

She spoke of Cherry, of course. No one could deny that the woman wore too much lipstick and rouge. But to point out such a thing right here on the church lawn? Why?

"I'm just saying, you're always telling me you want me to dress like a lady," Lottie said. "To put on dresses and such. I would think you'd be happy, Mama. I'm surrounded by fine ladies on every side. I've grown to care for them, and they for me."

"These women are anything but fine. They are what the Bible refers to as worldly."

"Worldly?" Lottie shook her head. "Now I'm really confused. Didn't you send Winifred off to Denver to experience the world? Wasn't that the sole purpose?"

"The Bible teaches us that there's a difference between being in the world and of the world," Mama said. "These women you brought to our fair town are *of* the world, not just in it."

"But, Mama, that's hardly a fair judgment call on your part. You don't even know them. You haven't given them a chance."

"I know everything I need to know. Did you see that one woman with the red dress?"

"Patricia?"

"Heavens, I don't know her name, and I don't care to. She was sidling up next to the mayor before church, making herself at home. His wife told me all about it during the opening hymn, and she wasn't smiling at the time, trust me. Women around here don't like the idea that female strangers are encroaching on their men."

"Encroaching? You make them sound like hunters."

"If the shoe fits." Her mother fussed with her belt. "Many are on the prowl even now."

Lottie felt her face grow warm again. "Patricia dropped her fan, and he reached to pick it up for her. I saw the whole thing."

"Likely she dropped the fan on purpose to get him to lean down and fetch it for her so that she could show off her—her... well, never mind all that. The whole thing was simply disgusting. Nelda Hennessey told me all about it. And what in the world was wrong with that one girl during the sermon? The one with the brown hair? I actually heard her crying. Crying. For everyone to hear."

"She was moved by the sermon, Mama."

"Moved? More likely she was coming under condemnation after hearing Reverend Brighton's message. Anyone with the decency to come to church needs to behave appropriately. You don't see me crying in church, do you?"

"No." Lottie sighed. *Me either. Though, I'm about to, if you don't stop this right now.* "Mama, I happen to know that Cornelia has been moved by the scenery on the mountain. God is using it to draw her to the faith she had as a child."

"I find it shocking that she's how old?—twenty-five, at least—and hasn't been to church since she was a child. That just tells you what kind of people we're dealing with here, Lottie."

"You can't blame them for that, Mama. Most of them weren't raised in church. They have no idea how to behave."

"What sort of person doesn't know how to behave in the house of the Lord?" Her mother crossed her arms.

"I'll tell you what kind." Althea Baker said. "A heathen. That's what you've brought to town for this theatrical of yours, Lottie. Heathen women."

Another rush of anger swept over Lottie. "No." She spoke with a trembling voice. "They're just wonderful women—loved by God—who don't understand the process of churchgoing."

Off in the distance, several of the ladies began to sing *Amazing Grace*. Lottie found it ironic, at best. Thank goodness they had no idea they were currently the topic of conversation. Otherwise they might've chosen a different song.

Mrs. Parker joined them at that very moment, her face lit with a smile. "That singing does a body good. Those sweet girls are such a blessing, aren't they? We're just so tickled to have them here."

Lottie's mother grumbled something under her breath.

"As I said, I've found them to be pure delight." Mrs. Parker's grin spoke of her feelings on the matter. "I've had such a wonderful time, getting to know them. And how fun to see all of them in church. What better place to share the love of the Lord?" Her eyes misted over and she dabbed at them with the back of her hand. "Sorry about that. I'm getting to be so emotional in my old age. But isn't it wonderful, seeing them seated together where they can hear the hymns and listen to a solid Bible lesson, one they're sure to remember for the rest of their days? What a blessing."

Althea shifted her position and placed her hands on her hips. "More like a curse."

Mrs. Parker's countenance changed at once. "Why, whatever do you mean?"

"You know perfectly well what I mean, Penelope. Those

girls have been sent here by the enemy to stir up trouble, just like Bathsheba was sent by the enemy to tempt King David."

"Actually, Bathsheba was minding her own business when David lusted after her," Mrs. Parker said. "So she certainly can't be blamed for his sin. And I can't imagine you—a wonderful, godly woman—would believe that these ladies are anything but a gift to our little community. Why, they're God's response to our prayers to save the lodge."

"You watch and see." Althea's eyes narrowed to slits. "They will bring division. The people will take sides for or against them."

Mrs. Parker looked stunned. "What sort of person could possibly take sides against them? Whatever have they done to deserve that?"

"I'll tell you what they've done." Althea proceeded to give Mrs. Parker a lengthy list. Lottie did her best to ignore the sarcasm in her voice.

When she ended, Mrs. Parker walked away, speechless.

Lottie's mother tugged on Lottie's shirtsleeve. "Lottie-Lou, don't dillydally. I've prepared lunch at home. I expect you to join us for a change."

"I have to hang the cast list on the door, Mama," she said. "We promised it would go up at noon, and it's only eleven-fifty. I have to wait until noon to post it, so please go on without me."

"Well, you do what you need to do. Althea and I have much to discuss before our meeting with the Women's League tomorrow."

"O-oh?"

"Yes." Mama clucked her tongue as she watched Fanny and Jeb Otis talking. "Indeed. We local women will need to band together to accomplish our goal, I believe." She muttered something under her breath then turned to resume her conversation with Althea.

With her nerves leading the way, Lottie walked toward the door of the church.

Mrs. Parker joined her in short order. "What in the world do you make of that?"

"They're opposed to the women coming to church." Lottie shook her head. "I can't make sense of it, to be honest. I thought the local folks would be thrilled to see the women in church, but I guess I was wrong."

"Well, if that doesn't beat all."

Seconds later, the women gathered around Lottie, most somber in appearance. She longed to say something encouraging but couldn't think of the right words.

Cherry sighed. "Lottie, I know your heart was in the right place, inviting us to your church and all—"

"But I don't believe any of us want to come back." This comment came from Prudy, who stood nearby with tears in her eyes. "You won't believe what a couple of the women said to me. And I was just trying to share the story of what happened to me up on the mountain yesterday."

"And you should've seen the look the mayor's wife gave me earlier." Patricia shivered. "All because I dropped my fan."

Lottie did her best not to sigh aloud. "I'm so sorry, ladies. I have no idea what happened here."

"What happened is that a bunch of holier-than-thou women made some assumptions about me," Patricia said. "About *us*. And they're not going to rest until they've either remodeled us or driven us out of town on a rail."

"Well, I certainly don't think it's that bad," Lottie said. "Honestly, I'm sure it can all be ironed out."

She tried to lace her words with confidence, but they came out shaky just the same. In fact, everything about today made her quiver. If this morning's church service was any indication of things to come, she'd be better off staying in bed with the covers pulled over her head.

* * * * *

GILBERT LISTENED FROM A SAFE distance as Lottie's mother ranted and raved. He could hardly believe the venom she spewed. He'd just about worked up the courage to approach her when his mother came up beside him.

"It's not worth it, son," she whispered.

He turned to face her, his hands trembling. "You heard them."

"Yes." She put her hand on her chest. "And frankly, I'm stunned. I knew that some of the women would be put off by a couple of the ladies, mostly Sharla and Patricia. Their dresses are a little, well, you know. But I figured the women of Estes Park were kindhearted enough and would keep in mind the Bible story the reverend used in his sermon today."

"Let him who is without sin cast the first stone," Gilbert said through clenched teeth.

"In this case, it would be 'Let *her* who is without sin,' but that just proves the point, doesn't it?" his mother said. "None of us is without sin. And I daresay, the anger we're feeling right now could lead to sinfulness on our part if we're not careful."

"Right now I don't want to be careful." Gilbert released a sigh, and part of his anger went with it. "But I will be. It's the right thing to do. Lord, help me guard my anger."

"He will help you, son." His mother patted his arm. "And in the meantime, you and Lottie have a lot to do. It's noon, you know."

"It is?" The church bells rang as if to answer his question, and he headed Lottie's way, a smile plastered on his face. No point in letting her know how upset he was. Not when they had so much left to do.

Moments later the two of them posted the cast list on the door of the church. Dozens of folks gathered around to see who got which part. The women edged their way to the front, Fanny leading the pack.

"What a madhouse," she hollered out above the crowd of would-be cast members.

A madhouse, indeed. Once the locals got involved, a group of nearly forty people pressed in to see the list. Some cheered, others just appeared a bit dazed. Gilbert looked on, a little overwhelmed.

"I've never even heard of half these character names, Lottie," Cornelia said. "Flossie must've changed the script completely."

Lottie's confident smile lifted Gilbert's spirits. "Yes, completely," she said. "But trust me when I say that Flossie and I came up with the perfect plan, and you're all in exactly the right parts."

"Still…" Cornelia's brow wrinkled. "I'm playing the part of Paige Turner?"

"And I'm Miss Bea Haven?" Cherry laughed. "Appropriate. All my life I've been accused of that very thing."

Gilbert kept his mouth shut. In light of what Lottie's mother had shared earlier, the folks in town saw Cherry as a loose woman. Perhaps giving her the part of Miss Bea Haven hadn't been the best idea on Lottie's part.

"I like my character's name too," Grace said. "And I'm so glad that you noted it's a dancing role. I can hardly wait."

"I can't believe I got the part of Miss Information," Hannah said and then laughed. "It's going to be so much fun."

"I think you'll enjoy that part," Lottie said. "Miss Information is always confused and passing on the incorrect information to people. It's a comedic role."

"I'm so glad you didn't give me a funny part," Prudy said, her voice low. "I prefer a small part like Shirley Knott."

"Oh, it's not a small part at all," Lottie explained. "In fact, Shirley Knott holds the key to solving the mystery in the show, so you'll play an important role." She turned to face the group. "You all will. It's going to be wonderful."

"So, let's see…" Margaret read the cast list aloud. "Grace is Jenna Rossity; Fanny is playing Alice Well. Jeb Otis is Abel N. Willin. I'm playing Penny Less. Sharla is Sarah Bellam, Patricia is Ellie Gant, Flossie is Sadie Word. Augie is Earl E. Bird, Chauncy is Hugh Dunnit, and Gilbert is Justin Credible." She listed the other character names, including the parts to be played by several of the local children and their parents.

Gilbert nodded, though he argued internally over Lottie's decision to put him in one of the larger roles. Still, what could he do about it now but play along?

And so, with the cast decided, there was only one thing left to do—get rehearsals under way and pray that the Women's League didn't butt their noses in where they didn't belong. With his heart in his throat, Gilbert decided that forging ahead was really their only solution.

TEN

A SITUATION AT THE STANLEY

Oscar Wilde once said that life imitates art. In an ironic twist of fate, we at Parker Lodge have witnessed this firsthand. Even as we prepare to dive into our first rehearsal, we've seen heroes and villains emerging, and not just the sort one might find on the stage. How will our story end? Well, stay tuned to find out! One thing is sure and certain— without a villain, the hero has nothing to overcome! And so we forge ahead, ready to prove that right overcomes might, David really does defeat Goliath, and a passel of females—out-of-towners, no less—truly have the interest of Estes Park at heart. Will you join us in our quest to right injustice, both onstage and off? —Your friends at Parker Lodge

ON MONDAY MORNING Lottie paced the lobby of Parker Lodge, her thoughts in a whirlwind. She turned to face Gilbert, her heart in her throat. "What can be done?"

"I don't know." Gil stopped his work of fixing the broken windowsill and faced her. "Are you absolutely sure you heard right? There's no doubt in your mind?"

"Oh, I heard right. Mama said the Women's League would be meeting at the restaurant in the Stanley Hotel at noon today to put an end to our theatrical once and for all." She took a strand of hair between her fingers and began to wind it around until it caused pain.

"But why? I just don't understand."

She could hardly stand the thought of sharing what she'd heard through Mama, but she had no choice. "Gil, brace yourself. I dread telling you what folks are saying, but you must know."

"I can take it. Just tell me."

"They're saying…" She squeezed her eyes shut and swallowed hard. "They're saying that Parker Lodge has turned into a—a…" She couldn't say the word.

"A theater?" He shifted the hammer from one hand to the other.

"No."

"A force to be reckoned with?"

"No."

"A pie parlor?" This time his voice cracked.

"N–no." She finally managed the rest. "A—a brothel."

"A what?" He stormed across the lobby, his face now red. "A—a…what?"

"You heard me, Gil. They think we've brought the women here for…well, for other purposes. Theatrics, yes, but not the kind on a stage." Speaking the words made her feel sick, inside and out.

"Tell me you're making that up." The hammer slipped out of his hand and landed with a crash on the wooden floor. "Tell me it's some sort of a line from the play or something."

"I–it's not." Her mother's words replayed in her mind. She couldn't stop them, no matter how hard she tried.

Gilbert swooped down and picked up the hammer, which he placed on the newly built windowsill. For a moment he said nothing.

"Are—are you all right?" she asked.

He turned to face her. "Of course I'm not all right. You're telling me that folks are calling my family's lodge a house of—of—"

"Ill repute." She shivered as her mother's words resurfaced.

"And how, pray tell, did they come to this conclusion?"

Lottie wanted to comfort him, wanted to throw her arms around his neck and whisper, "It's going to be all right" in his ear. Instead, she blew out a long breath and tried to still her racing heart. "Who knows what goes on in their minds? Mama said it was the only thing that made sense. I guess she got wind of the fact that some of the fellas are actually paying for the women's keep."

"The women's *keep*? Is that what she called it? The men are just chipping in for food and such. Nothing more."

"Well, of course," Lottie said. "You know that and I know that, but Mama and Althea Baker don't. I mean, I tried to explain it, but my words came out all jumbled. They had me so addlepated, I could hardly explain things in a sensible fashion."

"Lottie." He took her hand, looking her straight in the eye. "Are you sure you heard them say the word 'brothel'? Maybe you misunderstood. Maybe they said 'hostel.'"

Lottie shook her head. "I wouldn't make up something like this, Gil. Apparently yesterday morning after church, Althea Baker heard Jeb say something about how he's paying a heavy price to keep the women here. That's what got this rumor started."

Gilbert groaned and dropped her hand. "It's not like that."

"I know. I heard him say that he's selling Katie Sue to help out with the women's financial upkeep, and I understood what he meant, of course. But you'll never convince my mother or Althea. You know how they are. They believe what they want to believe, and I'm afraid it's too late to change their thinking now."

"Do you think Jeb caught on to their suspicions?"

"I'm sure he's oblivious, and that's a good thing. If he knew the Women's League suspected his...behavior...I think it would really hurt him."

Gilbert flinched. "Well, of course it would. Any of the fellas would be shaken by this. I can't even imagine what Phineas will do if he gets wind of it."

"I'm praying he doesn't."

"So, about the Women's League, what's their plan of action? What are they going to do with these suspicions of theirs?"

Oh, how she hated to share this next bit of news with him. And yet she must. "I heard Mama mention Althea's nephew, Thad. He's a highfalutin lawyer now, you know. Lives in Loveland."

"Well, yes, but..." Gilbert stiffened and his eyes grew wide. "Wait a minute. Why in heaven's name do they need a lawyer? If they're so sure we're running a brothel, why not go straight to the sheriff? If we were really guilty, he could come and arrest us and shut the whole place down. They have to know that."

"They know Sheriff Carnes would laugh them out of town, I guess. But Althea's figured out some legal angle to close down the show. Least, that's what Mama said." She released a sigh. "I don't know, Gil. I only know that everything is unraveling. It's going to be bad enough if the women hear about the accusations against them. If they find out there's a lawyer involved, we'll be up a creek without a paddle."

"Maybe." He picked up his hammer and took a few more swings at the windowsill. When he finally stopped, he lowered the hammer and glanced her way, a hopeful gleam in his eyes. "Maybe we'll just have to figure out a way to swim against the current."

"What do you mean?"

"We'll have to beat them at their own game. I'm not talking about letting things get ugly. Just saying we won't go down without a fight. But we'll have to be strategic. Ultimately, we don't just want to wins over the Women's League; we want to pray and ask the Lord what to do. He'll show us. Remember the story of David and the mighty Goliath."

"These women are a force to be reckoned with, for sure," Lottie agreed. "Who would've ever thought women could raise such a ruckus?"

Gilbert paused for a moment then snapped his fingers. "That's it, Lottie! You've given us the answer. We'll raise a ruckus by asking Augie to put articles in the paper. That's the answer."

"I don't understand."

"He can share our journey every step of the way. Put our story in print. We can also sneak bits of information into the handbills we place around town. We'll be like young David fighting the mighty warrior, only this time we'll be defending the honor of Parker Lodge. The honor of my family. What do you think of that?"

"I pray it works."

"It will, but you're right. We need to pray."

"I have been already," she said. "And I won't stop."

"Good. But we've got to figure out what to do about the ladies."

Gilbert's gaze narrowed. "You know what I think? I think those women in the League are jealous of them."

"Jealous?" The strangest shiver ran down Lottie's spine as she spoke the word.

"Yes, jealous of the out-of-town ladies. Most are young and pretty and very talented. They've swept into town, and the attentions of the men are turned to them."

"Well, maybe that's partly it," she said. "But they're also put off by how Sharla and Patricia dress and by how much makeup some of the ladies wear. Plus, too, you have to understand that there's a certain mystique about people in show business. These are theater women, you know. Mama thinks that women with worldly experience are…" She paused to choose the right words. "Well…"

"Loose?" The word came from behind Lottie. She turned to find Fanny standing there. "Is that what your mama thinks, Lottie? That Parker Lodge is overrun with loose women?"

Lottie sighed. "Yes. Unfortunately, yes."

"This is not the first time I've seen this sort of behavior," Fanny said with the wave of a hand. "And I'm sure it won't be the last."

"So what do we do about it?" Lottie asked. "How do we win them over? And why in the world would they see all of you as a threat, anyway?"

Fanny chuckled. "Oh, honey, you have a lot to learn."

"What do you mean?"

"Women are far more trusting of men than of other women. They see women—especially smart, younger, talented women—as competition."

"Competition?" Lottie paused. "I guess I see what you mean."

"This will blow over in time, I can assure you." Fanny's stomach rumbled. "Oh, that reminds me, I really came in here to ask you about lunch. Some of the women are wondering."

"Ah. We haven't approached Mama with the pie-parlor idea yet," Gilbert said, "so she's none the wiser. She's fixing sandwiches for lunch. They should be ready soon. But I'm afraid tonight she's preparing her pot roast and it's a bit, well..." He sighed.

"I see. Well, I'll tell the ladies to eat up at lunch," Fanny said. She wrinkled her nose. "When do you suppose Jeb will take over the cooking?"

"I don't know," Lottie said. "If he gets wind of what's been said about him, he's liable to stay away. All the men are."

"Over my empty stomach!" Fanny looked aghast. "You just leave it to me, sweet girl. I'll get that fella to do the cooking if it's the last thing I do."

Lottie nodded but was far too busy watching Gilbert as he headed off without saying good-bye.

Where are you going, Gilbert Parker? And why aren't you taking me with you?

* * * * *

GILBERT MADE THE WALK to town at double the usual speed. No time to dawdle, what with so much to do. Stopping by the *Mountaineer,* he shared his vision with Augie, who agreed to help and even came up with several article ideas on the spot.

After offering his thanks to his good friend, Gilbert decided to stop by the Stanley Hotel, knowing that the ladies from the Women's League were meeting for lunch. What he would say to them, he had no idea. Perhaps the Lord would give him the words in the moment. He would head off those judgmental ladies at the pass. Put them in their place. Perhaps, in doing so, he could tell Augie that the articles wouldn't be necessary.

As he walked, Gilbert thought through the situation from start to finish. Oh, how he hoped Jeb and the other men didn't catch wind of the latest gossip. Those poor fellas had already faced enough challenges in their lives. They didn't need the likes of Althea Baker coming after them. And Gilbert needed the men. They were now funding the show with their contributions, after all. With their current level of investment, he had to keep them happy.

Gilbert arrived at the Stanley Hotel at twelve forty-five. From the front lawn he gazed up at the magnificent white hotel—a true architectural wonder. The owner and proprietor, Freelan Stanley, stood on the elevated front porch talking to an older gentleman in a wicker chair. Gilbert made his way up the stairs, willing his racing heart to slow down. When he reached the porch, he waited until Mr. Stanley finished speaking with the hotel guest before clearing his throat.

"Mr. Stanley, sir."

Mr. Stanley turned his way and extended his hand. "Young Parker. How are you? What brings you into town? Lunching with us?"

"Hadn't planned on it. I just came by because..." Hmm. How did a fella go about saying that he came to talk some sense into unreasonable women? "I understand the Women's League is meeting here today."

"Ah." Mr. Stanley nodded. "I see. Yes. They arrived about an hour ago, looking quite determined. I didn't dare interrupt them, even with a friendly hello. They're meeting in the restaurant. Our chefs have prepared a wonderful salmon croquette, by the way. It's quite delicious."

It sounded delicious, of course, but all this chatter was slowing things down.

"You really should stay to lunch," the hotel owner urged. "The chef has been working all morning in preparation. My mouth has been watering for the past hour."

"I'll think about it. But, sir, I—"

"Please do. I'm nearly ready to eat lunch, as well. You'll join me as my guest." Mr. Stanley's conversation shifted to the weather and finally back to where they'd started. "Now, what about that lunch, young man? You getting hungry?"

"I'm starved, and lunch sounds wonderful. But before I can eat a bite, I have to see a woman—or rather, a room full of women—about a matter of some urgency."

The older man's brows elevated. "Well, you should have said so right away. Sounds intriguing. Do you need me to come along to protect you? I've seen that Women's League at work. They're quite formidable."

"They've met their match in me, sir."

Mr. Stanley laughed. "I do believe they have, young Parker. Well, get in there and give them what for. I'm not sure what they've done, but they'll undo it the moment they see the look of determination in your eye."

"I hope it's that easy."

As he entered the hotel, Gilbert glanced around the expansive foyer. Long, wide hallways with rich dark wood floors caught his eyes. A grand, sweeping staircase. Luxurious carpets. Quite a contrast to Parker Lodge.

He got a little turned around looking for the restaurant, what with so many guests coming and going on all sides. All around him, men, women, and children scurried to and fro. Gilbert couldn't squelch the feeling of envy rising up in him. When would Parker Lodge see this kind of patronage? Would guests ever show up, or would he and his mother lose everything they'd worked for?

He finally garnered up the courage to enter the dining hall, which he located to his left, just beyond the grand staircase. He would share his heart with these women once and for all. He would make them see the light.

Stepping inside the semidarkened room, he took a moment to allow his eyes to adjust. Though women abounded, none of them appeared to be familiar. Gilbert spoke with a waiter, who informed him that the Women's League had just ended their meeting and their members had left in a hurry. And in a bad mood, according to the waiter. So much for putting a stop to things. Looked like Augie would have to run those articles after all.

After telling Mr. Stanley that he wouldn't be able to stay for lunch, Gilbert made the lengthy walk back to the lodge, sharing his impassioned speech with the trees. Along the way, he passed Jeb and Phineas at the entrance to Jeb's property. He paused when they flagged him down.

"Fellas." He offered what he hoped would look like a confident smile, which neither man returned.

"Guess you heard what all's bein' said about us." Phineas's face grew tight.

"The lies those Women's League ladies have been spreadin' around town have ruined my reputation." Jeb kicked the dirt with the toe of his boot.

"You can't listen to 'em, fellas," Gilbert said. "You know that. And besides, Augie's going to run some pieces in the paper to let folks know what we're really up to."

"Cain't say as the women will believe it, even if they read it in the paper," Phineas said. "My sister stopped by this morning." He crossed his arms. "Nearly took my head off."

"And my mother is a member of that league." Jeb's gaze remained riveted to the toe of his boot. "She's forbidden me from participatin' in the melodrama."

"Your mother has forbidden you?" Gilbert didn't know whether to laugh or cry at this proclamation. Surely a man approaching fifty didn't need his mama's say-so to act in a play.

Jeb shrugged. "She's seventy-two years old. Do you think for one minute I'm gonna cross a seventy-two-year-old woman? Besides, you've never seen her when her temper gets to flarin'. It ain't purty. Let's just leave it at that."

"My sister's the same way," Phineas said. "This could get ugly quick, if we're not careful."

"So what are you fellas saying, exactly?" Gilbert asked. "Are you backing out?"

"Just sayin' we're not comin' to rehearsal until the stink dies down," Jeb said. "Don't want to risk it."

"Not coming?" Gilbert paused. "But how are we going to move forward without you?"

"We'll have to figure out some way to do this without folks talking."

"What difference does it make, really?" Gilbert asked. "They're just a bunch of women with nothing better to do than stir up trouble. You can either play into their hands or link arms with us and beat them at their own game."

This seemed to get the men's attention.

"Sounds like you've got some sort of plan," Jeb said. "Out with it."

"Come tonight and I'll explain."

"Just don't know that it's worth the risk," Phineas said again. "My sister tells me the Women's League has hired a lawyer."

"Let's not worry about legalities just yet," Gilbert said. "I feel sure that lawyer-talk is just a scare tactic anyway. We need to rest easy and keep moving forward with the show. You fellas want your investment to be secure, don't you?"

"Well, sure." Phineas's brow wrinkled. "Don't want to lose my money."

"Me neither," Jeb said, his expression somber. "Especially after, well…" He fell silent.

"Come to rehearsal tonight and let's get to work. We'll stick together and put on the best show this valley's ever seen."

Gilbert left the duo scratching their heads. Whether or not they would show up for tonight's rehearsal, well, that was yet to be seen. Until then, he could only pray that the Lord's will would be done, and that David wouldn't quiver too badly as he looked the mighty Goliath in the eye.

ELEVEN

TROUBLE BUBBLES AT BIG THOMPSON RIVER

Practice makes perfect—at least that's what we at Parker Lodge are counting on. As we set out to rehearse our upcoming theatrical, which Mrs. Parker has taken to calling Trouble Bubbles at Big Thompson River, *we are assured of two things: 1) anything that's worth doing is worth doing well, and 2) working together as a family is the only way to get the job done. So, let trouble bubble. With our arms tightly linked, we will forge ahead, ready and willing to meet all challenges so that our patrons can experience the best possible show.*
—Your friends at Parker Lodge

On Monday evening at ten minutes till seven, Lottie whispered a silent prayer for the Lord's favor then carried her script into the dining hall at Parker Lodge to set up for their first melodrama rehearsal. Until the very last moment, she didn't know for sure if the men would come.

Chauncy showed up first, God bless him, followed shortly by Augie, who seemed more enamored with the ladies than bothered by the latest gossip in town. As usual, he wore his finest clothes and had even waxed his mustache for the occasion. He looked the part of Earl E. Bird, the show's notorious villain, no doubt about it. Well, except for the huge smile on his face every time he glanced at a couple of the ladies.

Not that all of them had smiles on their faces. Fanny and several of the others still grumbled about the pot roast they'd eaten—er, tried to eat—for dinner. Lottie didn't blame them for voicing their complaints aloud. Maybe, if all went well tonight, she could ask Jeb about taking over as chef. If he showed up for rehearsal, anyway.

A couple of minutes after seven, he eased his way through the back door. Lottie gave him a warm hug and thanked him for coming. Phineas arrived moments later, hair combed, face shaved, and wearing what appeared to be a new shirt. He slipped in through the kitchen. Lottie appreciated the men being extra careful. With all the scuttlebutt from the ladies in the Women's League, no doubt they felt put on the spot.

She flashed a reassuring smile at the fellas then turned her attention to the whole group. "Folks, I'm so glad you're here tonight. We've had a rough day, as many of you have heard. I hesitate to mention it, but I'm of the opinion that we should keep things out in the open. There appears to be some opposition to our melodrama, but I feel sure things will quiet down shortly. We have to keep forging ahead, focusing on the task set before us. Agreed?"

Several of the ladies hollered out, "Agreed!" but Phineas and Jeb did not. In fact, they scooted down in their chairs and looked more concerned than ever.

From a chair at the front of the room, Fanny waved her hand.

"Lottie, before we start, there's something I'd like to say. I believe I speak on behalf of most of our cast members." She rose and turned to face Gilbert, who sat nearby. "Young man, I know you probably aren't keen on all of us knowing your family's business."

Gilbert squirmed in his chair.

"I don't mean to put you or your mother on display or bring you any kind of embarrassment, but I've noticed that you don't have a lot of customers around here. I want to do something about that. Now, I can't speak for the other ladies, but as for me, I'm going to do everything I can not just to save this show, but to save your family's lodge as well. If it means staying up all night sewing costumes. If it means spending all my free hours building the set. If it means working round the clock with the fellas so that they can memorize their lines…whatever it takes. I'm in."

"Me too," Margaret chimed in from behind her.

"Count me in," Cornelia said.

"I've always loved a challenge," Cherry added.

Gilbert looked on, red-faced but smiling.

One by one the women added their names to the list. They would merge forces and put on the best show in town…or they would die trying.

Though grateful for their dedication, Lottie certainly hoped it was the former and not the latter. She also hoped the men would add their voices to the fray. For now, at least two of them seemed more likely to bolt than to commit to linking arms with the ladies.

When they finished, Gilbert rose and gave them a nod. "Ladies, I can't tell you how grateful I am. I only wish my father could've been here to see such a display of support." He paused and cleared his throat. "Thank you for your patience with us as we move forward. This melodrama is a first for us, so we're breaking new ground."

"And we're thrilled to have your support," Lottie added, her heart now soaring. She shifted gears and moved into the rehearsal time. The cast members gathered around the tables in the dining hall for what Flossie called a roundtable reading—a straight read-through of the script from start to finish.

Most of the ladies took to their new roles with little trouble, but several of the fellas stumbled a bit. Perhaps their acting skills were better suited off the stage than on.

Still, how wonderful to hear them read through the whole script—that funny, melodramatic script. God bless Flossie and Fanny for their hard work in coming up with it all. Now, if only the set and costumes would come together as easily. For now, Lottie would take what she could get, and an excellent first rehearsal went a long way in lifting her spirits.

The evening ended on a high note. Literally. Cornelia rehearsed her solo, an operatic number that Flossie and Fanny had come up with that was sure to please the crowd. By the time they parted ways, even Phineas and Jeb were in good spirits. And when Fanny and Jeb lingered in the doorway to say their good nights, Lottie had her first real glimmer of hope that the ladies might, indeed, fall for the men. A few of them, anyway. Not that any of the women had figured out the real reason the fellas had brought them to Estes Park. Oh no. Phineas and the others would go to their graves with that secret. Still, with Jeb looking so nice in that starched blue shirt, Fanny appeared to be smitten.

Instead of going straight home after rehearsal, Lottie headed to the kitchen to put together a midnight snack for the ladies. By eleven forty-five, all but Prudy and Cornelia were assembled at the large kitchen table to eat the cold cuts, cheese, and bread Lottie had prepared.

Fanny tugged at the sash on her robe. "I don't know about the rest of you, but I'm starving. Ravenous, in fact."

"Don't you think Mrs. Parker will find out we've done this?" Sharla asked.

"Not if we clean up after ourselves."

"She's going to notice the missing food." Cherry reached for a couple of slices of bread and began to load them with ham and cheese.

"Nope." Lottie reached for the fork to jab a piece of ham. "Gil picked up the food in town this afternoon on the sly." She didn't tell them what a sacrifice it had been for him to come up with the extra money. For now, they would simply enjoy the feast set before them. "I'm only sorry you ladies have to eat so late at night."

"Oh, don't worry about that." With the wave of a hand, Fanny dismissed her concerns. "I've been a member of dozens of midnight supper clubs over the years."

"Me too," Patricia said.

"And me." Grace took a tiny sliver of meat and the smallest slice of cheese.

"Midnight supper club?" Lottie glanced at the ladies, confused by the expression. "What's that?"

Fanny slapped together her sandwich then took a big bite. She spoke around the mouthful of food. "Folks in the theater are accustomed to eating late, Lottie." She swallowed then took a drink from her glass of milk. "Think about it. Most of us are in the theater until eleven at night."

"Or later," Flossie said. "By the time we get out of our costumes and makeup, it can be midnight or after."

"Hence the name midnight supper club." Fanny took another bite, a contented expression settling over her. "Some of the best restaurants in New York stay open way past the middle of the night."

"Atlantic City too," Flossie added.

"I can't even imagine such a thing," Lottie said. "Here in Estes Park, our businesses close in the late afternoon or early evening. There's not a restaurant in town that stays open past nine o'clock. Well, unless you count the saloon. And they don't serve food."

"We had the yummiest delicatessen just a block or so from the theater where I performed in my last show." Cherry sighed. "They had the best pork tenderloin sandwiches in town. So my friends from whatever show I happened to be working on would head over there every night after the curtain closed." She licked her lips. "I still say midnight suppers are best." Another bite of her sandwich brought a look of sheer delight to her face.

Grace lifted her sandwich for a bite. "So you see why the late night hours don't bother us."

"Food is food, no matter when it's eaten." Flossie lopped a dollop of mayonnaise onto her bread.

"Still, I do hope Jeb will agree to act as chef so we don't have to keep these late hours going," Lottie said. "You ladies might be used to it, but I'm not."

"What's going to happen with Jeb?" Flossie asked. "Do you think he'll take on the job of chef once the rumors die down?"

"Oh, I think he will." Fanny offered a suspicious grin. The ladies turned her way and she shrugged. "What? I'm just saying that a woman's gotta do what a woman's gotta do to get a good meal. And if it means whispering a few sweet nothings in a man's ear, well, then, so be it."

"Fanny!" Flossie plopped her bread down on a plate, which clattered against the table. "Tell me you're not flirting with a man to get food out of him."

Fanny shrugged. "I'd probably flirt with him anyway. That Jeb is one handsome hunka beef, isn't he?" She giggled, and before long the women joined her. Well, all but Lottie, who couldn't get over Fanny calling Jeb a hunk of beef.

"I just hope he doesn't pay much attention to those Women's League ladies." Sharla's nose wrinkled. "If we have to wait for those biddies to stop gossiping before we can eat a hearty home-cooked meal, we're going to starve." She glanced at Patricia and Cherry. "We all know that women like that thrive on gossip."

Lottie did her best to turn the conversation around. No point in letting it slide into negative chatter about the townspeople. Besides, with their stomachs full and a great evening of rehearsal behind them, the days ahead looked sunnier than ever.

* * * * *

THE NEXT MORNING Lottie met with Gilbert's mother in the kitchen to broach the subject of the pie parlor. She found Mrs. Parker with a broom in hand, sweeping under the table.

"Strangest thing," the older woman said. "I found bread crumbs on the floor this morning. And there was a slice of cheese under the table."

"O–oh?" Lottie reached for the dustpan and held it in place as Mrs. Parker swept the crumbs into it. "Odd." She didn't say more. Instead, she took the dustpan to the trash bin and emptied it.

Mrs. Parker put the broom aside and washed her hands at the sink. "If I didn't know any better, I'd say that son of mine is getting into my food after hours."

"Well, he is a growing boy." Lottie gave her what she hoped would look like a convincing smile as she put the dustpan away.

"Someone talking about me in here?" Gilbert entered the room and reached for a biscuit from the tray.

His mother slapped his hand. "After you got into my food last night, you don't need any breakfast."

"W–what?" His mouth dropped open.

Lottie gave him a wide-eyed stare and hoped he would take the hint. "I told her you were a growing boy," she said.

Mrs. Parker laughed. "Remember when you were fourteen? You used to sneak into the kitchen every night for food."

Lottie suspected that had little to do with a growth spurt and everything to do with his mother's poor cooking skills. Still, she didn't say anything.

"I've always enjoyed raiding the pantry." He kept a straight face as he grabbed a biscuit and took a bite.

"Well, guard yourself," his mother said. "Remember, we're feeding a group now. We need to hang onto every bit of food we can."

He raised his hand—the one with the partially eaten biscuit—

as if taking an oath. "Mama, I can promise you I will not return to your kitchen in the middle of the night to steal your food."

Lottie bit back the laugh that threatened to bubble up. No, indeed, he would not. He wouldn't dare show up with so many ladies in their robes and slippers.

As she prepared gravy for the biscuits, Mrs. Parker began to hum "'Tis So Sweet to Trust in Jesus," and before long Gilbert was singing along. Lottie would've joined them, but her singing skills left something to be desired.

"Mrs. Parker," she said after the song ended, "I want to mention something to you that one of the ladies suggested."

Gilbert's mother turned her way. "What is it, Lottie?"

"The day the ladies arrived, you made a chocolate pie."

"Yes." Mrs. Parker smiled. "And I plan to make coconut tonight."

"Fanny will be delighted. She fell in love with your pie. She's been singing your praises ever since."

Mrs. Parker's cheeks turned the loveliest shade of pink. "Well, isn't that nice. I've often heard that my pies are quite tasty, especially the chocolate and my special coconut recipe. Oh, and my apple. I do believe it's my favorite. Next to the peach, of course…when peaches are in season."

Lottie whispered a prayer for God's help before plowing ahead. "Fanny had a great idea," she said at last. "She thinks we should start a pie parlor."

"Pie parlor?" Mrs. Parker's brow wrinkled. She gave the gravy another stir. "What's that?"

Lottie shot Gil a frantic look and he nodded, ready to take the conversation from here.

* * * * *

GILBERT SWALLOWED the last of his biscuit and joined the conversation. "It's a bakery of sorts, Mama. One where you could sell your pies to locals and tourists. Fanny came up with the idea. Parker's Pie Parlor. Don't you love it?"

"Well, yes. And I love the idea of spending my days baking, of course. But how can we run a pie parlor and feed all these women at the same time? I'm already swamped with work here at the lodge, not to mention the hours I spend in the kitchen."

Gilbert made sure the tone of his voice remained positive and upbeat as he shared the plan, one with more than a few ulterior motives. "Ah, well, we've been thinking about that too. Because you're truly the only person we know whose baking skills rise above the others—pun intended—and we feel as if it makes more sense for you to take on that task as the head baker."

"Well, yes, but what about the meals? They are—"

"Exhausting you," Gilbert threw in.

"True." Mrs. Parker sighed.

"Now, hold onto your hat, Mama," Gilbert said. "You might be surprised when you hear who wants to take over the cooking. Jeb Otis."

She clasped her hands together. "Merciful heavens, what a brilliant idea. I've been after that man for years to help me out in the kitchen."

"You—you have?" He could hardly believe it.

"Yes. Have you ever tasted his potato salad?"

"Last Saturday, in fact."

"He's got a talent, that one. And he knows it. We've spoken about it, of course. But to think that he would take the time to prepare meals so that I could bake pies…what a wonderful gesture of kindness on his part." She snapped her fingers. "I know! The first pie I bake I can give to Jeb as a thank-you for his kindness."

"Perfect." Gilbert beamed.

"I do love baking." She grinned. "And I have often thought how fine it would be to spend more time doing it." Her grin disappeared. "Though, I must say, it's hard work. Hope I'm up for it."

"How would you like to have a helper?" Lottie asked. "Hannah has told us that she loves to bake as well. From what I can gather, she's quite proficient at it."

Gilbert didn't think the joy on his mother's face could grow any more animated, but she proved him wrong. "I believe we could make that work."

He laughed. "You're not worried about her compulsion with cleanliness? Baking is messy business, and she's liable to get discombobulated when the flour starts flying."

"Surely we can get beyond that." With the wave of a hand, his mother dismissed that idea. "We'll get along just fine, mess or no mess. Send her my way and I'll put her to work." She poured the gravy from the pan into a large bowl.

Lottie helped prepare the tray of biscuits. "Speaking of work, several of the women have agreed to take turns tending to the rooms and doing laundry. Fanny and Flossie couldn't wait to volunteer."

Gilbert didn't add the real reason for Fanny's willingness to do laundry. She promised to do so only if Jeb agreed to cook her meals.

"Where will we put the pie parlor?" his mother asked. "Do we really have the space?"

"I had an idea about that," Gilbert said. "Our lobby is double the size it needs to be. Much of it is wasted space. How would you feel if we added a glass case where you could place the pies on display? That way they would be the first thing folks saw when they came in the door."

"Sounds wonderful. People are won over by what they see and smell," Mrs. Parker said. "I'll make sure the aromas get them when they walk in the door. And a glass case to display the pies would be perfect." She reached for her apron and slipped it on. "Why are we standing around here talking? I have a lot of baking to do." She headed to the other side of the kitchen, talking to herself about pie recipes.

"We completely forgot to tell her about the recipe contest," Gilbert said. "And about naming some of the pies after the characters in the play."

Lottie grinned and her green eyes took to sparkling, something he couldn't help but notice. "Oh well. The day is young. I'm just relieved she didn't mind Jeb doing the cooking."

"Same here."

Lottie sighed. "Gil, I hate to admit I'm envious of you, but I am. Your mom is so understanding."

"She is, for sure." He couldn't help but agree.

"I love my mama," Lottie said, "but there are times when she makes me feel like—like…"

"Like what, Lottie?" He leaned in close to her, overwhelmed with compassion when he saw the sadness in her eyes.

"Like a misfit." Lottie's eyes misted over. "Now that Winnie has gone to Denver, Mama's sole focus is on me."

He reached for Lottie's hand. "That's a good thing, right? I mean, all these years you've pined for her attention. She doted on Winnie."

"I thought I would enjoy it, but I don't. She's after me to

change—in every conceivable way. The way I dress, the way I wear my hair…everything."

Gilbert gave her hand a squeeze. "In spite of all the teasing you receive, I think you're wonderful just like you are." He meant it. Every word.

"I—well, I guess she wants to turn me into a lady instead of a tomboy."

He chuckled. "Ah. Sounds like she's been listening to Phineas and the others. Well, don't change too much, Lottie. I might not recognize you."

"As if I could change that much." She paused to think through her mother's words. "She's not keen on my overalls and my short hair. She says I'll never find a husband." She clasped a hand over her mouth. "I can't believe I said that out loud."

Gil chuckled again. "Lottie, you're beautiful. You always have been. You'll have no trouble finding a husband, trust me." He winked. "I'm sure Jeb or any one of those other fellas would marry you in a heartbeat."

"W–what?" She pulled her hand away and her eyes grew wide.

Gil couldn't help but laugh. "Oh, the look on your face! I wish I had a photograph. It's priceless."

"Well—you—but—you said—and it was so—"

"Rude." He grinned, but just as quickly feelings of shame washed over him. "I was just teasing, Lottie. About the fellas, I mean. Truth be told, I'm a little worried that some fella is going to sweep in here and steal you away. Then what will I do?" He suddenly felt sad—genuinely sad. "Promise me you'll never leave Estes Park."

"I—I can't promise that."

"Are you saying you're thinking of going...like your sister?" Panic wriggled its way down his spine at the very idea.

"Well, no, but if Mama says I should stay with Winifred in Denver next spring, what choice will I have?"

"All the choice in the world. Talk to your pa. He'll understand. He's a rational man. You can't go anywhere, Lottie. I—I need you." More than he dared say. "This whole melodrama thing is more than I can handle on my own. And now the pie parlor...it's going to be a lot of work."

"I'm sure it will pay off in the end. It's going to be great, Gil. And your mama was beside herself. Did you see the smile on her face?"

"I did."

"It's funny that she accused you of eating in her kitchen last night." Lottie giggled.

He lowered his voice and leaned in to whisper, "Speaking of which, do you think she's on to us? Do you think she realizes what we're really up to here?"

Lottie drew so close, he could feel her breath warm on his cheek. "I don't know," she whispered in response. "But we'd better be careful. And sneaky."

"Sneaky." He stared into Lottie's beautiful face, his heart now thumping madly. "Yes. Sneaky."

In that moment, Gilbert Parker was struck with the craziest notion. Where it came from, he couldn't say. But the closer he drew to Lottie's face, the more the idea latched on. Finally unable to control the incessant pounding in his heart, he did the only thing that made sense under the circumstances.

He kissed her.

TWELVE

A Love to Die For

All over town, folks are coming up with suggestions for titles for the upcoming melodrama. So far we've heard from several of our local men with titles like Chaos Behind the Curtain *and* Egg on His Face in Estes. *Nice try, fellas, but our story has a strong romantic thread, so we're hoping for something the ladies will appreciate too. Our world-famous actresses are trying their hands at the title. Just yesterday Fanny McAlister suggested* A Love to Die For. *We will continue to ponder this title—and many more—as the rehearsals continue. In the meantime, grab your sweetie and c'mon out to Parker Lodge, where you can enjoy a home-cooked meal from our new chef, Jeb Otis.*
—Your friends at Parker Lodge

GILBERT TOOK A GIANT STEP back from Lottie, stunned at what he'd just done. Stunned, and a little horrified. Whatever had possessed him?

Lottie stepped back as well, her loose blond curls framing her now-red cheeks. "G–Gil?" Her giggles filled the room. She said his name again, a smile lighting her face.

"Lottie, I…" He tried to make sense out of what had just

happened. He'd never before thought about kissing her. He'd been swept away by some unseen force, no doubt. But what could he do about it now? "I'm so sorry."

"S–sorry?" The smile on her face faded at once. "You're sorry?"

"Well, you know what I mean. I shouldn't have done that. I—I didn't plan it."

"Of course you didn't." She giggled and leaned in to whisper in his ear, "That's what makes it all so lovely."

"Still, I…" He stopped talking when his mother entered the room, singing "A Mighty Fortress Is Our God." She stopped cold when she saw them. "Well, what have we here? Are you two in cahoots against me or something?"

"W–what?" Gilbert took a step back. "No. Of course not."

She gave them a strange look. "I leave the room for a minute and you take to whispering?"

No point in arousing suspicions. Things were awkward enough already. "Oh, we were just talking."

"Mm-hmm." She pointed at Lottie. "That would explain why she's blushing."

"Am I?" Lottie felt her cheeks and smiled. "Is it warm in here?"

"Could be." Gilbert's mother grinned. "Someone turn on the oven while I was out? I get the feeling the temperature went up while I was away."

"I—I don't think so." Gilbert shrugged and tried to play innocent. Oh, how he longed to back up the clock, to make the last two minutes of his life go away. In one fell swoop, his emotions had gotten the better of him and he'd managed to confuse both Lottie and his mother. Not that he could do anything about it now.

"Well, I guess I'd better get to work." He led the way out of the room and Lottie followed closely behind. She reached to slip her fingers through his, and he struggled to know what to do to discourage her without hurting her feelings. Turning to face her, he released a slow breath. "I'm really sorry about what just happened, Lottie."

"You are?" Wrinkles appeared around her beautiful green eyes.

"Yes. No. I mean, do you understand what I'm saying?" He didn't want to hurt her feelings, of course, but he needed time to think things through.

Apparently so did Lottie. She turned on her heel and ran toward the door, muttering something about how she needed to go home to fetch her script. Why she needed her script at seven thirty in the morning was beyond him. Unless perhaps it contained some sort of clue for what was coming next. Right now...well, right now he had absolutely no idea where things were headed.

* * * * *

LOTTIE RAN ALL THE WAY HOME, her heart in her throat. Her emotions vacillated between extreme joy and genuine confusion. When she reached the road leading to her house, she paused for breath. Turning in silly circles, she chanted, "He kissed me... he kissed me!"

Her thoughts rushed backward to that moment, that glorious moment. In that instant, as his lips touched hers, everything she'd longed for, every dream she'd dreamed, every daisy petal she'd plucked, was fulfilled.

But why had he apologized? Was he sorry he'd kissed her, or just embarrassed?

Surely just embarrassed.

Oh, but how wonderful that moment had been! How unexpected. How totally blissful. In all the years she'd dreamed of their first kiss, it had never been so perfect. She giggled, realizing he'd kissed her in his mother's kitchen. As she relived the moment once again, she picked up her pace and tried to figure out why, for the life of her, she'd made such a mad dash for home. Wouldn't it make more sense to go back and kiss him again?

Laughter wriggled its way out once more as she imagined what that would be like and how, from this point on, she would be able to kiss him again and again.

By the time she reached the house, Lottie had forced herself to calm down. No point in arousing suspicions with Mama. No doubt she would have enough to say even without this latest news.

Sure enough, her mother met her in the front hall, her brow wrinkled. "Lottie? I thought you were working today."

"I am, Mama, but I realized I left my script at home."

Her mother studied herself in the front hall mirror as she donned a green satin hat. "I thought rehearsals were at night. Why rush home now?" She tied the hat sash then glanced Lottie's way.

Lottie did her best to still her racing heart. "Oh, well, there's a lot to do today and I was afraid I'd forget. Decided I'd better get the script before the ladies finished their breakfast." She forced a smile.

"The ladies. Humph."

Lottie cringed. She hadn't counted on another nasty encounter with Mama, not on a day when she'd just been kissed. She'd rather grab her mother by the hand, tell her the good news, then dance around the foyer together in celebration of the fact that, finally, Gilbert Parker had come to his senses.

Not that Mama would consider it good news. Her view of the Parkers had clearly changed now that the actresses had arrived.

"Lottie, I asked you a question." Her mother's voice interrupted her thoughts.

"I'm sorry, Mama. I was lost in my thoughts."

"Yes, I can see that. But it's an important question, one that warrants an answer. I have a right to know—what goes on over there at that lodge?"

"What goes on?" She raked her fingers through her curls. "What do you mean?"

"You know perfectly well what I mean." Her mother's stern gaze in the mirror did nothing to control Lottie's nerves.

"Mama, I don't. If you mean how do I spend my days, I spend them working." *When I'm not kissing Gilbert Parker.* "I help Mrs. Parker tend to the rooms and do the laundry. I also work with Flossie—a really nice lady from Atlantic City who's helped me a lot with the melodrama script. In the evenings, of course, we have rehearsals. I'm directing the play."

"So you've said." Her mother gave her hat a satisfied pat. "But I sense there's more to your story."

"More to my story?"

Her mother turned to face her. "Lottie, it's time to tell me the truth. I deserve to know what's really happening over there."

"I–I've told you the truth—as much as I know of it, anyway." *Well, except the part about being kissed, but this probably isn't the time.*

"You don't find it suspicious that nearly a dozen women were brought into town and have been boarded in the same place for an extended period of time? You don't find it equally as odd that the town's men are suddenly making daily trips over to the lodge to visit these women?"

Lottie felt the blood drain from her face. "Mama!" She eased her way into the large, overstuffed chair. "Mama, the things that you and Mrs. Baker have implied about those wonderful ladies…it's awful. You must know how wrong you are."

"What's *wrong* is their actions," her mother said. "And that's why the Women's League plans to see it stopped. We won't rest until those ladies head back out of town where they belong."

"But, Mama! You have to realize how important this show is to the Parker family. They're…" She wanted to add "in bad shape financially" but didn't want to give her mother more to gossip about. Looked like she had plenty already.

"I wish you would just forget about that play, Lottie-Lou," her mother said. "It pains me to see my daughter link arms with people of ill repute. No telling what sort of evil behaviors will rub off on you."

Lottie gazed at her mother, astounded. "That's the most ridiculous thing I've ever heard. And they're not women of ill repute. Why, many of those ladies are the finest, kindest people I've ever met."

Her mother muttered something under her breath. "If I thought your father would back me up, I would insist you stop working with that Parker family until they've shut down that—that…" She released a breath. "Anyway, until those women have packed their bags and vacated the premises."

All the joy of the morning fizzled out of Lottie as she stared into her mother's angry eyes. Funny how one person could change her mood so drastically.

"I have to get my script, Mama." She turned toward the stairs.

"Althea and I are meeting for breakfast at the Elkhorn, so I won't be here when you come back down," her mother said. "Her nephew is due to arrive later today, and we have a lot to discuss."

"I see."

Just two words, but they were all Lottie could muster.

She trudged up the stairs, her heart as heavy as lead. She felt the sting of tears but brushed them away. Nothing—not even Mama—could ruin a morning as lovely as this one.

Moments later, with script in hand, she headed back down the stairs. True to her word, Mama had disappeared. Not that Lottie minded. She didn't have it in her to face another confrontation. When she saw her father on the front porch, she cringed. Would he scold her as well?

No, in his usual fashion, he swept her into his arms and planted a kiss in her curls. "Well, g'mornin' Lottie-Lou. I thought you were working over at the lodge today."

"I am. I'm headed back there now." She held up her script. "Just had to come home to fetch this."

"Ah. I see." His eyebrows elevated in mock villainous style. "The infamous melodrama." A chuckle followed. "Ironic, isn't it?"

"What?"

"That you're directing a melodrama for the stage while your mama and Althea Baker have decided to write a real-life one."

"The mess with the Women's League, you mean?"

"Is there anything else?" He grinned. "Don't worry, sweet stuff. This will blow over. I feel sure of it."

"Mama's really gone overboard this time, Pa. Have you heard what she's saying about the women staying at the lodge? She's stirred up a lot of trouble, and none of it is true."

"I've heard." He squared his shoulders. "And trust me, I've done my part to convince her she's wrong, but she won't hear of it. You know how she is when she gets her mind made up. To her way of thinking, the whole thing smells of sin and corruption."

Lottie shook her head. "How did it come to this? We just wanted to have a simple little theatrical to raise money for the lodge. Bringing in real actresses seemed like a magnificent idea at the time, and I have to say I'm more convinced now than ever. I wish you could've seen them at rehearsal last night, Pa. They're amazing. So good that they almost make the fellas look like they can act too." She gave a nervous laugh. "Almost. Anyway, we're blessed to have them."

"No doubt." He turned to wave at Dave, the ranch's foreman. "Though, I can't believe they stayed after getting such a cold reception at church yesterday."

"Not only have they decided to stay, they know about the Parkers' financial woes and want to do all they can to help." Lottie's eyes misted over. "See what I mean? They're such wonderful women, and they're being unfairly judged."

"Sounds like it," he said. "But let's go back to what you said about the Parkers' financial woes." He paused and gave her a penetrating gaze. "They're really in trouble?"

"Yes, Pa. It's been a struggle since Mr. Parker passed away. Keeping the lodge open, I mean."

He headed toward Dave, who continued to wave from the east pasture. "It will kill Gilbert to have to shut that place down. It was his father's dream for as long as I can remember."

Lottie followed on her father's heels. "Yes, I know. And that's why I've been working so hard to help them come up with ways to bring in money. Don't you see? When they hurt, I hurt." She paused. "I hope you don't misunderstand what I'm about to say, but I almost look at the Parkers as family. Now that Winifred is gone to Denver, I find myself more and more drawn to Gilbert's family. I mean you and Mama no disrespect. Honest and true. But I enjoy—"

"Helping folks out." Her father slipped his arm over her shoulders. "That's such an admirable trait, Lottie-Lou. Have I told you how very proud I am?"

"Yes." She smiled. "But would you mind telling Mama? She thinks I'm a—a..."

"A what?"

Lottie wanted to use the word *madame* but didn't dare. "A person who brought unsavory women to town," she said at last. *And if she knew I let Gilbert kiss me, she'd probably question my reputation even more.*

Her father slowed his pace. "Honey, I'm sure the Lord will show us His true purpose for those women being in Estes Park. I feel pretty sure it has nothing to do with a play. If what Phineas and some of the other men have said is true, they're here as potential brides. You know he's been calling them *wedding belles*, don't you?"

Lottie gasped, horrified at what he'd heard. "Pa, it's not really like that. I mean, it sort of is, but not really. The fellas thought maybe if they brought women to town, some of them might end up finding brides in the batch, but it's not like these are arranged marriages or anything like that. I'm no marriage broker, trust me. If I were, I would've landed myself a husband by now."

He chuckled. "Don't go marrying yourself off. I've already lost one daughter to Denver. Don't want to lose my last remaining child to a husband. Not just yet, anyway."

He continued walking and Lottie trudged along behind him. "Pa, can I ask you a question?"

"Sure." He flung open the gate to the pasture and stepped inside. "What do you need to know?"

"Are you ashamed of me?"

"Ashamed?" He glanced her way, eyes wide. "Whatever makes you ask a question like that, Lottie?"

She stepped inside the gate and he closed it behind them. "I don't know. I just wonder if you think I'm an embarrassment to the family in some way."

"I could never be embarrassed by you. You're my little girl. I'm proud of you."

"Wish everyone felt that way," she mumbled.

Her father grabbed his gloves from a nearby fence post then pressed them on and gestured to Dave, who worked just a few yards away, branding the cows. The stark smell of burning flesh permeated the air as, one by one, the hot brand hit the backside of each animal.

She remained rooted in place as her father joined Dave. "What do you think of the new brand, sweet stuff?" her father called out from the corral. He pointed to the brand on a cow's rump. "We're expanding the business, so we need a newer, more modern brand.

Folks from here to Texas will know they're eating Sanders' beef."
A broad smile followed.

"That's nice, Pa." She sighed. Clearly, he didn't get the point, or
he wouldn't be talking about cows right now.

Her gaze landed on a cow with a brown patch across its left side.
Something about it gave her reason to pause. She squinted, trying to
figure out why she suddenly felt ill at ease looking at it.

The cow let out a somber *moo,* and she reached over the side of
the corral to pat her on the side. "Don't worry, old girl. You'll be in
Texas soon, served up as a steak on some cowboy's table. All of this
will just be a distant memory."

Another moo came from the cow.

"I know, I know. Well, look on the bright side—Texas is much
warmer in the winter than Colorado. And who knows, maybe I'll
end up going with you."

Yes, a trip to Texas sounded mighty good right about now.
Mighty good. In Texas, no one suspected her of being a woman of
ill repute. No, in Texas, folks were kind and courteous to strangers,
unlike the ladies from the Estes Park Women's League.

Then again, if she went to Texas, she wouldn't be able to kiss
Gilbert Parker. Well, that settled it. She would stay in Estes Park.

"Guess I'd better be going, Pa."

"Keep a stiff upper lip, Lottie," he said and then turned back to
his work.

She gave the cow one last glance, a niggling fear setting in.
Even in a field with dozens of cows milling about, something about
this one tugged at her heart. After a moment of pondering, she
realized why.

"Oh, no!" She turned to her father and pointed at the cow, horrified by her revelation. "Pa? Is that...?"

He nodded. "Yes, sweet stuff, it is. But I paid a fair price for her, and Jeb really sounded like he needed the money. I wanted to help him out."

"Oh, Pa!" Lottie didn't try to stop the flow of tears. With her heart in her throat, she ran all the way back to Parker Lodge.

THIRTEEN

FOILED AGAIN

Folks, we decided to offer a primer on the melodrama, for those who are unfamiliar with its components. A good theatrical has a story line with several twists and turns meant to leave the audience members on the edges of their seats. As for the characters, you will find a strong hero—charming and handsome, of course, but slightly flawed. The story's heroine will discover her strengths through the many trials she faces. And the villain? Well, like all villains, he/she threatens to destroy the hopes and dreams of the other characters. When does this villain appear? We're learning that adversaries abound even before the curtain rises. To find out more, you will have to purchase a ticket. They will be available for purchase starting the first week in July.
—Your friends at Parker Lodge

WHEN LOTTIE ARRIVED BACK at Parker Lodge, she found the ladies finishing up their breakfast. Her heart skipped to her throat when she saw Gilbert seated next to Cornelia, who gushed over him as he shared the plan of action about the pie parlor. Cornelia, in typical fashion, hung on his every word, her eyelashes batting with abandon.

Lottie tried to get Gil's attention. She wanted to talk with him about Jeb and Katie Sue, but clearly now was not the time. Maybe she could catch him later in the day.

Flossie approached with a let's-get-down-to-business expression on her face. "Lottie, we've sent Grace to town to shop for fabrics for costumes. She should be back in an hour or so, and I'd like to take advantage of the time to show you some sketches she's done. Costume sketches, I mean. She's quite good, and we're lucky to have her."

"Costumes? Already?"

"Well, of course. I've learned the hard way that waiting until the last minute for costumes is always a bad idea. The actors and actresses need to become familiar with their props and costumes long before opening night. Doing so will make them more comfortable. So, I figured we might as well get a start on the sewing."

Lottie's mouth gaped. "But the money…I mean, we don't have a budget for costumes just yet."

"Never you mind that." Flossie waved her hand. "I took out a line of credit at the general store. Figured we'd have the money to pay for the fabrics and other essentials by the time the bill came due."

A wave of nausea passed over Lottie. She pinched her eyes shut and counted to three. When she opened them, Flossie still stared at her.

"So what do you say? How are your sewing skills?"

"Oh, you know…" She fought to find the words. *Terrible. The worst in the county.* She said nothing, of course. No point in alarming Flossie any more than necessary.

And so, with Gil and Cornelia chatting merrily about the pie parlor, Lottie shifted her attentions to costumes. In fact, as Cornelia's giggles resonated across the room, she thanked the good Lord above that she had something else to think about.

"What do you think of this costume for Justin Credible?" Fanny laid a sketch in front of Lottie.

"I think it's amazing." She picked up the paper and stared at the costume. "Do you really think we can make this?"

"Of course. We've learned quite a few tricks of the trade over the years, so I feel sure we can pull it off." Flossie shuffled through the pages until she came up with one that featured a gorgeous green gown. "And what about this one? We envision this to be the dress Patricia wears in a scene near the beginning of the show. Do you like it?"

Lottie gasped. "Oh, it's the prettiest dress I've ever seen." Her heart quickened as she stared at the picture. *What would it feel like, to wear a dress like that?*

Grace arrived in short order, loaded down with fabrics wrapped in paper and tied up with string. One by one she revealed the colorful pieces, giggling the whole time. She held up a piece of dark blue fabric and smiled. "I thought this color would look good on Chauncy." Her cheeks turned pink. "I think he'll make a nice dance partner for the square-dancing scene. He's not the most graceful fella I've ever met, but he's quite handsome, if you think about it."

"Honey, if you have to think about it, he's not handsome." Fanny chuckled. "But I think I see what you mean."

Lottie got a kick out of that one. Her thoughts traveled back to Gil, of course. Wasn't he the handsomest man in Estes Park? And didn't he have the softest lips? She did her best not to giggle as she relived the morning's kiss once again.

"With some of these men, you have to look past a few things—whiskery faces, hair in need of trimming, rugged clothes and boots. But I think I'm learning that some things are worth looking past." Grace smiled. "Does that make sense?"

"Yes, of course. Sounds like that's just a fancy way of saying you shouldn't judge a book by its cover." Fanny winked. "Sometimes the story inside is really lovely, if you take the time to read it."

"Oh, I'm taking the time to read it." Grace's hand went to her mouth as if to cover up the words she'd just spoken. A giggle followed as she pulled her hand away. "Well, you know what I mean. And I can honestly say that the cover is looking more and more handsome with each passing day, as well."

Lottie reached over to pat her on the arm. "I suspected as much."

"I've asked him to come early so that we can rehearse that big dance number. It's been giving him a little trouble." Her cheeks turned the prettiest crimson color. "He seemed happy to oblige."

"No doubt." Lottie wanted to say so much more. She wanted to tell Grace that love was grand, that heroes really did exist, whiskery faces or not. Every time she started to open her mouth to share her thoughts, however, she remembered the expression in Gil's eyes when he gazed at Cornelia. That stopped her cold.

Flossie headed off to the kitchen to fix a cup of tea, and Fanny gave the ladies a concerned look. "I do wonder if all this talk about love is bothering my sister."

"Why would it?" Grace asked.

"Oh, honey, Flossie was in love once. You've heard me refer to a production we did back in '03, no doubt. It was really more of a vaudeville act. We traveled with several other actors, of course. One of them was a handsome fella named Gene Westin. Let me tell you, that man was something special to look at."

"Really?"

"Oh yes. He had the prettiest eyes I've ever seen on a fella, and his perfect mustache looked like something out of a picture book. In one of the little skits we did, he played the part of a general in the War between the States. Flossie fell head over heels for the fella. I've never seen her so happy."

Lottie could hardly believe it. Flossie...in love? "So what happened?"

Fanny sighed. "The show ended and she never worked up the courage to share her feelings with him. I think everyone knew they were meant for each other, but no one piped up and said anything. We ended up getting hired by the traveling show while he went off and did his own one-man show. At first we thought we'd be separated from Gene for a few weeks. But weeks turned into months, and months turned into years. We found out some time later that he had married one of the girls in the chorus line. Honestly, I think it broke Flossie's heart, though she never speaks of it."

"How sad." Grace's lips turned down in a pout.

"Sadder still to live your whole life locked up by pain when the true source of your problem is the unwillingness to let go of what might've been." Fanny's eyes filled with tears. "You don't know how many times I've wanted to tell her that living in the present is for the best. I truly think she's still pining away for that man."

Ironic. Hadn't Gilbert wasted precious time, pining away for Winifred?

"We don't always get a second chance to say what should've been said the first time around. That's why I believe we should share our feelings while we have the chance." Fanny gave everyone a nod then got back to work.

Flossie returned shortly, and Prudy joined them minutes later. The ladies spent the next hour working hard. With Grace's help, they cut out paper patterns for the various costumes and got busy pinning them to the fabrics. The work distracted Lottie and kept her from thinking about Gil. Mostly.

Around eleven o'clock, a yummy aroma permeated the room.

Fanny glanced up from her work and sniffed the air. "*Mmm.* Do you smell that?"

Lottie paused and drew in a breath. "Yum. Mrs. Parker and Hannah have already started making pies. Smells like coconut."

"And something fruity," Grace added. "Maybe lemon?"

"I love lemon meringue pie." Flossie rubbed her stomach. "Hope we're able to keep on working with pies baking in the next room."

"Me too." Fanny looked worried. "I might just have to run in there and grab a slice."

"I have a feeling we're going to get used to the smell of pies baking after a while," Lottie said.

Grace nodded. "Yes, I heard Hannah say that she wanted to try her hand at a couple of new recipes. I can hardly wait."

Mrs. Parker came into the room minutes later, all abuzz with excitement. "Ladies, I hope you don't mind sandwiches again. I know we had them for lunch yesterday."

"And at our midnight supper club," Fanny whispered and then gave Lottie a playful wink.

"Hannah and I are just so busy with this pie-parlor idea that I haven't had time to cook anything," Mrs. Parker added. "But there's good news! Gilbert has reached Jeb Otis, and he will be cooking your dinner tonight. In fact, he'll be making all of your meals from this point on while I focus on pies."

Fanny let out a quiet, "Praise the Lord!" which Mrs. Parker appeared not to hear. Lottie concentrated on the fabrics, not wanting to give anything away with her expression.

"Anyway, I do apologize for the sandwiches," Mrs. Parker said. "But I understand Jeb will be roasting chickens for dinner and making his famous Southwestern beans." She turned on her heel and headed back to the kitchen.

Fanny sighed. "I always did love a man who could cook."

Hearing the words "man" and "love" caused Lottie to think about Gilbert once again, of course. In spite of her attempts not to dwell on him, she'd thought of little else all morning. Still, he was conspicuously absent from their little sewing party, no doubt busy elsewhere. Strange, that Cornelia hadn't offered to help with the sewing, either. Lottie tried to push aside the feelings of jealousy that wrapped themselves like tendrils around her heart every time she thought of the way Cornelia gazed at Gilbert.

Oh well. Soon enough everyone would know that Lottie and Gil were a couple. She hoped so, anyway.

The ladies took a break for lunch at noon, though Gil seemed to be avoiding Lottie. She couldn't quite make sense of it. Was he trying to keep their relationship a secret, perhaps? Likely. She wanted to take the seat next to him at the lunch table but found it occupied by Cornelia. Naturally.

Grace invited Lottie to join her at another table, and before long they were in an intense conversation about costumes once again. Flossie shared her plans to sew Gilbert's Justin Credible costume right away, explaining that the more they could get done before tonight's rehearsal, the better.

True to form, after swallowing down a bit of food, she got right back to work. Fanny and Grace seemed anxious to get back to it too. Lottie joined them for a while but eventually headed off to the cabins to perform her usual afternoon chores.

She kept a watchful eye on the clock as the hours ticked by and wondered what time Jeb would show up to cook dinner. He came whistling across the property around three thirty. Lottie managed to catch up with him before he entered the lodge.

"Jeb."

He turned and flashed a smile. "Hi, Lottie. Wasn't sure I'd see you till tonight at dinner."

"Yes, I've been here all day. Well, mostly. I had to run home this morning to fetch my script." She paused. "And that's what I want to talk to you about. When I went home, I…well…something happened. Or, rather, I saw something. Something of yours."

He gave her a curious look.

"Tell me what happened with Katie Sue, Jeb," she said after a moment.

"Katie Sue?" Jeb's eyes glistened. "What brought her up?"

"Jeb, I—"

He put up his hand and kept walking toward the lodge. "I don't want to talk about it. Let's just say she's moved on to higher pastures."

"Jeb, I know all about it. I saw her just this morning. My pa was…" She decided not to finish the sentence. If he knew Katie Sue was headed off to Texas to become some rich man's steak, it would probably be the end of him.

"What were you saying, Lottie?" he asked.

"Oh, well, I was saying that Katie Sue looked like she fit right in with the other cows." Lottie offered a strained smile.

He stopped walking and turned her way. "Breaks my heart to let her go. It really does. But what can I do? I needed the money for all of this…" He gestured at the lodge. "To help cover the costs of the ladies being here. I don't have extra money like some of the fellas, so I have to do what I can to get by."

Lottie placed her hand on his arm. "I can't imagine you without Katie Sue, Jeb. She's your most valuable possession."

He shrugged. "Not the most valuable. My friendships are more valuable."

"Still…" She followed him inside and watched as he went to work cooking the evening meal. Jeb never stopped talking, mostly about Katie Sue. He grew quite somber when the conversation shifted and he ended up talking about the losses he'd faced in his personal life—losing his wife and a young daughter to influenza many years ago. Lottie's heart grew heavy. No wonder he'd been so attached to Katie Sue. She really was all he had left. Hearing his testimony— as he called it—put everything in perspective.

At five thirty, Lottie headed out to the dining hall to help Flossie, Grace, and Fanny clean up the mess they'd made cutting out and sewing costumes, and at six o'clock, all the ladies gathered in the dining hall for their first real home-cooked meal.

"Anyone hungry?" Jeb stood before them with a platter full of roasted chicken.

"Are we ever!" Fanny sat at the table, her fork in one hand and her knife in the other. "Bring it on, Mr. Otis!"

Lottie had the strangest feeling that Fanny's words had some sort of double meaning. Based on the crooked smile on Jeb's face, the two had some sort of secret.

Not that Jeb's cooking skills were any secret. Why, the chicken practically melted in her mouth.

After the meal, Hannah and Mrs. Parker handed out giant slices of pie—some chocolate, some coconut, and some apple. Then, just about the time Lottie wished she could curl up for a long nap, it was time for rehearsal to begin. She helped Mrs. Parker and Jeb clear the dishes then called the room to attention by clapping her hands.

The cast members gathered around her, ready to begin. Still, one person was conspicuously absent. Lottie glanced around, confused. "Where's Gil?"

"He's in the other room, changing into that Justin Credible costume we've been sewing all day," Fanny said. "Grace wants to hem the pants so we can focus on the green dress tomorrow."

"I see." Lottie clapped her hands again. "Okay, everyone. We've got a lot to do tonight. We're going to block the first couple of scenes."

"What does 'block' mean, Lottie?" one of the local boys asked.

"It means I'm going to show you exactly where to stand on the stage and when to move. You want to do what comes most naturally to you, of course. That means you can't just stand there. You've got to match your movements to the character's personality and motives, if that makes sense."

Lottie spent the next few minutes talking about the various characters. Just about the time she got the actors onto the stage for the opening scene, a stirring at the door on the opposite side of the dining hall distracted her. Her heart gravitated to her throat when she saw a familiar young woman standing there with tears streaming down her face.

Springing from her seat, Lottie sprinted to the door. "Winnie?" She stared at her older sister, thinking for a moment she'd seen an apparition.

Winnie threw herself into Lottie's arms. "Don't ask me any questions, Lottie! And whatever you do, don't let Mama hear that I've been crying. She can't know that…" Her words faded away. "Anyway, she can't know anything's wrong. I want her to think I've come home for a little visit, that's all."

"All right." Lottie brushed loose hair out of her sister's eyes. "But when you're ready to talk about it—whatever it is—you can come to me. Promise?"

Winifred nodded and looked around the room. "I can see that you're really busy."

"We're just about to start our rehearsal."

"Yes. That melodrama Mama told me about." Winifred pulled out her hankie and dabbed at her eyes. "I heard all about it."

"No doubt. But remember, you can't believe everything you hear. We're having a wonderful time and it's going to be a terrific show, filled with villains and vixens."

"Villains and vixens." Winnie sighed. "Ironic. That's just what I found in Denver too." She dabbed the tears off her cheeks. "Oh well, enough about that. I can fill you in later. Do you think it would be all right if I stayed here and walked home with you later?"

"Sure. Gilbert will walk us both home after rehearsal," Lottie said. "He's been very good about that." She tried to keep her admiration for Gilbert out of her voice.

"Where—where is Gil?" Winnie looked around, a glimmer in her eyes.

A ripple of jealousy trailed across Lottie's heart. She dismissed it at once, realizing that Gilbert now cared for the right sister. "He's changing into a costume. I—well, I guess you should know that he's playing the hero. His name is Justin Credible."

Winnie smiled. "Well, of course it is. And isn't that just perfect for Gil?"

"Y–yes." Lottie took her sister by the hand and led her to a table near the stage. "I'll be sitting here to direct. You can join me."

Several of the ladies glanced Lottie's way, as if to ask the obvious, "Who is that?" but she didn't make introductions. Not yet. No, she'd better wait until after the rehearsal when Winnie got her emotions in check.

"All right, everyone, back to rehearsal." Lottie clapped her hands, ready to work on the melodrama. At least with the play, she had some idea of how the story might turn out.

* * * * *

GILBERT DID HIS BEST to remain patient as Grace pinned up the hem of his pants. He found the costume rather ridiculous but didn't say so. Sure, he'd imagined Justin Credible to be the swashbuckling sort, but the costume was a little over the top.

As Grace continued to work, he squirmed.

"Careful, or I'll stick you with a pin," she teased.

At least he hoped she was teasing.

"The ladies are going to love this." Grace rose and gave him a nod. "Let's go show them."

"Right now?" He took a step backward.

"Well, sure. We've been working all day so that we could get your costume ready. I think it will help the other cast members see just how real this show is if they can see a costume. It will motivate them to do their best."

"I guess."

Gil trudged along behind Grace, who flitted out into the dining hall. "Yoo-hoo!" she called out, getting everyone's attention. "I have someone to introduce." With great flair she turned his way, flung out her arms, and said, "I give you our hero, Justin Credible!"

A gasp went up from the crowd, especially the women. Cornelia came rushing his way, all smiles. "You're going to make the most handsome hero ever, Gil," she crooned.

He bit back a response. Something about the way she gazed up at him made him uneasy, especially after kissing Lottie this morning. Not that he minded Cornelia's attentions, necessarily. Had it really only been a day or two since he'd welcomed them? Now he just felt confused. Conflicted.

"I can't wait to see you on opening night." She gave him a little wink. "You're going to look just incredible." She giggled. "Get it? Justin Credible?"

"Th–thank you." Gil's thoughts were elsewhere, however. He looked through the crowd, smiling when he saw Lottie. The shimmer of wonder in her eyes was really all he needed to calm his nerves.

When she came close, he smiled. "So, how do I look?" He pointed to the crazy getup. "Too much? Too little?"

Lottie's wide-eyed expression warmed his heart. "Perfect. You're very…" She paused and her face turned red. "Hero-like."

"Thank you. I—"

"Gilbert? Is that you?"

The familiar voice caught him off guard. He turned and saw the woman who had held his heart in her hands for so many years, the very one who had left him in the lurch for a new life in Denver.

"Winnie?"

She threw her arms around his neck and gave him a tight squeeze, drawing the attention of nearly every lady in the room.

After a moment of awkward silence, Fanny cleared her throat. Gilbert managed to pull away from Winnie's embrace. He gazed into her eyes—tearstained eyes, no less—his nerves now a jumbled mess.

Lottie finally spoke up. "Everyone, this is my sister, Winifred."

"Well, land sakes," Fanny said. "I never would've taken you two for sisters."

Gilbert flinched, knowing those words would probably cause Lottie a bit of a sting. Few people saw the resemblance between Winifred's peaches-and-cream complexion and Lottie's freckled, sun-kissed face. And Lottie's short curls were no match for Winifred's upswept hair.

He'd no sooner had time to think this through when Cornelia stepped next to Winnie and gave her a piercing look.

Uh-oh.

The two women took to staring, as if trying to size one another up. And Lottie...poor Lottie. She just looked like she wanted to run from the room and never return.

Well, maybe he'd join her. Melodrama hero or not, right now Gilbert Parker felt anything but incredible.

FOURTEEN

FOILED AGAIN

Estes Park residents, what's your favorite kind of pie? Lemon meringue, coconut cream, strawberry, silk chocolate, pecan? You name it, we've got it! We at Parker Lodge have made it our mission to tantalize your taste buds as we open the brand-new Parker's Pie Parlor today at nine a.m. Come hungry...and bring a friend! Nibble on a slice of your favorite pie and enter your mama's pie recipe in our "pie of the week" contest. You could win the right to have your pie sold in our shop! And while you're here, pick up your ticket for our upcoming melodrama. Our show's director, Lottie Sanders, has suggested a new title: Foiled Again! *What's your suggestion? Let us know, and you might just win a free week's stay at the prettiest lodge on Fall River.*
—Your friends at Parker Lodge

THE FOLLOWING SATURDAY MORNING Lottie entered the new pie parlor, her nerves a jumbled mess. For days, Gilbert had hardly spoken to her, except to ask her questions about his role in the play. He'd spent every available moment with either Cornelia or Winifred cooing after him. The very thought of it made her sick. It also made her more determined than ever not to change her appearance. Who cared if she looked like a tomboy if Gil wouldn't even give her the time of day? Likely, he wouldn't notice one way or the other.

She walked into the kitchen at seven thirty, stunned to find Hannah's apron covered in white flour. And chunks of—what was that?—apples? The ordinarily tidy young woman glanced her way and grinned. "Oh, Lottie, look! I've been working on the apple pies. We open in an hour and a half, you know."

"I know." Lottie grinned back at her. "Are you nearly ready?"

"Yes. I know I've made a mess in the process, but I don't care. Working with these ingredients has liberated me." Her eyes filled with wonder. "Now I know how the suffragettes feel after one of their rallies—really and truly set free." She giggled and tossed a chunk of apple into her mouth. Swiping the back of her hand across her cheek, she left a floury mark. Her eyes twinkled with a merriment Lottie had never witnessed before.

"If they taste half as good as they look, we're going to have some happy customers," Lottie said.

"They're going to taste twice as good as they look." From across the room Mrs. Parker's cheerful voice rang out. "This girl is a wonder. You should taste the lemon meringue pies she made earlier this morning."

Ah. Lemon meringue. That would explain the streak of yellow across the front of the apron.

"Would you like a teensy-tiny taste?" Hannah held up a slice.

"Sure." Lottie reached for a fork. "Lemon is my favorite."

"Mine too," a familiar male voice rang out. Lottie turned to discover Doc Jennings standing behind her. "I've always been partial to lemon meringue pie. And chocolate pie. And apple pie." He listed the many kinds of pies that made him happy. Before long, he'd purchased three. And the pie parlor hadn't even opened its doors to the public yet!

By eight forty-five a line had formed at the door. Local folks—excluding the ladies from the Women's League, of course—waited their turn to buy pies. By ten o'clock, there wasn't a pie to be had in the kitchen. Not one.

Just after a delightful lunch, which Jeb prepared with Fanny's help, Lottie found Gil seated at the kitchen table, writing checks. She pulled up a chair and sat across from him.

"Gil, did you see?"

He glanced up from his work. "See what?"

"The pie parlor. It's a hit!"

He chuckled. "I saw Phineas and Doc Jennings walking off with a couple of pies each, so I figured things must be going well in there."

"Oh, it is. You won't believe what Hannah looked like, though." As if she'd heard her name, a messy Hannah emerged from the kitchen, all smiles.

"Wouldn't have believed it if I hadn't seen it for myself." Gil laughed. "But I've never seen her so happy. I've never seen any of the local fellas as happy as they look of late, either."

"I know. There's something in the air." Lottie giggled, feeling her earlier anxieties lift. "Can you feel it?"

"I can." He smiled at her. "And we have you to thank."

"O–oh?" She gazed into his eyes and, for the first time in days, dared to hope that he might still care about her.

"It's your hard work," he said. "All of this has happened because you were willing to go along with a plan of action. A crazy idea that I came up with. How can I ever thank you?"

"Gil, you don't have to. I'm having the time of my life. Well, except for the part where my mother's not speaking to me."

"I'm having the time of my life too. And I'm sorry about your mama." He smiled again. "But I need you to know how grateful I am. It's important that you know. Maybe..." He paused. "Maybe one of these days we can actually pay you a real salary. I'm not sure I could ever give you what you're worth. You've meant so much to me." He cleared his throat. "I mean, to the lodge."

"Ah."

Before she could say another word, Winifred entered the room with Cornelia at her side. Gilbert's gaze shifted upward to the two women, and his face lit in a smile.

"Why, Gilbert Parker, we should've known you would be in here." Winifred giggled. "Always working, aren't you?"

He shrugged. "There's a lot to be done."

"Of course." She slipped her arm through Cornelia's. "But it's such a pretty day outside. I was just telling my new friend here about that lovely little spot near the river where you and I used to go for picnics. I was hoping we could talk you into joining us for a little rest from your labors."

"Hmm." He glanced down at the bills then back at the ladies. "I need to pay these before day's end."

Winifred's mouth turned down in a pout. Seconds later, that pout turned into a smile. "Lottie knows how to do that, doesn't she? I'm sure she wouldn't mind." Winifred turned to face her and Lottie felt her heart grow heavy. "Would you mind, Lottie?"

The pleading look in her sister's eyes almost won Lottie over. Almost. For once, though, she held her ground. No more the accommodating little sister.

"Actually, I'm headed off to meet the ladies to sew some costumes. Sorry."

She rose and took several steps away from them, praying all the while that Gil would stick to his guns and pay the bills instead of joining them. Unfortunately, she heard the scraping of his chair legs against the floor and realized her battle had been lost. Minutes later, he disappeared out the door with Winifred on his right and Cornelia on his left, their girlish giggles echoing across the room.

Lottie sighed and plopped back down in her chair.

"You care about him, don't you?" The voice came from behind her. She turned to see Fanny standing there with Flossie behind her, holding several costumes. Grace entered behind Flossie, her arms loaded with fabrics.

"Oh, I…" Her words trailed off. She was embarrassed to speak her thoughts aloud in front of the ladies.

Fanny put her hand on Lottie's arm. "No point in trying to hide it, sweet girl. It's as obvious as the nose on your face. You're smitten with him."

Lottie sighed. "I am."

"I knew it." Grace dropped the fabrics on the table.

"Well, praise the Lord." Fanny grinned. "What a lovely match the two of you would make."

"No, we'll never be a match." *As much as I dared to hope.*

"Let's don't assume that, honey." Flossie draped the costumes over the back of a chair and took a seat across from Lottie. "You never know."

"I've cared about Gilbert Parker forever, but he's never noticed me." *Well, except for that one time when he kissed me. But he doesn't seem to remember doing that.*

"How could he not notice you?" Grace sat next to her and reached for her hand. "You're the star of his show."

Lottie found those words to be perplexing, at best. "What do you mean?"

"I mean you're center stage in his life—right in the very middle of everything that's important to him." Grace gave her hand a squeeze. "Why, you might as well have a spotlight shining on you. He would have to be blind not to notice you."

"Maybe I should rephrase what I said, then." Lottie paused to think her words through. "He doesn't notice me in the way I want to be noticed. He's been head over heels for my sister Winifred for as long as I can remember."

Fanny's nose wrinkled. "I see. Hmm. Never figured on that."

"It's true." Lottie rose and began to fuss with the costume. She held up the pretty jade-colored fabric and gave it a scrutinizing look. "I was just that annoying kid sister who tagged along on their heels when they were courting."

"Are they? I mean, are they still courting?" Grace asked.

"Oh, no. Winifred has moved away." Lottie paused, choosing her words carefully. "That is, she had moved away to Denver. Mama sent her there to stay with our cousin so that she could be introduced to proper society. She met her fiancé—well, the man who was her fiancé—during her stay in Denver. But apparently they have ended things. I know Mama isn't happy about the breakup, because the man is a successful banker. Very wealthy. He's everything Mama ever wanted for Winifred. Only, now she's coming back and my chances with Gilbert have come to an end. I might as well get used to the idea."

"But you don't know that, Lottie." Fanny slipped an arm around her shoulder.

"Could we just forget about this and get to work on the costumes?" Lottie asked. "I think I would feel better if we could."

"Of course, honey."

They spent the next couple of hours pinning and hemming. Finally, with everything on their list nearly done, Lottie turned her attentions to the new jade dress. "This is the prettiest one by far. Patricia is going to look wonderful in it."

"You're about the same height as Patricia." Flossie gave Lottie a pensive gaze. "We'll use you as a model so I know where to pin the hem."

"Oh, no. I could never wear the same costume as Patricia. She has such a lovely figure and I'm, well…" She pointed at herself. "A little top-heavy."

"Who could tell, with those overalls?" Flossie asked.

Grace nodded. "Yes, I daresay there could be a girlish figure under there. Only one way to find out." She handed Lottie the dress and then clasped her hands together. "Try this on for us, Lottie."

Finally, unable to squelch the idea, Lottie headed off to the powder-room to change into the gown. Once she got it on, Grace came in to fasten the buttons up the back.

"Lottie, you look gorgeous!"

"Do you think so?"

"Yes." Grace gestured for her to turn around. "This is just like a scene from *Pygmalion*."

"Pig who?" Lottie made a little turn and then stopped.

"*Pygmalion*. The stage play." Grace knelt down and began to pin the hem. "Ah, I know why you've never heard of it. It's only just been written by Mr. George Bernard Shaw."

"Don't believe I've heard of him."

Grace put her finger to her lips. "Don't let Flossie hear you say that. She'll call you a fraud."

"I *am* a fraud. I don't mind admitting it." A second glance in the mirror gave her reason to doubt those words, however. In this gown, she felt very much like a lady.

"No, you're not." Grace gave her a wink. "I daresay your acting skills are quite good. Otherwise no one would've believed you to be a true director. And it's clear you spend your days acting as if you don't care one whit about Gilbert Parker when, in fact, you are madly in love with him."

Lottie groaned. "Please don't say that to anyone else. Promise?"

"You don't deny it, then?" Grace's eyes twinkled.

"I've already told you how I feel about him." She squirmed as Grace continued to pin the gown. "Anyway, what is this pig story you were referring to?"

"Not pig. It's *Pygmalion*. Lovely story of a young Cockney woman in London who undergoes a physical and emotional metamorphosis when Professor Henry Higgins takes her under his wing." Grace continued to pin the hem, her fingers moving with swift assurance. Suddenly, she glanced up. "I daresay that's what's missing here."

"The pig?"

"The metamorphosis. The shocking transformation."

"You're saying I need to change?"

"I didn't say it, you did. You said that Gilbert didn't notice you as you are. That he looks right past you."

"Right."

"Then show him a different side of you." Grace put the last pin in place and rose. She stood alongside Lottie and they both gazed at their reflections in the powder-room mirror. "And before you give me that rehearsed speech about how he should love you just as you are, remember what you've already said—that he considers you the kid sister. It's time to show him that you're a grown-up woman." Grace leaned in and whispered, "You are, you know. Grown up, I mean."

"Y–yes." She swallowed hard. "W–what are you suggesting... exactly?"

"Just a few changes." Grace winked. "Nothing huge."

Lottie felt nauseated at the very idea.

"Do it for you," Grace said. "Not for Gilbert and not for the people who will be shocked. Do it to build your confidence. Do it because feeling like a lady is a grand feeling. I can help you with your posture so that you have a more ladylike pose. In fact, we could work on that right now." She took Lottie by the shoulders and led her through a few graceful walking steps.

"Now what?" Lottie asked.

"Now we give Gilbert a glimpse of you he's never had before."

"O–oh?"

"Yes. Come out into the dining hall dressed in that gown. We'll come up with a reason to get him in there. A real bona fide reason.

That way it won't look as if you're doing this to impress him. It'll be more natural-like." She paused then snapped her fingers. "I've got it! We'll tell him he's needed to hang a rod for the costumes. That's bona fide."

"I don't know, Grace."

"Sure. It's bound to work. He'll come in just in time to see you standing there, looking like a beauty queen, with Flossie hemming your gown."

"How do you know he'll come in at just that moment?"

"Oh, you poor, dear girl. You don't have a clue, do you?" Grace giggled.

"A clue? About what?"

"About men. Trust me when I say that we'll time things perfectly so that he arrives just as you're standing there dressed in this glorious gown, which matches your eyes perfectly, I might add. He will be swept away by your beauty."

"I don't know." Lottie paced the room. "Just seems so wrong, to pretend to be something I'm not."

"Something you're not?" Grace turned her around to face the mirror once again. "Lottie, give yourself another look. You are exquisite."

"I—I guess."

"Come with me. Let's show the other ladies." Grace took her by the hand and tugged her out into the dining hall, where she was met with gasps from Flossie and Fanny. Grace excused herself to go find Gilbert while Flossie got to work at hemming the gown.

After a few seconds of staring, Fanny clucked her tongue. "What were you hiding from, Lottie? Under those overalls, I mean?"

"H–hiding?"

"Yes. Clearly you were hiding something. Or maybe hiding *from* something."

"I don't know." She paused to think through her answer before speaking again. "I feel safe in overalls."

"Safe?"

"Well, for one thing, they hide my…" She paused and pointed to her chest.

"Your curves?" Fanny's eyes widened. "Honey, some girls I know would kill to be as blessed in abundance as you are." She chuckled. "And you have the tiniest little waist. I didn't have a waist like that even when I had a waist."

"It's just embarrassing."

"It's no sin to accentuate what the good Lord has given you. You're such a beautiful, vibrant girl on the inside. It's nice to see it showing on the outside too."

"I guess." Lottie felt a little nervous about speaking her thoughts aloud but did so anyway. "I guess I've been dressing the part of a wall-flower so that I would disappear into the background. Be nonexistent."

"Why?" Flossie glanced up from her spot on the floor.

"Never really thought about it," Lottie said.

Flossie gave her a motherly look. "Well, this is just a suggestion, of course, honey, but maybe it's easier to push people away by dressing differently. That way you're prepared ahead of time."

Lottie frowned. "I'm not sure I understand."

"Just suggesting—and that's all this is, a suggestion—that you've been dressing like a tomboy so that Gilbert *won't* take an interest in you. That way it won't hurt so much if he doesn't seem to notice you."

Lottie felt a quickening in her heart.

"Maybe you've done this to somehow protect your heart," Flossie said.

"I—I suppose it's possible," Lottie said. "Though I never did it on purpose." She shook her head as the truth set in. "It's true that I've always been afraid of being hurt."

Flossie nodded. "Sounds like you went to a lot of trouble to accomplish this."

"Maybe I did." She sighed. "Funny, how I did it without realizing why. Sounds so silly when I say it out loud."

"Rejection isn't silly," Fanny said. "Trust me when I say that we all know what it feels like. The sting of rejection can be painful, even years after the fact."

"Yes." Flossie nodded again. "I can attest to that."

"So can I." Fanny shrugged. "So, it appears we have something else in common, then."

"I guess we do." Lottie offered the ladies a warm smile. Her feeling of contentment lasted until she caught a glimpse of Gilbert entering the room. Then their eyes met and she saw the shock on his face.

Yes, suddenly she felt very much like a lady.

* * * * *

GILBERT STARED AT LOTTIE, completely captivated by the gown she wore. He'd never seen anything so beautiful. As pretty as the dress was, however, it didn't hold a candle to the girl wearing it. He saw her as if for the first time—the high cheekbones, the upturned nose, the winsome smile, the perfectly placed freckles. Oh, he'd observed those things a thousand times before, of course. Only, today they looked different. *She* looked different.

No, it wasn't the dress. Not really, though it did show off her figure in a way that startled him. No, there seemed to be something more. Standing here, appearing very much the lady, Lottie seemed more at ease than she had in all the years he'd known her.

And judging from the smile on her face, she recognized it too.

FIFTEEN

PERIL IN THE PEW

Friends, do you love stories of transformation? If so, then you're in for the time of your life when you come see the melodrama at Parker Lodge. Watch as characters—both on stage and off—transform before your very eyes. One moment meek and mild, the next filled with courage to face their foes. Who's transforming, you ask? Why, Miss Information, for one. She transforms from comedic sidekick to strong heroine material. And Ellie Gant, that one-time vixen; she transforms into an elegant lady that folks in town scarcely recognize. Yes, this show is filled with stories of lasting change. But isn't that just as it should be? Doesn't life afford us equally as many opportunities? Just something to chew on between now and opening night.
—Your friends at Parker Lodge

OVER THE NEXT SEVERAL DAYS, Lottie transformed in much the same way a butterfly nudged its way out of the chrysalis—one painful step at a time. It started with Grace's insistence that Lottie take a couple of her dresses, ones she claimed didn't fit now that she'd started eating Jeb's good cooking. Then Flossie, God bless her, gave Lottie a few lessons in posture. Fanny, always looking at the bright side, decided Lottie could use a few diction lessons, and Sharla, Patricia, and Cherry helped her with her hair.

"You know, those curls are delicious," Sharla said, brush in hand. "But your hair is actually a lot longer than it looks."

"Oh?"

"Yes, the curl pulls the hair up several inches, making it appear short. But it's really not. I believe it's long enough that it could be pulled up into a chignon."

Lottie didn't argue as the ladies went to work, transforming the messy curls into an upswept look that, truly, took her breath away in the end.

"Oh, Lottie." Cherry stood back. "You're such a beauty."

"I—I am?" She gazed in the mirror, completely mesmerized by the face staring back at her.

"Stand up, Lottie." Patricia took her by the hand and Lottie rose. "Turn around."

Lottie turned, the soft blue skirt swishing lightly. She'd never had a swishing skirt before and rather liked it. Indeed, gazing at her reflection in the mirror, she had to admit she liked just about everything about this experience. Well, almost everything.

Whether or not Gilbert seemed to notice this gentle transformation, she couldn't say. He seemed too preoccupied with Winnie and Cornelia to pay much attention. Sure, he'd said a couple of words to her at their last rehearsal, commenting on the dress she'd worn, but other than that he seemed not to notice.

By the time Sunday morning came around, Lottie could hardly

wait to go to church in her new blue dress. She'd somehow managed to talk Fanny, Flossie, Prudy, and Grace into meeting her there, but none of the other ladies would budge after the reception they'd received on their first visit. Lottie just kept praying. Surely the Lord could work it all out.

She arrived at the church early, ready for an encounter with the Lord. What she got was an encounter with Reverend Brighton.

"Lottie?" He took a seat in the pew next to her. "I had to look twice to make sure it was you."

"It's me." She offered a shy smile, which he returned.

"Well, you're a vision of loveliness. But then, you always have been." His fatherly smile offered assurance.

"Thank you." She felt her cheeks grow warm.

The reverend glanced back at the chapel door. "Look, I haven't really shared this with anyone but my wife, but I think what you're doing is admirable. Helping the Parkers raise the funds to save their lodge. Bringing the ladies to Estes Park and sharing the love of the Lord with them."

"Oh, Reverend." Tears stung her eyes. "You've made my day. My week. My month!"

He patted her on the shoulder. "Well, good. And just for the record, I believe the scuttlebutt going on with the Women's League is ridiculous."

"No doubt the enemy is stirred up," Lottie said. "The Lord has led these women from all over the country to our little town. He's entrusted them to us. Mrs. Parker says she believes that, instead of our going into all the world to spread the gospel, the Lord has brought the world to our doorstep."

"What an appropriate thought."

"Oh, Reverend, if you only knew everything. These women are meant to be here, in Estes Park. Some of them have never known the Lord, but I truly believe in my heart of hearts that they can find Him here, if folks will just reach out to them in love."

"Of course." He rose and paced the aisle, finally coming to a stop. "Lottie, I will add my prayers to yours. You know what the Bible says about the power of two people praying together."

"Thank you, Reverend. Those women need people who will share God's love. And now that I've gotten to know each one, it's so clear why He has gathered together these particular women for the show."

"Yes. And my wife has come up with an idea that she hopes will help your cause. She plans to enter a pie in that contest at the pie parlor. It's a key lime pie recipe. Very tasty. If she wins, every woman in town will know that she's linked arms with the Parker family. In other words, it will send a message to the masses." He smiled. "Or, as we said in seminary, 'That'll preach.'"

Lottie grinned. "How can I ever thank you?"

"Put in a good word for my wife's pie?" He chuckled. For a moment, anyway. His brow wrinkled as several parishioners came through the back door of the church and made their way up the aisle. The reverend lowered his voice. "I daresay, in the grand scheme of things, all of this has nothing to do with a made-up melodrama. It has everything to do with the very real drama that's transpiring right in front of us—one that doesn't require a stage or costumes or even rehearsed lines."

"I never thought of that," she whispered as her mother took the spot in the pew beside her.

"Never thought of what?" her mother asked.

Thank goodness, Althea Baker distracted Mama when she took the seat directly in front of them. At that very moment Grace, Prudy, Fanny, and Flossie arrived. They nudged their way into the pew next to Althea, who scooted down—not to make room, but clearly to avoid them. Fanny gave her a warm smile and a cheerful, "Happy Lord's Day!" to which Althea just nodded.

Minutes later Jeb and Phineas entered. Jeb took the seat in front of Fanny and Althea, and Phineas sat just behind Flossie. Lottie couldn't help but smile. Well, until she saw the expression on Althea's face as she noticed the attention Jeb was paying to Fanny. *Is she jealous?* What an interesting revelation.

As the organist played the opening hymn, Althea kept her gaze on Jeb, who kept turning to give Fanny quick glances. All of this Lottie observed from a couple of rows behind them.

Other than one moment when Fanny dropped a hymnal, the service was uneventful. Lottie wanted to go back to the lodge with the ladies for lunch but knew better. Sunday was family day, and with her sister back in town, spending time at home was more important than ever.

Less than an hour later, the Sanders family sat around the table while Becky, their cook, served up Sunday dinner.

"Smells good enough to eat, Becky," Lottie's father said with a smile.

"It's your favorite, Mr. Sanders. Steak." She put the platter on the table.

Winnie wrinkled her nose. "Eating beef really isn't good for my figure. In Denver I learned that beef is bad for the constitution and it adds weight." She took the tiniest sliver.

"That beef has given you the life you've craved from the time you were a little girl," her father said. "So eat up. I won't be hearing any more about how bad it is for you."

Winnie cut off a small bite and put it in her mouth then made a face.

Lottie reached for a big piece then added a scoop of mashed potatoes to her plate, followed by a hefty helping of Becky's home-grown green beans.

"You might want to slow your pace, Lottie," her mother said. "Becky has made a tasty custard for dessert."

"Actually…" Her father squirmed a bit in his seat. "I picked up dessert yesterday when I was in town. Well, not in town, exactly…" He took a bite of his steak.

Lottie's mother frowned. "You shopped for food? Well, this is a first!"

"I couldn't help myself. I'd stopped by Parker Lodge to have a little visit with Gilbert, and—"

"You went to Parker Lodge?" Lottie's mother dropped her fork. Her mouth hung open in an unladylike fashion. "Am I to under-stand that my husband actually went to that, that…" Her faced turned redder than the tomatoes on the salad.

"Now, Dorothy, calm down. It wasn't like that. In fact, nothing is as you've imagined. I simply went to the lodge to visit with Gilbert about a financial matter, and the smell of those pies in that new pie parlor of theirs was too much to take. I couldn't help myself."

"Well, I never!" Lottie's mother picked up her fork and took a bite of her salad, her gaze boring holes through her husband.

"No, I don't suppose you've ever really taken the time to get to know those ladies, now have you, dear?" He stared back in what appeared to be a showdown of wills.

Lottie glanced back and forth between them, intrigued. She was also more than a little interested in her father's comment about Gilbert. What sort of financial situation were the men discussing? Something to do with the melodrama, perhaps? Hopefully Gilbert hadn't told Pa about the line of credit Flossie had taken out at the general store.

"Honestly." Winnie rolled her eyes. "Is this what has happened since I've been away? Are the dinner hours always like this now?"

"Yes." Their mother turned to glare at her. "Ever since those women came to town."

"I met them, Mama," Winnie said with a shrug. "They just seem like normal girls to me. Nothing inappropriate or anything like that."

"They've seduced our men. I saw as much this morning in church."

"Wh–what?" Lottie could hardly believe her ears. "Just because Flossie and Fanny sat near a couple of the fellas, you think they've bewitched them in some way?"

"We will not discuss this at the table." Her mother gave her a stern look.

Lottie wanted to ask, "Then why did you bring it up?" but didn't.

Her mother took another bite of her beef then gazed across the table at Lottie's father. "I saw that we still have Jeb Otis's cow. How long will I have to go on looking at that beast before you ship her to Texas with the others?"

"Not sure." Lottie's father cut a large slab of steak then jabbed it with his fork. "Maybe I'll keep her around and make a pet of her. That's what Jeb did."

Lottie actually chuckled aloud. She'd never heard her father speak to her mother in such a forward way before, and it got her tickled. Giddy, even.

Her mother didn't seem quite as happy. "You're taking this all so lightly, Harold, but you need to keep your senses about you. Folks in town aren't taking this lying down. You know we've got a lawyer coming to town tomorrow morning to discuss our options."

"Lawyer?" Lottie's father looked up from his plate. "Who's he suing, the cow?"

"No." She laid her fork down and glared at him. "Not the cow." She closed her eyes, and Lottie watched as she counted to ten under her breath. Afterward, her eyes opened and she spoke calmly. "I have no choice but to live in a town that's divided; however, I will not dwell in a house that's divided. Either we come to some sort of agreement on this—this…issue, or—"

"Or what?" This time Lottie's father laid down his fork. "I would guard my next words very carefully, Dorothy. You don't want to say anything rash or speak out of anger."

This shushed her in a hurry. In fact, she didn't speak a word until it was time for dessert.

As soon as he finished his food, Lottie's father reached for the bell and rang it. Becky arrived moments later, wiping her hands on her apron.

"Yes, Mr. Sanders?"

"Becky, please bring that lemon meringue pie from the kitchen. I think I'll have a large slice." He rubbed his stomach. "I left just enough room."

"Yes, sir." She disappeared into the kitchen.

Lottie's mother huffed and went to the kitchen, returning with several glasses of custard. "*This* is our dessert."

"Looks wonderful, darlin'. I think I'll start with that." Lottie's father reached for a spoon and started eating the custard. Then, when Becky arrived with the pie—a gorgeous lemon pie with a meringue so high it looked as if it might just float to the skies—he took an extra large slice.

Lottie's mother muttered something under her breath but refused to take any pie.

"I daresay this is the best lemon meringue pie I've ever eaten," Lottie's father said between bites. "Might just need a second piece."

Lottie cut herself a slice and lopped it onto her plate then passed the pie to Winnie, who refused, saying she didn't need the extra pounds it might cause.

"You don't know what you're missing, Winnie," Lottie said. "This is Hannah's special recipe. She said it was her grandmother's."

"Hmm. Well, maybe just a teensy-tiny bite." Winnie cut a little sliver and put it on her plate. "Hannah, you said? Now which one is that?"

Lottie started to reply, "The one who's always clean and tidy" but stopped herself. These days, "Hygiene Hannah" was covered in pie dough and pecan pie filling.

"I'll tell you which one she is," Lottie's mother said. "She's the one over there drawing men away from their wives and tempting them to do…terrible things."

"Terrible things like buying pies?" Lottie's father quirked a brow. "I can't speak for the other men in town, but that's what she tempted me to do."

With a huff, Lottie's mother rose and threw her napkin on the table. "I've had about enough of this."

"Well, before you go, Dorothy, I had an idea."

She turned to face him. "And what was that?"

"Hannah told me they're holding a contest at the pie parlor. They're asking local folks to submit their pie recipes. One recipe a week will be chosen to be added to the menu."

"And?"

"And, you make a mighty fine strawberry pie. So, I was thinking…"

"You can wash that thought right out of your head, Harold Sanders. My pie recipe is famous in these parts, and it will not be turned into a joke at a place such as that."

She tore out of the room, her skirts swishing all the way.

"I'm sorry to hear that." Lottie's father took another piece of the pie then looked at the girls and shrugged. "That strawberry pie would easily make it on the menu. And I can see the name now: Sanders' Strawberry Pie." He took another bite, a pleasurable expression settling over him. "Mmm. We'll have to think about that, now, won't we?"

Winnie nibbled at her slice of pie then muttered something about how she needed to go to Parker Lodge to visit with her new friend, Cornelia. Lottie suspected her sister wanted to see someone else but didn't say so. Instead, full of beef and pie, she headed upstairs for a much-needed nap.

* * * * *

GILBERT PACED THE DINING HALL, completely worked up. If what Winnie had just said was true, Althea's nephew, Thad—the lawyer from Loveland—was due to arrive in the morning.

"Are you telling me he's going to file some sort of lawsuit against us? How can that be?"

"I don't know." Winnie wrung her hankie. "I can only tell you what Mama said, and she was plenty worked up when she said it. The Women's League is examining their options, whatever that means." She slipped her hand up to his shoulder. "What's going on around here, Gil? Things have changed so much since I left."

"Things have changed, yes, but they were only meant to change for the better. I don't have any idea what those women at the Women's League are thinking."

"I'll tell you what they're thinking." A strong female voice rang out from behind him. "They're thinking they will take us down. But they're wrong."

Gilbert turned to see Flossie standing just a few feet away. He took a step back from Winnie's touch, embarrassed to be caught in what might be misconstrued as a compromising position. "O–oh?"

"Yes. But we're not going to let them take us down, Gil. We're going to save this lodge, and the show will go on as planned. 'If God be for us—'"

"'Who can be against us?'" He finished the Scripture for her and then smiled, feeling a boost of confidence.

"Exactly. Now, get on over to Lottie's place and tell her she's needed here. We're going to have a meeting this evening, one to map out a plan of our own. That way, if Mrs. Baker's fancy lawyer-nephew does show up tomorrow, we're ready for him. Got it?"

He smiled. "Got it."

Gilbert turned and took off running for Lottie's house with Winnie on his heels.

SIXTEEN

THE BALLAD OF THE LONGS PEAK LADIES

Theatricals are known for their handsome heroes who rush in to save the day and weak, spineless damsels in distress. When was the last time you saw a melodrama with females who banded together to right the injustices they faced? We at Parker Lodge feel the time has come for a different sort of theatrical. Our damsels refuse to let their distresses get them down. Instead, they use them to propel the hero to be the man he was meant to be. And they do it all arm in arm, hand in hand. Estes Park, you just haven't lived until you've seen a band of feisty females in action! —Your friends at Parker Lodge

LOTTIE HAD ONLY SLEPT for an hour when Winnie came bursting into her bedroom, making all sorts of noise. Her sister's wide eyes clued her in that something was happening.

"You have to get up. There's going to be a meeting at the lodge, and you're needed. Gil's downstairs waiting."

"Gil, here?" Lottie yawned and stretched.

"Yes, it's important. You need to come with us."

Lottie swung her legs over the side of the bed, more confused than ever. "What sort of meeting?"

"I'm not sure," Winnie said. "But I don't think you want to miss this one, Lottie. Sounds like it's gonna be a doozie."

Lottie got up and dressed at once, not bothering to fuss with her hair. Minutes later, she, Winnie, and Gil entered the dining hall at Parker Lodge to find that Phineas, Jeb, Chauncy, and Augie had beaten them there.

"Must be really important." Lottie released a breath and tried to still her heart. She took a seat, and Flossie rose to address the room.

She started by clearing her throat then dove right in. "Folks, I guess it's apparent: the ladies in that Women's League are a force to be reckoned with."

"Don't I know it." Sharla rolled her eyes. "What've they done this time?"

"They're just up to their usual tricks, but they're bringing in the big guns. A lawyer is set to arrive tomorrow."

"A lawyer?" Cherry's brow wrinkled. "Whatever do they need a lawyer for?"

"We're not sure," Gil said. "But we want to be ready, just in case they're up to shenanigans."

Cherry fanned herself. "Gracious. The last time I saw a lawyer, he was serving me with papers from my ex-husband." She giggled. "Good riddance, I say. That louse was a noose around my neck. Happy to be rid of him."

Lottie was startled by this news. Then again, there were probably all sorts of things she didn't know yet about the ladies. Surely each of them had a story. Fear wriggled its way up her spine. Hopefully none of them were convicts or anything like that. Goodness, why hadn't they thought to check into that before bringing them to Estes Park? At once her imagination ran away with her. She envisioned several of the ladies being wanted by the law, and she pictured Althea's nephew—the high-powered lawyer—proving his case.

"Lottie, are you still with us?" Gil gave her a funny look, and she nodded.

"Y–yes. Sorry. Just thinking."

"Ah." Crinkles appeared around his eyes.

"I think it's time to take action," Flossie said.

"Isn't that what we're doing with the melodrama?" Margaret asked.

"And the pie parlor?" Hannah chimed in.

"And the handbills?" Lottie asked.

"Yes, and Augie's articles in the *Mountaineer* too. But I truly believe we've been brought here from New York, Denver, and Atlantic City to play a larger role than the ones we've been given on the stage."

"A larger role?" Patricia shrugged. "What do you mean?"

"We want to be a help to the Parker family, but the Women's League has been a hindrance. They've reared their heads, and I feel we must respond, though perhaps not as you might think. There are a million ways for a woman to get what she wants. All across this great country of ours, women are fighting to have their voices heard."

Fanny raised her hand in the air and let out a rousing, "Preach it, sister!"

"This is the part I don't understand," Lottie said. "Mama and Mrs. Baker are strong women. They both believe in women's rights. That's why I'm so perplexed by their current behavior."

Flossie pursed her lips. "Most folks think that only men are territorial, but I'm of the firm conviction that women can be even more so."

"What do you mean?" Lottie asked.

"We're encroaching on their territory, so they're kicking back by trying to make our lives miserable."

"They're succeeding too," Margaret said. "From all appearances, anyway."

"They will only succeed if we allow it." Flossie squared her shoulders. "And that's why we're not going to allow it. You hear me, folks? We're not going to let them lick us. They can bring in their important lawyer, but we won't go down without a fight. We'll stay here—at Parker Lodge—and put on the best theatrical this town has ever seen. We'll win the respect of those women and anyone else with any degree of suspicion." She gave Lottie a knowing look. "Are you in?"

"Do I have any choice?"

Flossie laughed. "Lottie, I'll make you a promise. Not only will we beat those women at their own game, but we will eventually win them over to our way of thinking."

"And how, pray tell, will we accomplish that?" Lottie asked.

"Ooh, I know," Margaret said, brushing loose strands of hair from her shoulders. "We can appeal to their materialistic side."

"Materialistic side?" Prudy didn't appear to be convinced.

Flossie crossed her arms. "What do you mean, materialistic side?" she said to Margaret.

"For women, going to the theater is all about who's wearing what," Margaret said. "It's an excuse to shop. When those women catch on to what's what, they'll want to outdo each other with their fancy dresses and hats and coats. You'll see."

Fanny shrugged. "Maybe. Not sure about that, though. If they show up, they'll be dressed in nice clothes, sure. But how do we get them here?"

Augie rose and addressed the group. "They'll show up all right, dressed to the nines. You'll see finery like you've never seen it. Want to know why? Because I'm going to run pieces in the *Mountaineer* about how to dress for the theater. The local woman will be rarin' to go, each one trying to outdress the other."

"Maybe." Fanny still didn't appear convinced.

Flossie didn't either, but she didn't seem worried. "Those women are the very last thing you need to worry about. They're not our problem. They're our answer."

Every eye in the room turned to her.

"Our answer?" Lottie couldn't help but voice the words. Since when was Althea Baker an answer?

Flossie now spoke with great passion. "Look, I know not all of you are going to agree with me. What I'm about to say might not even make much sense to you. But I'm a firm believer in the Bible, and the Bible says that we are to take possession of our territory."

"Take possession of our territory?" Sharla shook her head. "What does that mean? Are we going to war?"

"Maybe. Ever heard the story of Joshua at the town of Jericho? He marched around that city seven times, blew his horn, and the walls fell down." Flossie lifted her arms.

"And David facing the mighty Goliath," Fanny spoke up. "Surely you've heard that story."

"*That* one I know." Cherry chewed her fingernails. "But I still don't see what it has to do with us. I don't even own a slingshot."

"Well, I do." Flossie gave her a smile. "The Word of God is my slingshot, and it's one I plan to use. I'm going to give you gals some Scriptures to memorize. You're going to say them every day."

"Scriptures?" Patricia wrinkled her nose. "But I'm busy memorizing my lines."

"These lines are more important than any in a script. So get ready. We're going to start marching around Jericho—er, Estes Park—right away. Put your walking shoes on."

"Better yet, put your boots on." Lottie grinned. "I'll have all of you in cowboy boots before long, anyway."

Sharla mumbled something about how she didn't have any boots—and even if she did, she wouldn't be caught dead walking around the mountains in them—but Flossie kept going, regardless. She quoted Scripture after Scripture, honing in on one Bible story after another as proof that God could—and would—move on their behalf if they banded together.

"This is what theater people do," Flossie said. "We're a family. We're more than just a cast. These are the people you eat, work, and play with. And we've been brought together, as the Bible says, for such a time as this. So don't question why you're here in Estes Park. Just accept it and understand that God is up to something bigger than us."

Lottie saw that Phineas watched Flossie with an admiring look in his eyes. And when Fanny rose to share her heart, Jeb could hardly stay in his seat. The fellas definitely appeared to be enraptured with these strong female heroines who'd swept in to save the town.

And why not? As Lottie looked on—as she listened to Fanny's impassioned plea—she felt pretty enraptured, herself.

* * * * *

GILBERT LISTENED TO FLOSSIE'S SPEECH with renewed hope. Though he'd always trusted the Lord, he hadn't fully given over this situation to Him. He'd spent more time trying to come up with solutions on his own. But no more. The time had come. He would let go of the reins and march around Jericho. He would trust God in the same way Moses trusted Him at the Red Sea, the way David trusted Him as he stood before Goliath. And Gilbert would do it with a group of women—well, mostly women—who looked fit for the task.

At least, with those who were paying attention. As the meeting ended, Grace and Chauncy made their way to the stage, where she began to work with him on his dance steps. They'd been together a lot lately. So had Phineas and Flossie, who were now engaged in a conversation on the other side of the room. And Jeb and Fanny, who seemed like an odd but somehow appropriate fit.

Augie approached with a smile. "Gilbert, I just wanted you to know that I've got the perfect person to help me with the new fashion column for the *Mountaineer.*"

"Oh? Who's that?"

"Prudy."

"Prudy?" He glanced at the shy young woman who stood on the far side of the room chatting with one of the other ladies.

"Yes." Augie's face lit into a smile. "We've been discussing her love of writing. Did you know she's quite talented in that area?"

Gilbert took a seat and gestured for Augie to join him. "No. I wish I'd known. Lottie could've used her help with the script."

"Well, not that kind of writing." Augie gave Prudy an admiring look. "She's done several journalistic pieces in the various towns where she's lived. She's even written for the *New York Times*. Her clippings are great."

"Clippings?"

"Oh, sorry. Always forget that people who aren't in the business don't always understand the terminology. Clippings. When you've been published in the paper, you cut out the article and keep it in a file. Those clippings are shown to editors—people like me—to prove a history of publishing."

"Interesting. So…" Gilbert did his best to hide a grin. "She has nice clippings?"

Augie crossed his arms. "She's a wonderful lady, Gilbert. Very professional. I know she seems withdrawn, but she's not. The real Prudence comes out on paper. You might be surprised to discover that she's quite bold in print."

"That is interesting." He could hardly believe it, in fact. Still, if what Augie said was true, she would be the perfect person to write the articles, because she understood the women's point of view.

"Sometimes writing things down makes us courageous. In her case, she's far more outspoken on the written page, and that's a good thing. Finding a balanced reporter—one who doesn't come across as aggressive, but one who gets the job done—well, those reporters are hard to find. And when you do find one, you do your best not to let her—er, them—go."

"What are you saying, Augie?" Gilbert leaned his elbows on the table and gave his friend a closer look.

A smile turned up the edges of Augie's mouth. "Oh, just saying I have a lot to think about."

"Sounds like it." Gilbert extended his hand and Augie shook it. "Thanks for your help, my friend. It means a lot."

"You're welcome." Augie rose. "Now, if you don't mind, I've got to go see a woman about a newspaper job."

Gilbert chuckled. He sat alone for a moment, thinking through everything that had been said. From across the room he noticed Lottie glancing his way. For a moment, he hardly knew what to make of her. Standing there in that pretty blue dress with such a relaxed expression on her face and with her fashionable hairstyle, he hardly recognized her.

She approached the table and took a seat next to him. "In spite of everything we've been through up till now, I have such hope," she said and then smiled.

"Me too." A wave of guilt washed over him as he remembered the kiss he'd stolen from her. Oh, he wasn't sorry for it. Not really. Just sorry that he'd been so mixed up about it after the fact.

Lottie shared about the various romantic unions taking place around them. He didn't correct her when she reported that Augie had his eye on Margaret Linden. No point in stirring up more gossip. When she paused, he happened to catch a glimpse of Flossie. Something about her seemed different. Had Lottie noticed it too?

"All right, I just have to come out and say it," he finally managed.

"Say what?"

"Flossie." He glanced at the woman, who sat next to Phineas, laughing and talking. "She looks—"

"Younger?"

"Yes!" He turned to Lottie, stunned. "You've noticed it too. I thought maybe it was just me. Don't you remember what she looked like when she got here? I thought she was much older."

"I remember one of the fellas guessing she was a hundred and three."

Gilbert chuckled at the memory. "It's the strangest thing. Looking at her tonight, I would say she's dropped several years."

"I agree."

"And this might sound crazy, but she doesn't seem as wrinkled."

Lottie nodded. "I have a theory about that. She's not as tense. When she got here, she was wound up tighter than a clock. These days she's more relaxed. When you're anxious, it shows in your face. When you're relaxed, your whole countenance changes."

"Guess she's relaxed, then."

Sure enough, Flossie let out a little giggle, one that had Phineas turning red in the face.

"Wonder what's up with those two," Gilbert said.

"I don't know. But if you'd told me in the beginning that Phineas and Flossie would eventually see something in each other, I would've said you were crazy." Lottie grinned. "Sometimes the Lord has a plan we can't see."

"Yes." Suddenly Gilbert felt that same attraction to Lottie as the morning he'd kissed her. "Sometimes He does. Maybe we're just too busy or too distracted to notice."

"Yes." She gazed into his eyes, and his heart skipped to double time.

Just then Winifred came up to them, giggling. "Gil, you've got to come and see Cornelia's costume for the play. It's simply divine."

Winifred took him by the arm and pulled him up out of his chair. "You don't mind, do you, Lottie?"

"Oh, I..." She looked disappointed but didn't stop them.

Gilbert felt a strange reluctance at leaving her seated at the table without him. What right did Winifred have, interrupting their private conversation? Then again, he'd never been very good at turning her away, had he?

Until tonight.

"Winnie, if you don't mind, Lottie and I were in the middle of something. We'll have to talk later."

Winnie's eyes widened, but she didn't respond. Instead, she turned with a huff and headed back across the room to Cornelia.

Gilbert reached for Lottie's hand. "You were saying?"

"I was saying..." Her eyes filled with tears. "Oh, Gil, I'm just so happy. Everything's going right for a change."

Yes, everything was going right. And Gilbert couldn't help but think that things were only going to get better from here.

SEVENTEEN

HOT DAMES, COLD HEARTS

Folks, Alice Well down at Parker Lodge. No, you didn't read that wrong. Alice Well is the name of one of the characters in our upcoming melodrama. She will be joined by our villain, Earl E. Bird, played by Augie Miller, who—according to our sources—has announced his run for mayor in the upcoming election. We at Parker Lodge find this news Justin Credible. Oops. There we go again, introducing you to yet another character in our show. We try to keep things light here at the lodge, where rehearsals are in full swing. In fact, things are going so well that we will begin selling tickets for the show just one week from today. So save your nickels and dimes! We don't want you to come Penny Less. Oops. There we go again! Guess you'll just have to c'mon out to the show to meet these folks in person. —Your friends at Parker Lodge

ON MONDAY MORNING Lottie awoke in a blissful state. After last night's meeting, she could hardly wait to get to work. With all of her cast members linking arms, the show would be a rousing success and the lodge would be saved. And with Gil's hand in hers, they would prove that true love could win out, no matter the bumps and bruises along the way.

Her happy frame of mind lasted all the way to the lodge, where she found Mrs. Parker and Hannah baking up a storm in the kitchen. Lottie's smile widened even more when Gilbert walked in and gave her a cheerful "G'morning!" Indeed. It was a good morning. And nothing—and/or no one—could change that. This morning she held the world on a string.

"Oh, Lottie, I almost forgot..." Mrs. Parker reached into her pocket and pulled out an envelope. "The postman came by early this morning to deliver something for you."

"For me? Here at the lodge?"

"Yes. Look, honey." She pointed at the envelope. "It's from Denver. A Mr. Gerald Jefferson. Does that name sound familiar?"

"Not at all." Lottie reached for the envelope, fingering the expensive paper for a moment.

"It's addressed to Miss Lottie Sanders, director of *Predicament at Parker Lodge,* so it must be for you," Mrs. Parker said. "Open it, honey."

Lottie gingerly opened the envelope and pulled out a letter. She didn't recognize the handwriting at all, but she was quickly caught up in the message of the letter.

Gilbert leaned in close. "What does it say?"

The letter trembled in her hands as she read. "Oh, no. Oh, no!" Her stomach churned as she absorbed the note; then the paper fluttered out of her hand and drifted to the floor. She plopped into a chair and began to fan herself with the envelope. "This is terrible news. Terrible."

"Did someone die?" Gilbert took her hand.

"Only our show. Our reputation. Our…everything." Lottie leaned forward, her forehead dropping to the table.

As Gilbert reached down and snagged the letter, she looked up. He scanned it then shrugged. "Lottie, this isn't terrible news. A famous theater critic wants to come see our show. All the way from Denver, no less. Why, this could be the best thing that's happened to us. Think of the promotion we'll get in the Denver paper."

"Best thing?" She groaned. "I doubt it. This man has the capability of putting an end to our show before it even kicks off." She hated to state the obvious but had no choice. "Gil, have you been at the same rehearsals I've been to? Sure, the women are doing a great job, but…the men? They're lacking in so many ways." She paused to think about Jeb's latest attempt then shuddered. "All we need is for some big-name reporter to sweep in here and do a write-up blasting our show. We'll close that same night."

"What?" Flossie's voice rang out as she came into the kitchen. "Did you say a critic is coming?"

"Yes." Lottie groaned. "A Mr. Gerald Jefferson from the newspaper in Denver. I'll have to ask Winnie about him, but it sounds like he reviews most of the big shows in Denver theaters."

"Hmm." Flossie frowned.

"What are we going to do if the show opens to poor reviews? We're—we're…we're ruined!"

Lottie dissolved into tears, and Gilbert patted her on the back. "Hold your horses, Lottie. No one said anything about being ruined."

"They didn't have to. I can sense it…" She pointed to her midsection. "Right here, in my gut."

"What happened to all that positive thinking from last night?" he asked. "When we left here, we agreed to trust God to work out the details. He's the one who's going to save this show, not us. And if He's for us, as Flossie reminded us last night, who can be against us?"

"It's true. I did say that," Flossie acknowledged. "Though, I must confess I'm a bit worried about the quality of acting, so it is a little disconcerting that a theater critic is headed our way." She looked at them. "I know that a lot of the men said they could act—and we've been really patient with them as they've fumbled their way through their lines—but maybe it's time to require more of them."

"They're so kind to take on acting roles in the first place," Lottie said. "I just don't know how it would make them feel to be demanding. They're not benefiting in any way from being in this show."

Flossie quirked a brow. "I daresay they are benefiting. Being in this show has put them in the company of many a fine woman. And they're having the time of their lives. That much is clear. So, requiring more of them isn't asking too much. Their acting skills are lacking, at best. Jeb is the poorest in the bunch, but Phineas isn't far behind him." She reached down to grab a cookie from the tray.

"Doesn't take a trained eye to see that Jeb Otis is no actor," Gilbert threw in. "But he's doing his level best."

"Yes, but we have a paying audience," Lottie reminded him. "I mean, in theory we have a paying audience. No one has actually purchased any tickets yet, and that has me very nervous."

Now Gilbert looked nervous too. "I see your point."

"And if this theater critic shows up on the very first night, as this letter suggests, we'll be doomed." She leaned her elbows on the table, feeling the weight of the world on her shoulders. So much for taking her hands off and giving this situation to God.

"Not doomed, Lottie." Gilbert sat across from her. "Don't be so dramatic."

His words pinched. "Someone has to be," she said.

Flossie squared her shoulders. "This is a matter for prayer, and I, for one, promise to hit my knees. Just as soon as I have a little chat with Phineas and Jeb."

"A chat?" Lottie and Gil spoke in unison.

"Yes, if you don't mind. I think I'm the right person for the task, because of my many years in the theater. I can encourage them to take their acting more seriously. If I word things carefully, they won't be wounded."

"You don't mind?" Lottie asked.

"Not a bit. This won't be the first time I've had to give this speech." She smiled. "And besides, I daresay Phineas will do as I ask. He's, well, he's…" Her words drifted off as her cheeks remained the loveliest shade of pink.

"Yes, he is." For the first time since opening the letter, Lottie smiled. "He's a great fella, Flossie, and I think you're right. He'll listen to you. And you can give him some special acting lessons on the side."

"I think he'll enjoy the extra attention from you, to be honest." Gil laughed. "So I doubt you'll hear any complaints."

"Hope not. But I'll say a little prayer just in case." Flossie gave them a little wave.

No point in worrying about spilled milk, as Mama always said. Surely by the time the show kicked off the first weekend in August, the fellas' acting would improve.

Lottie only hoped they kept their acting to the stage between now and then.

* * * * *

GILBERT SPENT THE MORNING working on set pieces for the melodrama. He needed to stay focused on the task at hand, now that he knew a theater critic would be analyzing his work. No shoddy craftsmanship here. Of course, with Chauncy at his side, there was little chance of that. They worked together to build a backdrop for the first scene, Chauncy chattering all the while about Grace.

"Looks like you two are getting along well." Gilbert couldn't help but smile.

"Yep. This whole plan of bringing in brides is working out better than we hoped. I think Phineas is sweet on Flossie."

"I've noticed that." Gilbert laid down his hammer and stepped back to analyze his work. "And it's clear Fanny and Jeb are cozying up to each other, as well."

"Yep." Chauncy pieced together a couple of two-by-fours and reached for the bucket of nails. He put several in his teeth then spoke around them. "Ain't quite figured out who Augie's got in mind. That uppity Margaret gal is just his type, though."

"I wouldn't be so sure about that." Gilbert took his hammer in hand again. "He's been singing another lady's praises, as well."

"Oh, who's that?"

Before Gilbert could respond, Flossie came flying into the room, her face pale. Lottie followed directly behind with a group of women after her, all looking distraught. Gilbert stopped his work to listen.

JANICE HANNA

"What's wrong?" Lottie placed her hand on Flossie's arm. "Has something happened?"

"Something has happened, all right." Flossie's face contorted. "Only, I think you know all about it." She looked at the men, her eyes narrowing. "All of you."

"Know all about it?" Lottie looked alarmed, and Gilbert didn't blame her. "What do you mean?"

By now the other women had joined them, all talking at once. Gilbert could hardly make sense of it. Well, until Fanny's voice rang out.

"We know, Lottie." Fanny placed her balled-up fists on her hips. "Flossie told us."

"Everything," Margaret added.

"Yes, absolutely everything," Cornelia said, her eyes filling with tears.

Once again the women's emotional voices began to layer, one on top of the other.

Unnerved, Gilbert laid down his hammer and took a few steps in their direction, though he had a feeling he would end up regretting it.

"Let me just ask you a question." Flossie took over now, her gaze shifting back and forth between Gilbert and Lottie. "Were we brought here"—she gestured to the room full of women—"to marry the single men of Estes Park?"

"Uh-oh." Chauncy spit out his mouthful of nails, which hit the floor plinking and plunking. Instead of picking them up, he skedaddled out of the room.

Coward.

231

Gilbert wished he could do the same, of course, and all the more when he stared into the angry eyes of nearly a dozen women.

"Are we nothing more than a bunch of mail-order brides?" Flossie asked. "Is that what this is?"

"Wh–who told you such a thing?" Lottie looked as if she might be sick.

"Phineas." Flossie dropped into a chair and shook her head. "I went over to his place to talk to him about his acting skills, and things got ugly."

"Ugly?" Gilbert pulled out a chair and sat next to her. "What do you mean?"

"I guess he didn't take to my critique of his acting." Her expression tightened. "Though, I did my best to explain about the critic coming and all."

"There's a critic coming to see our show?" Margaret asked. "A professional one?" When Flossie nodded, she dropped into a chair and muttered, "Oh no!"

"What about Phineas?" Gilbert asked, his heart in his throat. "What did he say after that?"

"He got good and mad about my critique of his acting. He said he worked hard to get the ladies here and deserved better. I asked him what he meant when he said he worked hard to get us here."

"Oh dear." Now Lottie dropped into a seat and leaned her forehead on the table.

"And he said...?" Gilbert felt his jaw twitching as he anticipated Flossie's next words.

"He said that he'd paid good money to bring us all here and hadn't gotten his money's worth."

Tell me he didn't.

A gasp went up from the ladies. They gathered around the table in a cluster.

"Lottie? Gilbert?" Fanny looked back and forth between them. "Something you want to tell us?"

"Yes, tell us the truth, Lottie." Hannah's eyes filled with tears. "Was this whole thing some sort of hoax? Were we brought here under false pretenses?"

"You two have a lot to answer for." Fanny waggled her finger back and forth. "If even half of what Flossie says is true, then we've got a lot to talk about."

Lottie lifted her head, lashes damp. "I can't deny that the men have always hoped they would find wives from the group of women," she said. "But I can assure you, the idea of putting on a melodrama to raise funds for the lodge has always been the chief plan, though the men had other ideas. From the start I told them not to make assumptions, but you know how they are. They're anxious to marry."

Gilbert cleared his throat and the women all looked his way. His gaze shifted downward.

"Well, not anymore," Flossie said with the wave of a hand. "After the discussion I just had with Phineas, I daresay he will never marry. If his display of temper was any indication of his true personality, I don't know a woman who would put up with him. Especially not a strong woman like me."

"I didn't come to Colorado to get married." Cherry's eyes grew wide. "I came to do a show. Plain and simple."

"Wait a minute..." Sharla snapped her fingers. "Is *this* why the ladies in that Women's League think we're—we're..." Her face tightened. "You know." Another pause followed. "Do they think that of us because we were brought here for the men from the very beginning? In other words, do they know that the men paid money for us?"

Gilbert had just opened his mouth to respond when Grace interjected her thoughts on the matter.

"Well, they can lay those hopes to rest," she said, her eyes narrowing to slits. "Any thoughts I might've had about letting Chauncy court me just flew out the window."

"Same here," Fanny said. "If I'd known for a minute that Jeb had paid some sort of price for a mail-order bride, I would never have considered him."

Lottie groaned. "Honestly, ladies, it's not like that. And no, you're not mail-order brides. As I said, the men were just hopeful you might take an interest in them."

"Is this why we were made to sign that ridiculous contract?" Flossie asked. "So we would stay long enough to end up falling for the men?"

Gilbert sighed. "Look, ladies, I can't deny that the men felt they would need time to woo you. But you can clearly see that we primarily needed the time to put together a show. We've never done a show before, and—"

"Now I see why." Flossie gave him a sour look then turned her attention to Lottie. "You were never meant to be a director, and those men were never meant to be actors."

"You're wrong. I wanted to help Parker Lodge from the very beginning." Lottie dissolved into tears and Gilbert felt his heart grow as heavy as lead. She'd tried to tell him this was a bad idea and he hadn't listened. Now he had to pay the piper. Er, pay a room full of women. But how could he go about paying them back when the fellas had invested very real money into the show? If these ladies skedaddled and the show fell apart, everything would unravel. The lodge would have to close its doors and he would end up owing the men their investments back.

With the eyes of the women boring a hole through him, Gilbert rose. He'd just started to say something brilliant—though he hadn't quite figured out what—when his mother entered the room, her face ashen.

"G–Gil?"

He faced her, happy to be looking away from the women, though he had to wonder why she looked ill.

"Um, I think you'd better come with me."

"Come with you? Where?"

She fussed with her apron strings, her hands trembling. "To the pie parlor. We, um, have an unexpected guest."

From the expression on Mama's face, they weren't talking about a welcome guest. Gilbert went to her, and she leaned over to fill him in. "It's Thaddeus Baker, the lawyer from Loveland."

Perfect. Just what he needed to cap off the ideal morning.

EIGHTEEN

LOVESICK IN LOVELAND

What good is a theatrical without conflict? Good versus evil. Hero versus villain. A great melodrama must have all of the above. Of course, we would rather just get straight to the happily-ever-after part, but would that really leave the audience satisfied? Of course not! Patrons are looking for angst and lots of it! And do we deliver! Of course, this isn't the first story chock-full of conflict. Between now and opening night, we would like to encourage our upcoming audience members to read the original good versus evil story, starting with the book of Genesis and going all the way through to the book of Revelation. You will find that it, too, has a large cast of likable—and unlikable—characters.
—Your friends at Parker Lodge

Rushing out of the room on Gil's heels seemed the only logical solution to Lottie. She'd rather face a den full of lions than ten angry actresses with their penetrating glares. As she ran, she heard a couple of them making comments that stung—almost as much as Flossie's words about how she was never meant to be a director.

Only when she reached the pie parlor did she realize why Mrs.

Parker had called Gilbert out. Thaddeus Baker. Althea Baker's nephew. The attorney. Though she hadn't seen the fella in years, she would recognize him anywhere. Same haughty expression. Same businesslike attire. No, nothing had changed.

And yet, everything had changed.

She looked on as Thad extended his hand in Gil's direction.

"Gilbert Parker." Thad offered a strained smile. "It's been years."

"Yes." Gil shook his hand, but Lottie saw the tight expression.

"Is there a place we can sit and visit?" Thad asked. "I have some important things to discuss."

"My office is, well…" Gilbert stumbled over the words and then paused. Lottie knew why, of course. Gil's office was filled, top to bottom, with costumes for the show.

"Maybe we could find a place outside to sit and talk?" Thad said. "I noticed a table and chairs out by the river."

"That would be fine."

Lottie's heart continued to race as she tagged along on the men's heels. Mrs. Parker stayed put in the pie parlor to wait on customers but mouthed, "I'm praying!" as Lottie walked by. They needed those prayers right now. No doubt about it.

Thad paused at the river's edge and turned to face them. "Now, you two know me. Or at least you did when we were children. You know I don't really want to stir up more trouble."

"Well, that's good." Gil looked relieved. He leaned against a tree. "Thought maybe you'd come searching for some."

"No." Thad released a breath. "But, as you're probably aware, the Women's League has called me here to discuss a matter of grave importance."

A shiver ran down Lottie's spine. "I'm sure if we just talk sensibly, we can get to the bottom of this. It's all a huge misunderstanding, you see. There's truly no reason to get folks any more riled up than they already are."

"And they are, for sure." Thad's brow wrinkled. "Do you two realize that folks around here are convinced you are running a…well, a brothel? They think these women you've brought here are—"

"Some of the most precious women I've ever met." Lottie offered a smile.

"Ah." A smug look came over him. "Well, that may be, but the Women's League doesn't see it that way." He opened his briefcase and pulled out an envelope with several legal-looking papers inside.

"I think I'd better sit down." Lottie took a seat at the table and Thad took the spot to her left. Gil—heaven help him—sat on Thad's left, looking as if he'd like to drown himself in the river sooner than face this head-on.

Thad lost Lottie somewhere between the words "morality issues" and "prostitution charges." None of this made any sense. Had Mama and Althea Baker lost control of their senses, to take things this far? Why would they do such a thing?

Thad pressed the papers back inside his briefcase and closed it. He gazed at Gilbert then glanced Lottie's way too. "These ladies have asked me to draft a petition to present to the local business owners, which I plan to do only if this meeting with you does not go as I had hoped."

"A petition?"

"Yes. They're asking local merchants not to sell food or other supplies to you as long as the women remain at the lodge. I'm sure you understand."

Gilbert rose, his face now beet-red. "I don't understand. In fact, I will never understand. Why don't you say what you came to say, Thad? Tell us about this lawsuit you plan to file if we don't back down."

"Well, now, let's don't get ahead of ourselves." Thad set his brief-case on the ground next to him.

"Exactly. There won't be a suit because the Women's League has no case."

"Oh?" Thad rose. "I would beg to differ. The women are starting a petition to avoid filing a morality suit."

"Morality suit?"

"Yes. Allow me to cite Chamberlain vs. Maxwell, where the city of Pine Grove filed suit against a house of prostitution that was using a lodge as a cover."

"But we're not a—a…" Lottie couldn't even get the words out. She wanted to punch this fellow right in the face. To give him what for. Why, oh, why, was she wearing a dress and good shoes? Her overalls would've come in handy right now. She could've easily taken down this smug lawyer in her overalls and cowboy boots.

Gilbert rose and raked his fingers through his hair, leaving it, as he so often did, in a messy state. "Ask the reverend. He'll tell you what he thinks about their nonsense. Even the sheriff has told me that he thinks they're behaving like a group of bullies."

"I will be speaking to several key leaders in town when I leave here." Thad reached for his briefcase.

Righteous indignation rose inside of Lottie. "For your informa-tion, we're going to stand up to them, even if every merchant in town decides to close their doors to us. Even if they do file some sort of suit against us. Would you like to know why, Thad?"

The attorney remained silent, likely stunned by her outburst.

"Because right always wins over might. In the end, anyway."

"Yes," Gil chimed in. "So draft your petition. Fill it with your legal mumbo jumbo. Threaten away. Frankly, I don't care."

"I can see that this conversation has come to an end." Thad took off across the property then paused and glanced back at them. "You know, I had hoped to persuade you to end this melodrama nonsense and send those ladies packing. Now I can see that I have no choice but to draft that petition." He took several more steps toward the building then stopped and sniffed the air. "Why are they baking all those pies in there, anyway?"

"Why do you want to know?" Gil crossed his arms. "Are you going to petition us to shut down our pie parlor too?"

"Of course not. There's no law against baking." Thad took a couple more steps then stopped and sniffed the air again. "What sort of pie is that I smell? Smells almost like—"

"Apple streusel," Lottie said. "Fresh-picked apples, just the tiniest hint of cinnamon and nutmeg, with a laced crust better than Grandma could make."

This stopped him cold. "Hmm. My favorite." A couple more steps landed him at the door leading into the pie parlor. "I think I left my hat inside."

He slipped inside the door and Lottie followed behind him. To her surprise she found Winifred helping Hannah and Mrs. Parker with the pies. Winnie's face lit into a smile when she saw Thad. "Well, hello there. How can I help you this fine day?"

"Winnie Sanders." He reached across the glass counter for her hand. "Don't you remember me? Thaddeus Baker. We played together as kids when I came to stay with my aunt Althea."

"Oh, well, my goodness, yes." She grinned. "You're that pesky boy who used to chase me around the playground and call me names."

"Guilty as charged." He chuckled. "And speaking of guilty as charged, do you know what a fine mess these two have stirred up?" He gestured to Lottie and Gilbert.

Winnie dismissed his concerns with the wave of a hand. "Oh, pooh on all that. People are making such a fuss." She batted her eyelashes, which caused Thad to freeze in place. "Lottie has explained everything to me, and it's clear there's been a huge misunderstanding. You know how those women are—they make mountains out of molehills."

"Enough mountains to cause a lot of trouble," Lottie added.

Thad took a step back. "Still, they're prepared to take action, and they've paid for my services, so I have no option but to—"

"Oh, Thaddeus…" Winnie offered up a girlish giggle. "This is just silly. Tell them to drop it."

"I wish I could."

"I see. Well, in the meantime, why don't you try a slice of pie? I'm especially fond of the Sanders' Strawberry."

Lottie gasped. "Sanders' Strawberry?"

"Sure." Winnie gave her a wink. "Our family's recipe."

Thad's gaze narrowed. "You're telling me that your mother—the same woman who brought me here to represent her—has entered a pie in some contest Parker Lodge is running?"

"That pie was entered, and it won." Mrs. Parker glanced up from her work on the other side of the case. "I got the recipe early this morning and baked the pie myself. It's by far the best strawberry pie I've ever had, so I put it on the menu right away. Can't wait to share the news."

Winnie offered Thad a huge slice. He took the plate and stared at the gorgeous mound of whipped cream perched atop the bright red strawberries over a luscious graham-cracker crust.

"Well, now, this is problematic."

"What's problematic?" Winnie's nose wrinkled. "Surely you don't mean the pie."

He grabbed the fork and took a bite. His eyes fluttered closed and the most satisfied expression came over him. "Oh, this is good. Really, really good."

"I thought you said it was problematic." Winnie giggled. "You lawyers. You make no sense to me at all."

His eyes popped open. "I meant it's problematic because one of the women in the Women's League—your mother, no less—is apparently undermining their cause by cavorting with the opposition."

"Ooh. Cavorting. I've always been fond of cavorting." Winnie's eyes grew large. "But I do see how it could be considered problematic. Would you like a scoop of ice cream to go with that pie?"

"On the house," Mrs. Parker added and then smiled.

"I don't suppose it would hurt anything to have a scoop of ice cream."

"Perfect." Winnie went to work, scooping up a big white mound of homemade vanilla. "And if you don't mind, I'll join you so we can catch up on old times."

"Well, that would be nice."

She came out from behind the counter, her skirt swishing as she sashayed across the room. "Let's go outside. It's such a pretty day."

"Yes. Beautiful." His gaze remained fixed on Winnie as she headed outside, chattering all the way.

"Well, that was a close one."

Lottie turned to face Gil, who looked as if he might be sick.

"What did he have to say, son?" Mrs. Parker asked.

"He knows about the men fronting the money for the ladies to be here, and that seems to be the primary source of the problem." Gil paced the room. "I'm so scared he's going to find out about our primary investor."

"Primary investor?" Lottie and Mrs. Parker spoke the words in unison.

Gil's face turned red. "Yes. Look, I'm really not at liberty to say anything more. But you might as well know that a local investor has fronted most of the money for the set, costumes, handbills, and so on. What the fellas came up with went to food, as you know. That's what has the ladies so riled up, thinking the men are paying for, well, services."

"So, let me ask you a question," Lottie said. "Will this primary investor be named in the lawsuit, if the Women's League decides to sue?"

"I don't know." Judging from the wrinkled brow, Gil was just as worried about this as she was. "That would be really cruel. And not a very nice way to repay him for his kindness and generosity."

"We just have to make sure those ladies don't find out who he is," Lottie said. She turned away, the sting of tears in her eyes, knowing full well who'd funded the show. And the sooner she could get home to thank him, the better.

* * * * *

Gilbert continued to pace the pie parlor, his stomach in his throat. The attorney's threats had stirred up a hornet's nest inside of him, to be sure. Why, oh, why had he taken any money from the men? And how could he convince folks that things weren't what they looked like?

Lottie had tears in her eyes. "Gil, I've got to get back to the ladies and somehow convince them that things aren't as bad as they seem. It's bad enough having threats coming from outside. To have them coming from our cast is even worse. I've got to get back into their good graces. Even if they won't speak to the men, I think I can get them to trust me again. I hope."

"Well, maybe the men have misrepresented themselves to the ladies. I don't know. But I do know that those ladies don't even know how great those fellas are. No doubt Flossie thinks Phineas is just a simple farmer, based on the way he dresses. She has no way of knowing he's got a thriving cattle farm and a big fancy house. And Jeb might not have much money, but he makes up for it with those cooking skills. A woman like Fanny—please pardon me for saying this—but a woman like Fanny would really benefit from a fella who loved to cook. And Chauncy...well, I've never met a kinder man. His woodworking shop is doing well, especially during tourist season."

"What are you saying?"

"I'm just saying that the ladies wouldn't be getting the short end of the stick if they did end up marrying these fellas. I just hope their anger doesn't prevent them from whatever romantic unions the Lord might've had in mind all along."

"You're saying the Lord brought them here?"

"Flossie said as much last night during that passionate speech of hers. Less than twenty-four hours ago she stood in front of us and claimed that the Lord brought all of the ladies to Estes Park. Now they're ready to pack their bags and head back home. Either the Lord brought them here or He didn't. There's no gray area. No room for debate."

"True."

"The only thing that's changed is that the women are now questioning the men's motives. Other than that, everything is exactly as it was last night. We somehow need to convince the women that the men had their best interests at heart."

Lottie approached, and he noticed the trembling in her hands.

"Gilbert, there's one thing I have to know before I go back in there and try to patch things up with the ladies. It's been bothering me for days." She pulled him aside, away from his mother, and whispered, "Why did you kiss me the other morning?"

He opened his mouth to respond, but she kept going.

"It's clear you don't care for me. The only logical conclusion I can draw is that you were trying to lead me on. I feel I deserve an honest answer. Has this whole thing been a ruse from the start?"

"A ruse?"

Tears filled Lottie's eyes. "It felt very real," she whispered. "But now I have to wonder if that kiss was part of some sort of scheme the fellas put you up to, to get me to go along with you about the melodrama. Am I right?"

"Well, I..." His words faltered. "Look, Lottie, maybe at first I wanted to win you over to my way of thinking. The fellas suggested I flatter you a little bit. Offer some manly charm to convince you."

"Manly charm. Humph." She snorted.

"I did want to win you over, sure, but somewhere along the way…" He paused, his heart in his throat. *Somewhere along the way it stopped being a game and became real.*

She balled up her fists and placed them on her hips. "You once told me that we needed women with staying power. Do you remember that conversation?"

"Of course."

"Well, maybe I've overstayed my welcome."

"What?" He reached for her hand. "No. Lottie, please. What are you saying?"

"I'm saying that I've had enough. I see that you're…" She paused, tears now streaming. "That you're still enamored with my sister. And Cornelia. When they walk into the room you completely forget I'm there. I see how it is, Gil. I'm not stupid. You only want me around because I'm a hard worker. That's all it's ever been."

"Oh, Lottie." He shook his head and fought for the right words.

"Anyway, I've had it. You've made it clear you don't want me around here anymore."

"Of course I do. That's crazy talk."

"Why do you want me?" She crossed her arms and stared him down. "Why?"

"Because, I…" He raked his fingers through his hair and paced the room. "I can't imagine Parker Lodge without you in it." Now he fought back tears. "You bring life to the place, Lottie. The guests love you. The locals love you. I…"

She leaned in close, but he couldn't get the words out. "Anyway, I—I don't know what would happen if you went away," he finally managed. He found himself completely tongue-tied as he stared into Lottie's beautiful face. Why, oh, why couldn't he just sweep her into his arms and tell her how he felt? Judging from her expression, she would probably smack him if he tried. Oh, but how he wanted to try. And so he leaned in, determined to replay that mesmerizing moment when he'd kissed her before.

Just as he leaned in to prove his feelings, she stepped back. "Gil, I—I don't know what to think." Turning on her heel, she ran from the room.

NINETEEN

Jilted in the Jitney

As opening night draws near, we at Parker Lodge feel it only fair to warn our audience members that our melodrama's story continues to intensify. When a script is carefully crafted, it will always contain one scene, one inevitable moment, where the hero appears to falter, where it looks as if he won't come through. Do not be alarmed! This is only a ploy on the part of the scriptwriter. Any writer worth his salt knows that he must tease his audience with the "How can this possibly work out?" scene. Why torment the audience members in such a fashion, you ask? So that they get their money's worth. And we at Parker Lodge are keen on you getting your money's worth. Get your tickets before they sell out! Special rates for members of all local civic organizations, including the Women's League. —Your friends at Parker Lodge

GILBERT WALKED OUT OF THE KITCHEN, his heart heavy. A walk by the river would do him good right about now. Unfortunately, he discovered that Lottie had already beat him there. Oh well. He'd take a jaunt into town. Meeting up with the men was key to figuring out a plan of action. No doubt when they heard that the ladies knew of their plot—albeit mostly innocent—to marry them, they would react unpleasantly.

He stopped off at Phineas's house and found his friend seated in his parlor in low spirits.

Gilbert entered the room and took a seat across from him. "I know you had a fight with Flossie. Heard all about it."

"Yep. I figger the cat's out of the bag now." Phineas sighed. "Sorry about that, Gilbert. My temper got the best of me and I said some things, well, that I shouldn't have."

"Understandable."

"So I'm guessing Flossie told the others?" Phineas's brow wrinkled.

"Mm-hmm." Gilbert didn't add any of the particulars.

"I see. Figgered as much." Phineas sighed. "Well, what do we do now?"

"Now we go to town and meet with the other men. We're the ones who started all this. We've got to be the ones to end it."

"You don't think it's too late for that?"

"Nope." Gilbert rose. "Not as long as I'm alive and well. I still believe very much in what Flossie said last night—God can turn things around. Trust me when I say that I quoted a few of those Scriptures from Flossie's list on the way over here. No matter how bad things get—lawsuits, petitions, angry women—I still think God will have His way in the end."

"Well, amen." Phineas rose also. "When you put it like that, I have no choice but to go to town with you."

"Thanks."

Moments later they set off, bound for Augie's office. Along the way they stopped at Jeb's house. Poor Jeb. Until they clued him in, he had no idea the ladies were even mad. The same was true with Chauncy, who got the news when the men stopped off at his woodworking shop in town. Both men seemed devastated to learn that the women they'd grown so attached to were now angry at them. The only one who seemed to take the news in stride was Augie, who sat at his desk at the *Mountaineer* nodding as the story unfolded.

"I figure we've got to pay the piper," he said at last. "Did we or did we not cook up a scheme to bring those ladies to Estes Park in the hopes that they would marry us? And did we or did we not invest in the show, hoping those ladies would end up in our arms?"

All the men sighed in collective unity.

"Yeah." Phineas kicked a wad of paper with the toe of his boot. "Guess yer right."

"But it ain't like we advertised for brides, exactly," Jeb said. "And we didn't exactly pay to bring them here. No one twisted their arms or nuthin'."

"They came in good faith, thinking we only needed—or wanted—them to act in a melodrama." Gilbert leaned against the wall, grateful for something to hold him up.

"Now we've created a little melodrama of our own," Augie said. "Only, we don't have a script, so it's unclear what's coming next." He paused. "But one thing's for sure—what Flossie said last night is truer than ever. We do need to band together and pray."

"Fer what, exactly?" Phineas asked. "Pray that Flossie doesn't shoot me at tonight's rehearsal?"

"She won't," Augie said. "She's a consummate pro. A theater buff. She'll be all business at that rehearsal tonight. What we need, fellas, is a way to prove to the ladies that we've made fools of ourselves." A smirk followed as he added, "Shouldn't be too hard."

"They're already convinced, sounds like." Jeb sighed.

"Yes, but they also need to know that we have their best interest at heart," Gilbert explained. "That, they don't know. And they also don't know how sorry we are, or the logic behind why we came up with the idea in the first place." He paused. "Not trying to white-wash what we've done. Just saying our motivation wasn't bad. They need to know that. The whole town needs to know it."

Phineas still looked downcast. "How do we prove it to 'em?"

"Not sure." Gil shifted his position. "I just know that we need to start by praying. That's why I wanted to meet with you fellas before the rehearsal. Seems like prayer is probably our only answer. And boy-howdy, do we need it. That lawyer showed up today."

"I know all about it," Augie said. "He stopped by here on his way to your place. Something about a petition that the local business-men are supposed to sign to boycott Parker Lodge."

"Are we gonna keep on yammerin', or are we gonna pray?" Jeb pulled off his hat. "'Cause we could stand here all day talkin' and not put a dent in the problem."

"True, true." Gilbert glanced around the room at his good friends and bowed his head. Surely, with God's help, this mess they'd made could all be turned around.

* * * * *

LOTTIE PULLED OFF HER BOOTS and socks and stepped into the shallow waters of Fall River, overcome with emotion. First the scene with the ladies. Then the visit from the attorney. Now this? Had she and Gil really just turned on each other?

Common sense kicked in. He'd never really cared about her at all. That much she now understood. That kiss—that unexpected moment of bliss—was all a ruse. All to appease Phineas, Jeb, Chauncy, and Augie. To keep her on his team.

Would she stay on his team, or would she run?

Lottie kicked the water, splashing it high into the air. "That's what I think about what you've done to me, Gil." She kicked the water again. This felt good. Several more kicks got her anger out.

Afterward, she sat on the bank of the river, watching the water as it rushed by. Seemed like she always ended up here when life's frustrations got the best of her—at the water. Here, in this place, she felt free. She gazed at the water as it ran downstream at a rapid pace, headed to the vast unknown. Nothing stopped it. And when she stood in it, the current tugged at her and gave her courage.

Oh, how she needed courage! And peace. Lottie began to pray with great passion, her heart overflowing—with anger, at first, and then genuine compassion.

By the time she calmed down, her decision had been made. As much as she wanted to run for the hills, the only decision that made sense was to stay put. After all, they still had a rehearsal in a few hours, and their little melodrama would forge ahead, no matter the obstacles.

She put her boots back on, praying all the while. She quoted a couple of the Scriptures Flossie had given them as she made her way back to the dining hall. When she arrived, she found Flossie seated with Fanny at one of the tables. The other ladies were nowhere to be seen. Flossie glanced up at Lottie with tearstained eyes and gestured for her to come closer.

"Lottie, I—I spoke in haste. I…" Flossie's voice cracked and she swallowed hard. "I didn't mean what I said—that you weren't meant to be a director." She looked up and brushed tears from her eyes. "In so many ways you've been a better director than I could've been. You've held your temper in check when others would've lost theirs. You've been nothing but kind to everyone and patient to those who've struggled with their lines."

"In short, you're the real deal, Lottie." Fanny stood and wrapped Lottie in her arms.

In that moment, the dam broke and Lottie began to weep. "I—I—I did—didn't want the fellas to make assumptions. I told them so from the beginning. Trust me, I did."

"Oh, you poor dear girl." Flossie rose and rushed her way, joining the circle. "I know you're not behind all of this. It's those…those men. They need to be strung up for what they've done." She squared her shoulders. "But we have no choice."

"O–oh?" Lottie's tears came in force now.

"Yes." Flossie smiled and whispered, "We must finish what we started."

"You—you really mean that?" Lottie could hardly believe it. "You're going to stay?"

"Well, of course," Fanny said. "What they've done is terrible, but it doesn't change the fact that we came here to do a show to save Parker Lodge. If we ever needed to prove that, once and for all, it's now. We *must* plow forward, for the sake of every woman who's in it. We have to prove to this community that we are women of our word, women who mean what they say and say what they mean."

"Just one thing, Lottie." Flossie put up her hand. "I think it's only right that we limit our time with the men to the hours of rehearsal. They need to know that what they've done is wrong, and that there's a need to come clean and make apologies to all involved. I won't waver on this."

"None of the ladies will," Fanny said. "Though they've all promised to be civil to the men, for the sake of the show."

"For the sake of the show." Lottie sighed and swiped her eyes with the back of her hand. "I'm very grateful, and I know that, ultimately, Mrs. Parker and Gil will be too." She offered a weak smile. "I'm sure, when all is said and done, we'll look back on this and laugh."

"Hmm. Hard to picture." Fanny shrugged. "But if you say so."

Lottie headed off to find the other ladies and, after a few tears and some lengthy conversation, assured them that no one expected any of them to get married or to stay in Estes Park beyond the length of the show.

After convincing them of that fact, she made her way down to the pie parlor, where she filled Mrs. Parker in on the situation.

Mrs. Parker gave her a hug. "Oh, Lottie. I knew trouble was brewing. I could sense it. I'll be praying for all involved."

"Thank you. We need those prayers."

Lottie went through the motions of doing her daily chores, only pausing for a moment when Jeb arrived to start cooking dinner for the ladies. He took her hand and gave it a squeeze and promised to keep his distance from the others. When the dinner hour arrived, he stayed in the kitchen. None of the other fellas showed up, including

Gil. Thank goodness, they all came just in time for rehearsal. Not a word was spoken about the morning's events. Everyone had a "let's get down to business" attitude.

Lottie somehow made it through the rehearsal, though the tension in the room was so thick, she could've cut through it with her pa's bowie knife. The only time the ladies spoke to the men was onstage, in character.

Other things kept her distracted, as well—the visit from Thad Baker, for one thing. Would the local merchants really sign that petition? Why, oh, why wouldn't Mama and Althea Baker just give up and send their lawyer back to Loveland where he belonged?

Of course, the situation that burdened her the most was the one with Gil. Many times she caught him glancing her way. Still, she kept her distance. After what he'd put her through, she'd rather just keep to herself, thank you very much.

The rehearsal ran smoothly and Lottie caught a ride home from Phineas to avoid having to be alone with Gil. By the time she crawled into bed, her head ached. The nighttime hours were spent tossing and turning, with intermittent prayers being offered up. Still, she didn't feel a sense of peace. In fact, she felt so ill upon awakening that she decided to stay home until the evening rehearsal.

Downstairs, she heard her parents quarreling, and she sighed. Couldn't she escape the drama even at home? She'd hoped to talk to her father about the money he'd invested, to thank him for his kindness. Guess that would have to wait.

A rap sounded at the door, and Winnie opened it and stuck her head inside. "Sounds like there's trouble brewing downstairs."

"There's trouble brewing everywhere." Lottie sighed again.

Winnie took a few steps into the room and sat on the edge of the bed, a pained expression on her face. She gripped Lottie's hand and gazed into her eyes. "There's something I need to say to you."

"Oh?"

"Yes." She took a deep breath. "I haven't been a very good big sister, and I want to apologize for that. Being away put things in perspective. Then, when I came back, everything was topsy-turvy."

"What happened to us, Winnie?" Lottie asked. "We used to be so close when we were little."

A tear trickled down Winnie's cheek. "Lottie-Lou, do you have any idea just how jealous I've been of you?"

"Jealous…of me?" Lottie could hardly believe it.

"Well, of course, you little runt. You've always had Pa's heart. You've been his favorite from the very beginning. That meant Mama focused more on me."

"I think she deliberately avoided me because she was ashamed of me," Lottie said. "And maybe…" She paused to think through the words. "Maybe that's partly why I dressed the way I did. Maybe I figured if I dressed my own way she wouldn't pressure me to be like her."

Winnie's nose wrinkled and her voice lowered to a whisper. "Do you want to know the real reason I went to Denver, Lottie?"

"Of course."

"It wasn't to meet men, though I was certainly open to that idea. It was…" She sighed. "To get away from my life here. To get away from what folks expected of me."

"What they expected of you?"

"I'm convinced Mama wanted to shape me into her image," Winnie said with a shrug. "And I very nearly let her. She wanted a high-society daughter, one who would marry a well-to-do man. And I thought I could go along with her plans." She lowered her voice again. "Have you ever just had enough?"

"Have I?" Lottie fought the laughter that threatened to betray her. "Yes, Winnie, I've reached my limit—with people and with things. And I certainly understand what you mean when you say you didn't like being pressed into someone else's mold. I'm convinced—" She fought for the words. "In spite of everything, I still believe that God has great plans for our lives. If I mess up, He's capable of—of…'"

"Readjusting the plan?" Winnie grinned. "Well, speaking of that, it's another reason I came in here before going down to breakfast. I have the perfect solution for the situation with Thad Baker."

"You do?"

"Well, sure. He's only going to be in a town for a few days, so we'll have to move quickly. But I think we need to pair him up with one of the ladies from the lodge. He looks like the marrying sort, don't you think?"

"Oh no you don't," Lottie said. "We're already facing a mess because the fellas tried to plot a little matchmaking. We don't dare start with an attorney, of all people. Why, his aunt would have a conniption if she found out."

Winnie tapped her lips with her index finger, clearly lost in her thoughts. "I was thinking about Margaret Linden. She would make the perfect lawyer's wife, don't you think?" She gave Lottie a wink. "It's an ideal situation for both. She'll get the big, fancy house, and he'll get a society woman with a nice wardrobe who will look perfect on his arm at charity events and such."

Lottie had to admit, the idea did hold some merit. Still, she couldn't think about such things right now. After all, Thad Baker had come to town to represent the opposing side. He was probably passing that petition of his around town even now.

"You just let me do what I do best." Winnie giggled, clearly oblivious to Lottie's inner turmoil. "If there's one thing I know how to do, it's snag a fella." A sigh followed. "Of course, keeping them is a little tougher, but I'm going to get better with that over time. I can feel it."

From downstairs, Mama's voice rang out, laced with anger.

"You going down there?" Lottie asked.

Winnie sighed. "Guess we have no choice."

Together, they made the descent into the dining room, where they found their mother pacing. She pointed her index finger at Lottie. "I blame you for this."

Great. Someone else blaming something on me.

Lottie gazed at her mother and sighed. "What is it, Mama?"

"You and that—that pie kitchen. You had to go and do it, didn't you?"

"Do what?"

"Enter my recipe."

"W–what? Mama, I—"

Lottie's father cleared his throat. "Dorothy, before you say another word, you need to know that I did it, not Lottie. She didn't even know about it."

"You—you what?"

"I entered the strawberry pie in the contest and it won. The Sanders' Strawberry has received a place of honor behind the glass case at Parker's Pie Parlor. Isn't that exciting?"

Mother looked as if she might burst. "Harold, how could you? You've subjected me to shame and ridicule from the other ladies at the league. I'll never be president now."

"Shame? How could it be shameful? Did you not hear what I said, woman? Your pie was chosen. Everyone in town will see our family name on the wall at the pie parlor."

"Yes, that's the problem. Everyone in town will see, and they will all think that I submitted it. I'm going right over to that lodge and demand they remove it at once."

"You'll do no such thing."

Lottie gazed back and forth between her parents, wondering how this would end.

"They have no legal right. I didn't submit that recipe. It's been stolen from me."

"Dorothy, think carefully about what you're doing."

"I am thinking. I'm thinking that they've taken my recipe— a private family recipe—and used it to their own advantage to raise money for that brothel of theirs. What they've done is illegal."

"No." He stepped in front of her, a firm look on his face. "What *I've* done is perfectly legal."

"We'll just see what Thad Baker has to say about that."

"He will say that you don't have a leg to stand on."

This certainly piqued Lottie's interest.

"What do you mean?" Her mother dropped into a chair.

"I mean, you can fuss and fume all you like, but there will be no lawsuit over that pie. Would you like to know why?" He walked across the room and took his seat at the head of the table. "Because it was never your recipe to begin with. It was my mother's."

Lottie couldn't help but notice that Mama's face paled.

"Merciful heavens. I'd forgotten."

"Well, I hadn't. It's been my favorite pie since childhood. And the Sanders name is my mother's name—a name I'd like to see honored, now that she's no longer with us. So, if you don't mind, I'd like for folks in town to know that Sanders' Strawberry Pie is the featured pie of the week at the lodge. And I would appreciate it if you would call off those hounds who might try to ruin my fun."

The room grew silent. Well, silent until Winnie knocked over the pitcher of cream and Becky came in to clean up the mess.

Lottie plopped down in a chair, overwhelmed. With so many other real-life messes to tend to, a glass of spilled milk seemed small in comparison.

TWENTY

REVENGE IN THE ROCKIES

Friends, are you ready to be swept away to worlds yet unknown? Ready to travel to the highest heights? When you attend the upcoming theatrical at Parker Lodge, our set design will transport you to parts of the globe you have only imagined. You'll be amazed at the intricate handiwork and the exquisite paint colors. Our hats are off to Chauncy James, local woodworker, who designed and crafted most of the set pieces, including the backdrop of mountains. They are so lifelike, you can almost sense the weight of the clouds settling in around them. Speaking of clouds, there's been a heavy fog over our area of town for some time now. We're praying it lifts soon. In the meantime, we continue to lift our eyes unto the hills. —Your friends at Parker Lodge*

JUST TWO WEEKS BEFORE the debut of the melodrama—which Lottie had taken to calling *Revenge in the Rockies*—she made a decision to take the ladies back to the mountains for the day. They could all use a break from their labors, and she felt sure the beauty of their surroundings would invigorate them and put things into perspective.

It would provide the necessary respite from their heavy load and get them away from the men for a while.

Well, all the men but Gil. She needed him to get them there, after all. This time the journey up the mountain on the trailer was made in near silence. Traveling without Jeb and the other fellas wasn't as much fun, but Lottie didn't mind. Keeping their distance from the men would serve the ladies well, at least for now.

They arrived midmorning at Longs Peak, and she felt herself breathing more evenly. Hopefully the ladies would sense the peacefulness of the place and begin to let go of some of their bitterness toward the men.

They quickly set up a picnic spot. Cornelia turned around in circles, her eyes wide as she gazed at the mountains in the distance.

"This scenery. It's…magnificent." Grace's eyes misted over. "The colors here are unlike anything I've ever seen before. I'm not sure why they move me like they do, but the blue sky, the green grass, the white snow on the sandy-colored mountains—it's breathtaking. Makes me wish I could paint. Only, I'm not sure I could recreate the colors. And I certainly couldn't capture the majesty of all of this. The mountains are…" She shook her head. "There really are no words to describe them."

Lottie stared at the clouds, which hung low over the mountain peaks. "I know, because I've tried for years. You should read my journal. I've tried to write poems about the mountains, but they fall short every time."

"I'd love to see them anyway. I'll bet they're much better than you think." Grace gave Lottie an admiring look. "Don't sell yourself short, Lottie. Promise me?"

"I—I won't." She hardly knew what to say next, so instead of speaking she turned her gaze to the mountain and fought to hold back the tears that threatened to erupt.

"I said it that first day we came to the mountains for a picnic...." Cornelia's voice trailed off to a whisper. "I can almost *feel* God when I'm here." She turned to face Lottie, tears covering her lashes. "Isn't that odd? I mean, there's no church, no steeple, no stained-glass windows. But God is as close—maybe closer—than ever." She brushed away a tear and shrugged.

"That's not silly at all." Lottie placed her hand on Cornelia's arm. "We're always drawn to things of beauty, and what's better than God's creation? It's grander than any man-made building. And I think the reason we sense His nearness in the mountains is because they're so majestic. When we look at them, we realize that only God could have created something so—so..."

"Incredible?" Cornelia said.

"Yes." She smiled. "Incredible. I like to think that God reached down with His fingertip and created the canyons and valleys then folded His palm to pull the mountains into place."

"What a fascinating image." Cornelia's eyes misted over. "I guess I never took the time to think about where the mountains came from."

A familiar Scripture flitted through Lottie's mind, one she'd memorized as a child. She spoke the words aloud: "'For, lo, he that formeth the mountains, and createth the wind, and declareth unto man what is his thought, that maketh the morning darkness, and treadeth upon the high places of the earth, the Lord, the God of hosts, is his name.'"

"Lottie, that's beautiful." Grace whispered the last few words then turned her gaze back to the hills.

Lottie's thoughts drifted to her childhood, to the many times she'd quoted that Scripture. "It's a verse from the book of Amos, in the Old Testament. It's always been dear to me."

"It's perfect." Cornelia's damp eyes now sparkled. "It makes me wonder what took me so long to consider the fact that there is a God...at all."

"He's there all right. And He's a magnificent Creator, isn't He?" Lottie sighed. "That's how we know we can trust Him. If He took the time to create such a lovely backdrop for our lives, I have to believe He cares about the very details of our lives as well."

Cornelia sighed. "I've tried so hard to create a good life for myself and yet..." She shrugged. "Things don't always work out like I hope they will. I can't tell you how many times I've gotten my hopes up and then had them dashed. It happens all the time in theater. And in love too." She gave a little shrug.

"That's where trust comes in, I suppose."

"I guess." Cornelia took a few steps across the field, holding up her hem as she stepped across a tiny stream of water. "Until I came here, the only mountains in my life were the obstacles...the things that got in my way. Seemed like I faced them at every turn."

"The Bible says you can speak to those mountains and they have to move."

Cornelia gave her a funny look. "Speak to the mountains? What does that mean?"

"It means those obstacles in your life don't have to be obstacles. If you have enough faith, you can speak to them and they will move."

"Interesting." Cornelia turned to face the nearest peak and hollered, "Get out of my way, mountain!" which brought a handful of the other ladies running.

"What's all the ruckus over here?" Fanny asked. "Thought maybe someone fell in the creek."

"No." Cornelia smiled. "Just yelling at mountains."

"Hollering at the mountains, eh?" Fanny grinned. "Are they echoing back?" She slapped herself on the knee and laughed.

Lottie did her best not to roll her eyes. Instead, she focused on the group and smiled. "Ladies, before we have lunch, I want to show you something. I'm going to take you for a walk to the edge of Longs Peak so we can look down on the most beautiful sight in the world."

Prudy shook her head. "You ladies go on without me. I'll just stay here and set up."

"But why?" Lottie asked. "It won't be the same without you."

Prudy busied herself setting up a picnic area. She opened the basket and pulled out the quilt, which she unfolded and placed on the ground. "I'm sorry, but I just can't make myself do it."

"Whyever not?" Lottie put her hand on Prudy's arm.

"Because I've always been terrified of heights." Prudy visibly trembled. "In fact, I've always been terrified...period."

"Where does that fear come from?" Fanny asked.

Prudy settled onto the blanket then put her hand over her forehead to shield her eyes from the sun as she looked up at them. "I think..." She paused and her gaze shifted downward. "I think it goes back to my childhood. I was raised in such a poor home. My father died when I was three, and my poor mama..." Prudy dabbed at her eyes and grew silent.

Grace settled onto the quilt next to her.

"You've never a met a woman more gripped with fear," Prudy whispered. "She always anticipated the worst, and in the end, well…"

"What happened?" Grace asked, her voice filled with tenderness.

"In the end she took her own life."

Lottie gasped. She dropped to her knees next to her friend. "Oh, Prudy. You poor thing." She threw her arms around the young woman's neck, unable to hold back her tears. In spite of everything she'd been through with Mama, she couldn't imagine losing her. Not for a moment. Why, the very idea made her heart feel as heavy as lead. How ever had Prudy endured such a devastating blow?

"You precious girl." Fanny eased her way down and joined the circle. Before long, all the ladies sat together on the quilt.

Prudy gazed off in the distance, her eyes still brimming with tears. "Because I was the oldest, I had to care for my little brothers and sisters. Only…" She shook her head, tears now tumbling down her pink cheeks. "Only, I failed. And the one thing that scared me most—losing them—actually happened. They were taken to the children's home, away from me, away from the only family they'd ever known." She cried in earnest now.

Lottie tried to think of something to say but couldn't. Oh, how her heart broke at this revelation. Finally, when Prudy's sobs slowed, she knew just what to say. "Estes Park is a place of healing."

"What do you mean?"

"Well, you might not know this, but when Mr. Freelan Stanley, the man who owns the Stanley Hotel, came to town, he had consumption. The doctors didn't give him much hope. After being in Estes Park for a short time, he recovered. The Lord healed him. He

used the town to accomplish it. Well, the town and the mountains."
She gestured to the beautiful peaks nearby. "But this isn't just a place
for the healing of bodies. It's a place for the healing of souls."

"W—what do you mean?" Prudy swiped at her eyes with the back
of her hand.

"The kind of healing I'm talking about is spiritual in nature."

A couple of the women shifted their position and looked elsewhere. Clearly they didn't wish to discuss this. Oh, but she must
forge ahead. Hadn't the Lord opened the door for this conversation?
Surely He had a plan.

"Please hear me out." Lottie glanced from woman to woman. "I
know the ladies at the church didn't make the best first impression,
but I hope you can put that behind you."

"They left a bitter taste in my mouth, to be sure." Prudy's shoulders slumped forward.

"We need to forgive them and move on, for only in doing so
will we all receive the kind of healing we seek." Fanny rose and took
Prudy by the hand. "I know it's going to be hard, but I want you to
come with me to the edge of the mountain and look down."

"I—I can't."

"We won't let anything happen to you," Fanny said.

"That's right." Lottie nodded and extended her hand. "We just
want you to see that you can let go of your fears. God can heal you
of that. And as He does, He will show you things you've never witnessed before. Are you willing to give it a try?"

Prudy hesitated then said, "I'll walk with you for a while and
decide when we get close. Is that fair?"

"More than fair."

Prudy took Lottie's hand and rose. Lottie led the way along the familiar path to the edge of the peak. How many times she'd made this journey as a teen. What joy she'd found in the beautiful view. Today, she offered up a silent prayer that Prudy would find that same joy, that same sense of release.

They reached the outskirts of the overlook in less than thirty minutes. As they got closer to the edge, Prudy held back. When Lottie encouraged her to move forward, she shook her head. "I'm sorry, Lottie, but I just can't."

"I won't make you, of course. But it makes me really sad, because the view is unlike anything you will ever see elsewhere. Truly."

"Do I have to get right up to the edge?" Prudy asked.

"No. There's a spot where we can stand, probably twenty yards or so from the edge. And trust me when I say that I'm not going right to the edge, either. Just close enough to get a good look at the view."

"Maybe I could come a few feet closer." Prudy slipped her arm through Lottie's and took a few tentative steps. "Not too close." She squeezed her eyes shut as they walked out onto the overlook.

"I promise we won't get off the trail," Lottie said. "Just to the point where you can see down. All right?"

Prudy nodded and kept walking. A few paces later, Lottie stopped. They were quite a ways from the edge, but even from here, the valley opened up in front of them in all of its beauty.

"Open your eyes, Prudy," she whispered.

Prudy shook her head.

"When you're ready, dear," Fanny said. "Trust me, you don't want to miss this."

Prudy opened one eye and then the other. She closed them right away and looked as if she might be sick. Her face turned ashen and she trembled so badly that Lottie wondered if she might faint dead away. Little good that would do. In that moment, goose bumps covered Lottie's arms. She felt the presence of the Lord as never before and, at His nudging, began to sing:

"I'm pressing on the upward way,
New heights I'm gaining ev'ry day,
Still praying as I'm onward bound,
'Lord, plant my feet on higher ground.'"

Prudy's eyes opened. "Oh, I love that song. Must've heard it as a child or something." She released a slow breath. Her eyes fluttered shut again. Lottie continued to sing.

"I want to scale the utmost height
And catch a gleam of glory bright;
But still I'll pray till heav'n I've found,
'Lord, lead me on to higher ground.'"

Fanny and Prudy added their voices to hers as she sang the chorus:

"Lord, lift me up and let me stand
By faith on heaven's tableland;
A higher plane than I have found,
'Lord, plant my feet on higher ground.'"

By the time they finished the chorus, Prudy's eyes were fully open. She gazed at the magnificent scene before them.

"Oh my goodness!"

"Told you." Lottie grinned. "It's quite a view, isn't it?"

"Yes! Oh my." Prudy slipped her arm out of Lottie's and put her hand over her mouth. "This is the most glorious thing I've ever seen." She pointed off to the west. "And look! Is that a rainbow?"

"I think so." Lottie squinted to get a better look. "Yes, that's a rainbow. We see those a lot in the mountains. Really adds sparkle and shine to the whole portrait, doesn't it?"

"Yes. Oh, yes."

Lottie sighed. "You know, I was once jealous of all of you. You've traveled all over this big wide country of ours, and I've never left Colorado."

"Aw, you sweet girl." Prudy gave her a hug.

Lottie gazed out over the majestic scene God had painted before her, overcome with emotion. "But ladies, I've been to the tops of mountain peaks and I've waded in rapid rivers. I've fished for trout in a lake so beautiful that it made you dizzy. I've seen sunsets so brilliant that they make the most beautiful painting pale by comparison. I've watched an eagle swoop so low that I thought he would pick me up and fly me off to the skies. I've seen rainbows over canyons and fields of wildflowers. I have rarely left Estes Park—certainly got no farther than Loveland—and yet I feel I've had enough adventures to last a lifetime."

"Well, my goodness." Tears sprang to Prudy's eyes. "Lottie, you should write all of that down and give it to Augie for the paper. Words like those would draw tourists in from all over."

Lottie smiled. "Maybe I will." She began to hum, and before

long the words to the hymn flowed from several of the ladies, their voices almost angelic against the backdrop of the mountains.

> *"Lord, lift me up and let me stand*
> *By faith on heaven's tableland;*
> *A higher plane than I have found,*
> *'Lord, plant my feet on higher ground.'"*

With tears streaming, Lottie felt—literally felt—the Lord bringing healing, not just to Prudy, but several of the others as well. And, in that moment, as heaven kissed earth, she truly understood what it meant to speak to the mountains.

* * * * *

GILBERT WAITED AT THE PICNIC SITE, wondering what in the world could be taking the women so long. Lottie had been so distant of late. Had she deliberately gone off away from him just to torment him? Being away from her proved to be exactly that—torment.

At one in the afternoon, the ladies came down off the mountain, singing a familiar hymn, one he'd loved since childhood.

Strange. They looked different from before. He'd never seen that many tear-filled eyes.

"What do we have here?" Gilbert rose from the quilt and took several hurried steps in their direction. "What happened up on that mountain?"

Prudy stopped singing and glanced his way. "Gilbert, we—we had church!" She erupted into tears but managed to smile through them.

"Had church?" He looked Lottie's way and she nodded.

The women began to sing once more, and before long he joined in, praising God for planting his feet—and their feet—on higher ground.

Gilbert couldn't be sure what had happened up on the mountain, but he had the strongest sense it would be the first step toward bringing the people of Estes Park together again.

TWENTY-ONE

LOVELESS IN LOVELAND
TIPS FOR COURTING

Fellas, if you plan to bring your gal to the melodrama, you might want to take a few tips in courting her proper-like, so that she arrives with a happy heart. When a cultured man courts a lady, he calls her sweet names and opens doors for her. He plays the part of a gentleman in every situation, public and private. Most of all, he lets her know—in any and every way possible—that he has feelings for her. No beating around the bush when you're in love, fellas. Just get right to it. Tell her how you feel, then let the chips fall where they may. Once she's accepted your gestures of love, she'll link her arm through yours and come with you to see the show. We're looking forward to seeing you there. —Your friends at Parker Lodge

The women arrived back at Parker Lodge late in the afternoon, just as Jeb arrived to start dinner. Lottie couldn't help but notice the expression on Fanny's face as she laid eyes on him. For a moment, the woman seemed to come alive. His face lit up too. Just as quickly, their smiles faded. They parted ways—Fanny going to her cabin and Jeb to the kitchen.

The other ladies left too, most heading to their various rooms.

"What are you going to do between now and suppertime, Lottie?" Grace asked. "Go back home for a couple of hours?"

"I still have some chores to tend to." She yawned. "Wish I had time for a nap."

Grace yawned as well. "Now see what you've got me doing?" She giggled. "I'm tired too. Why don't you come to my room and sleep for a few minutes before doing your chores? I'm sure Mrs. Parker won't mind. The pie parlor has been closed for hours, so she's not on double-duty or anything."

"True." Lottie looked at the CLOSED sign on the pie parlor door. "I'll rest for a while." She followed Grace and a few others to their cabin and climbed into an empty bed. But instead of sleeping, the ladies told funny stories and made Lottie laugh until her cheeks hurt.

A knock sounded at the door, and Fanny popped her head inside.

"What are you ladies up to in here? We can hear you laughing all the way in our cabin." She stepped inside with Flossie behind her. "What are we missing?"

"Come and join us." Lottie patted the edge of her bed. "We're telling stories."

"Good ones, it sounds like." Fanny quirked a brow. "You talking about the men or something?"

This got another laugh out of the women.

"No," Lottie said. "But I could, if you like. What would you like to know?" She felt her cheeks grow hot. "Not—not that I know a lot about men, of course."

This got another laugh.

"Tell us about Phineas and Jeb and the other fellas," Flossie said. "What were they like before we got here? What are their stories?"

"Ah." Lottie paused. "Well, all the men were different back then. Phineas used to be a little grumpy. Well, actually, a lot grumpy. And bossy too. I think it's because he had no one else to talk to. Guess that's what happens when you live alone on a cattle ranch. You get used to bossing the animals around."

"Speaking of cattle, what's the situation with Jeb and that cow of his?" Fanny asked. "I've never seen a man so heartbroken over losing an animal before. You would've thought he'd lost his pet dog or something."

Lottie sighed. "Loneliness, I suppose. I guess you ladies don't really know this, but there was a time—not so long ago, I might add—when Jeb threatened to jump off Longs Peak because the Widow Baker wouldn't give him the time of day."

"Althea Baker?" Fanny snorted and smacked the bed with her hand. "That's so funny. Why, they're total opposites."

"I told him that many a time," Lottie said. "But he wouldn't hear it. Back then, he only had eyes for Althea."

"And now?" A smile turned up the edges of Fanny's lips.

"Now he's quite happy he didn't jump off Longs Peak." Lottie reached to give Fanny a warm hug.

"I'm glad he didn't." Fanny giggled. "I've got to tell you, when he takes to playing 'Swanee River,' my heart just goes to pitter-pattering. Nothing touches me right here"—she pointed to her heart—"like that man's saw." A lingering sigh followed, along with the fluttering of eyelashes.

Lottie fought to hold back the laughter.

"Before you ladies came to town, the men were sour most of the time," she said. "They didn't have a lot to laugh about. Now they're behaving like total strangers. I'm telling you, I don't recognize them half the time, and it isn't just their clothes and hair. Their manners are different. Everything is different."

"A good woman will do that to a man," Grace said and then sighed. "Not that any of us women have spoken more than a word to the men in weeks." A pause followed. "Still, Chauncy's been awfully sweet to me, in spite of my coldness. I don't know how much longer I can go on being rough on him." She glanced around the room at the other women. "What about the rest of you?"

Fanny's gaze shifted to the window, and Flossie shrugged.

"Don't rightly know," Flossie said. "Guess everything has to work according to God's plan. I'm not going to fight it, but I'm not going to force things, either. We'll just rest easy and see what He's got up His sleeve."

A rap sounded on the door and Fanny hollered out, "C'mon in and join the party."

Margaret stepped inside, looking half-asleep but fully frazzled. This certainly got everyone's attention.

"Anyone seen Prudy?" Her words were strained.

"Prudy?" The women spoke in unison.

"I figured she'd be hidden away in her room till supper, reading a book or something," Lottie said. "Why?"

Margaret shook her head. "No. When we got back from the

mountains, she rushed to the room and changed into her prettiest dress. Even fixed up her hair. Said she had to go to town."

"Go to town?" Again, several of the ladies spoke in unison.

"Surely not." Lottie yawned. "Maybe she just went for a quiet walk to think through all that happened up on the mountain. She needs time to absorb it all."

"No. It's a quarter of six and she's missing. But there's more."

Lottie sat up straight. "More?"

"Yes. I don't know if you've been noticing the commotion outside, but the fellas are here—Phineas, Jeb, Chauncy, and Gilbert. They're cooking something up."

"In the kitchen?"

"No. In the dining hall. I saw them hanging a curtain and putting in some set pieces that I've never seen before. When I went in to ask them about it, they shooed me out of the room."

"Interesting," Fanny said. "Very interesting."

"Yes, well, before I left the room, I overheard Chauncy say something to Phineas about how worried he was that Augie hadn't shown up to help them. I don't know what those men are up to, but I think we're going to find out very soon."

Lottie's thoughts shifted as fear kicked in. "I sure hope Augie shows up for rehearsal. You don't think he's backing out, do you?"

"Hope not, but he has been acting a bit strange lately," Fanny said. "Has anyone else noticed it but me?"

"I have," Flossie said.

Lottie nodded. "Me too. Of course, he's announced his run for mayor, so that probably has something to do with it."

"Well, he's certainly been away from the lodge a lot," Flossie said. "Barely shows up in time for curtain call."

"Between running the paper and running for office, he's up to his eyeballs in work." Lottie shrugged. "Least, that's my guess. I hope he's not losing interest in the production. His part would be the most difficult to recast." She sighed. "Goodness, I do hope he's not jumping ship. We really need everyone—every single person. And now with Prudy missing...I don't know. Sounds like tonight's rehearsal is going to be rough, for sure."

"I say we get ourselves dressed and show up for supper early." Fanny sprang from the bed and ran for the door. "Meet me in the dining hall in fifteen minutes, ladies."

They all flew into action, each woman headed to her own room. Lottie and Grace remained in Cedar Lodge, along with a handful of others, who all helped Lottie make sense of her messy hair and wrinkled dress. Then, with curiosity mounting, she led the way to the dining hall, where they found Gil, Phineas, and Jeb working together on some sort of unfamiliar backdrop.

"Gil?"

He turned around, his face red. "Lottie. You ladies are early. We're not ready for you."

"What are you doing?"

"S–something."

"I can see that."

He took her by the hand. "Look, we've planned something special, but we're not quite ready. We've got a little supper show cooking up, but I'd be grateful if you didn't say so. Jeb made lasagna. Put it in the oven nearly an hour ago, so it's probably almost ready. Mama's gonna dish it out so that he can stay here with us for the..." His words drifted off. "Well, the surprise." Wrinkles appeared on his brow. "'Course, we're not sure how we're going to pull off this surprise without Augie. He's a key player."

He'd no sooner spoken the words then Augie rushed into the room. "Whew! I barely made it."

Gil wiped the sweat from his brow. "You scared us to death, Augie."

"Well, something came up at the office. Pretty big story brewing that required my attention. But I'm here now and that's all that matters."

"Yes, well..."

Behind her, Lottie heard several of the ladies talking at once. She turned to discover that Prudy had arrived at last. Rushing her way, she gave the young woman's hand a squeeze.

"You frightened us."

"I'm so sorry about that."

Lottie gazed at the beautiful dress Prudy wore. The perfectly upswept hair. The blush in her cheeks. Very odd.

Then again, everything about this day had been a bit odd, hadn't it? And yet, she'd never seen the Lord work so swiftly... or smoothly. Perhaps the time had come to just relax and let Him prove, once and for all, that He made a far better director than she ever could.

* * * * *

GILBERT RUSHED AROUND, finishing up the set pieces and costumes while his mother scooped helpings of lasagna onto the ladies' plates. Once they settled into their seats, he met with the fellas behind the makeshift curtain.

"Well, this is it," he said. "Everyone ready?"

Jeb stared at him, wide-eyed. "Ready as I'll ever be."

Phineas sighed. "Gilbert, are you absolutely sure this idea was God-inspired? I have to think it's a little on the crazy side."

"I'm tellin' you, fellas, the idea is inspired. Trust me."

"Hmm." Phineas did not appear to be convinced.

"How do I look?" Jeb pointed to his mismatched costume pieces and Gilbert laughed.

"Perfect. Fanny's going to find you hard to resist."

"Oh, I hope so."

Gilbert pulled off his hat—a crazy, colorful number Chauncy had found—and offered up a prayer for God's help and mercy. If they ever needed help from on high, it was now. Then, after giving the fellas a couple of last-minute instructions, he made his way to the front of the curtain to face their audience.

Stage fright gripped him…until he saw Lottie's face. Somehow just gazing into those gorgeous green eyes gave him courage to go on.

"What've we got here, Gilbert?" Fanny called out. "A parlor show?"

"Of sorts." He cleared his throat. "Ladies…" He looked at several of the local cast members who had arrived as well. "Friends, we've got a little something to share, something we've created for your entertainment and pleasure. We give you *Loveless in Loveland*. Curtain, please!"

The curtain opened—well, sort of, anyway—to reveal a cockeyed set and four fellas dressed in the wackiest costumes known to mankind. They'd pieced them together themselves, using scraps of fabric and pieces of other costumes from the real melodrama. Not that it mattered. The sole purpose here was to garner the attention of the ladies, nothing more.

And apparently, they succeeded. The women laughed and clapped, which only served to put smiles on the faces of his actors.

The men dove into gear, acting out the little script they'd all been working on for days. Hopefully the ladies would see the story inside the story—about a group of repentant men who were woefully sorry for the pain they'd caused the women they loved.

Gil smiled as his heart flooded with joy. The woman he loved looked on with wonder—and a bit of horror—in her eyes. Oh well. By the end of the show, she would know how the men felt. All the women would know. As for how they responded—whether or not they would join in the fun—well, that was up to them.

* * * * *

LOTTIE SAT GLUED to her chair, watching as the silly little skit played itself out. The fellas took on the roles of sinners, sorry for their misdeeds and overly dramatic in their apologies both to the Lord and the ladies. She got the message of the story. And from the whoops and hollers of the women around her, they got it as well. The fellas were trying to apologize for what they'd done. They acted out their shame and their apologies.

The show reached its climax when Gilbert, the evil villain, tied all four of the other fellas to the train tracks. There they remained, struggling against their ties, as Gil let out an evil laugh. Not a very believable evil laugh, but a good attempt on his part, anyway.

He stepped to the front of the stage and gazed at the audience. From backstage someone began to make train sounds—an unconvincing whistle followed by clacking noises. Mrs. Parker popped her head out from behind the curtain and Gil gestured for her to hide once again.

This got another chuckle out of the ladies.

"Folks, can you hear the train coming?" Gil's expression grew more animated as he spoke to the audience. "It's just around the bend and comin' fast. These fellas are sure to meet impending doom unless..." He gestured to the audience. "Unless some fair damsels come to the rescue.

"Who will rescue these poor, helpless men in distress from a sure and certain death—a death of the heart and soul?"

An awkward pause followed, accompanied by a couple of the ladies clearing their throats.

Finally someone stirred. "By gum, I will!" Fanny rose from her seat and raced to the stage, where she made quick work of untying Jeb. He swept her into his arms and gave her a kiss right there in front of the audience. A roar went up from the crowd and Lottie found herself laughing and crying all at the same time.

Mrs. Parker peeked out from behind the curtain once again, causing the train noises to stop. Gil gestured for her to continue, which she did.

"Can you hear it, folks? There's still a train coming around the bend, and three men remain tied to the tracks. Who will save them? Is there not a woman in the room with a compassionate heart?

"Ooh, my turn!" Grace shot out of her seat and raced to the

stage, all gracefulness put aside in the passion of the moment. She couldn't seem to get Chauncy's ropes untied, but he helped her, and the two ended up in each other's arms. Lottie watched, transfixed, her heart going almost as fast as that silly train clacking.

"And yet two remain." Gil's voice intensified. "Are there no fair damsels willing to risk their lives for the sake of the men they love?"

"Well, shoot. When you put it like that…" Flossie trudged onto the stage and made quick, steady work of untying Phineas, who planted a kiss on her that made every woman in the room—single or married—blush.

"And now only *one* remains…" Gilbert stressed the word *one*. Lottie watched Augie, wondering what would happen next. She had her suspicions, of course, but couldn't be sure.

Two women rose at once—Margaret Linden and Prudy Stillwater.

Prudy took a step in Margaret's direction, put up her hand, and said, "Oh no you don't, sister. He's mine!" Then she raced for the stage.

This, of course, got a spectacular cheer from all in attendance. Well, all but Margaret, who sank back into her chair with a wounded look on her face.

By now, all the folks in the room were on their feet, clapping and laughing. Lottie joined them, her heart so full she could hardly stand it.

Still, one fella on stage had not asked to be rescued.

She stared up at Gil, who glanced her way with a smile. Whether or not he wanted her to untie him from the proverbial tracks remained to be seen. But at least several of the other ladies would have their happily-ever-afters.

For now, that would have to be enough.

TWENTY-TWO

IN APPLE-PIE ORDER

We at Parker Lodge are in the final days of rehearsal for our melo-drama, which will open to the public this Friday night, just three short days away. Ticket sales have far surpassed our expectations, and we can hardly wait for our audience members to enjoy the antics of Sadie Word, Hugh Dunnit, and the rest of our cast. Much work has gone into the show, but there is still much to be done. Lights, costumes, set pieces—we're in a flurry here at Parker Lodge as opening night approaches. But never mind all that! Whenever we get stressed, we head to Parker's Pie Parlor for another slice of that amazing Sanders' Strawberry Pie, our featured pie of the week. It's a little piece of heaven on earth. Why not enjoy a slice while you watch the show with your sweetie? See you soon! —Your friends at Parker Lodge

THE WEEK LEADING UP TO the August first opening was pure chaos. Lottie's thoughts remained a jumbled mess as she fought to keep things straight. Sets. Costumes. Lines. Ticket sales. The hovering issue with the Women's League. Every time she needed to escape, she closed her eyes and pictured herself standing on the edge of the mountain, looking out over that breathtaking scenery. At once, she felt her nerves settle down.

As for the petition going around town, she had it on good authority—Augie's—that few businessmen had been willing to place their signatures on it. She took this as a very good sign. Another thing had her hopeful, as well—ticket sales. Folks had come in droves to purchase tickets for the melodrama.

Not everything was coming together, of course. Mama was still hopping mad over the pie issue, and all the more when she saw that the news had been spread across town on the latest Parker Lodge handbill. Not that Lottie had been home much. She'd spent most of her days at the lodge, working against the clock, to prepare for the show.

With just three days left, she found herself worried about something new. Something unexpected. She told Gil all about it at breakfast.

"I'm really worried about Hannah."

"Hannah?" He looked up from his scrambled eggs, concern in his eyes. "Why?"

"She's not well. I don't know if you noticed how frail she looked at last night's rehearsal. She's paler than usual and has an upset stomach. She's also complained of feeling a bit woozy."

"Nerves?" Gilbert asked

"Maybe. I'm not sure. I stopped by her room this morning and she asked if we could call Doc Jennings."

"Did you send for him?"

"I did. He should arrive anytime now. I just hope she's okay.

I'd hate to think of what might happen if she's truly ill. What if she's contagious? We could have an epidemic on our hands. With the show opening in just three days, we can't risk exposing the entire town to some sort of disease."

"Lottie." Gilbert chuckled. "I don't want to take your concerns lightly, but how did this go from Hannah not feeling well to the town succumbing to an epidemic?"

"I don't know. Just worried, I guess. She prepares pies, so I suppose it's possible that she's passed along whatever she's got to others in town." Lottie chewed the nail on her index finger but stopped when she realized Gil was watching her. "I'm already worked up because of my mother. Things at home are awful." Lottie sighed. "I had a long talk with Pa recently, and he, well…I guess you already know."

"I do?"

"Well, yes. And so do I, of course. He's the one who's funded the show. I knew it the moment you said a local investor had offered to help."

The relief on Gil's face was evident. "He's been such a blessing, Lottie. You have no idea."

"He's always been far too good to me."

"And now to me." Gilbert sighed. "He even took care of the line of credit at the general store."

"That's my father for you." Lottie smiled. "He said he'll smooth things over with Mama, but I don't know. I just feel like I'm walking on pins and needles. Probably nerves. There's so much to do."

Gil put his hand on her arm. "Lottie, take a deep breath. We've come this far. We're going to be fine."

She'd just started to respond when Doc Jennings arrived with medical bag in hand.

"Where's our patient?" he asked, a worried look in his eyes.

"She's in the Chalet Suite," Lottie said. "I'll walk you there."

"Has she been out in the heat? Eaten anything unusual? Running a fever?"

"Well, we've all been out in the heat—going from the cabins to the dining hall, that sort of thing. But nothing out of the ordinary."

"Hmm. I've seen quite a few others on the outskirts of town who have influenza. Sure hope that's not it."

"Does it present with stomach pain and shakiness?"

"Sometimes." He pursed his lips. "But let's not worry unnecessarily, Lottie. Could be she's just exhausted. Those symptoms you're describing would fit. Has she been working harder than usual?"

"Has she ever. Have you tasted the pies she's been baking?"

Doc Jennings rubbed his extended belly. "You have no idea. I've been by several times over the past month to purchase pies. Loved the chocolate one, but I've got to say, the persimmon pie is my favorite."

"That's Hannah's favorite too."

"Yes, I know. We spoke at length about it when I came on Monday. Strange that she's taken ill so suddenly. She seemed fine then." A concerned expression passed over him. "But with your big theatrical coming up it's more important than ever to make sure she's not contagious."

"That's what I told Gil. Don't want to start an epidemic."

"You're wise to be cautious, Lottie. Many people don't pay attention to the potential spread of germs. I'm glad you're aware of the possibilities." His brow wrinkled. "At any rate, it's a good thing you called."

They stopped in front of the Chalet Suite and Lottie knocked on the door. She heard a faint "Come in" and turned the knob.

They found Hannah in bed, fragile and pale. Doc Jennings headed to her side at once, the concern on his face palpable. "Tell me what's going on, Hannah." He reached for his stethoscope. "What are your symptoms?"

She released a slow breath. "Well, after staying up really late to rehearse last night, I got out of bed early and made my way to the kitchen to start baking, as always. Only, this morning I felt light-headed and strange. My head is swimming and I'm a little shaky."

"I see." He pressed the stethoscope against her back. "Go on."

"Well, I've been so thirsty. Nothing quenches my thirst, really. And my vision is a little blurry." She looked panicked as she shared this information. "That's not normal, is it?"

"Coupled with some of your other symptoms, perhaps. Tell me, have you noticed any weight loss?"

"My dresses are a bit loose." She blushed as he moved the stethoscope to her upper chest. "I just attributed it to working. I haven't had time to eat much."

"Take a deep breath, Hannah."

After listening for a moment, Doc Jennings put his stethoscope back in his bag and continued his exam, focusing on her ears, nose, and throat. "Let me ask you a question," he said when he finished. "You told me that you haven't eaten much."

"Well, not much real food, anyway." She giggled. "You know

that I've been working in the pie parlor." Her cheeks turned pink. "Well, of course you know. You've purchased three pies from me over the past couple of weeks."

"Um, yes." He cleared his throat.

Lottie couldn't help but laugh.

"Let me ask you this, Hannah," Doc said. "Have you been sampling the pies?"

"Sampling them? I've eaten little else but!" She laughed. "Someone has to taste them to make sure they're good. Why, just yesterday I had a slice of our new banana twist pie and the persimmon as well. Before that, it was the cinnamon streusel and the coconut cream. The day before that—"

Doc Jennings put his hand up. "Say no more. I believe we've found our answer."

"We have?" Her eyes widened. "You can tell me. I won't be afraid. Am I going to…I mean, is it fatal?"

He chuckled. "Hardly. In fact, I daresay with a few days of regular food and no sugar, you'll bounce right back. I'm guessing your blood sugar is high, Hannah. Far too high, which would explain your odd symptoms."

She sat up. "I'm not dying?"

"No." He reached to grip her hand and gave her a look so tender that even Lottie felt the emotion behind it. "I'm not sure what I would do if that were the case. So, please do as I say and eat a solid meal. Refrain from sugar." He turned to Lottie. "Can you arrange for some sort of meat and vegetables to be brought here to Hannah? No potatoes or other starches and no breads. Just proteins and green vegetables, please."

"Of course. Jeb is cooking brisket, and I have it on good authority he's got a big pot of green beans cooking too."

"Perfect. I'm going to suggest some vitamin tablets. We'll have someone from the pharmacy bring them out. And drink plenty of water. You need to wash that sugar out of your system."

"Can I...can I still be in the show?" Hannah's voice trembled.

"If you're feeling up to it, of course. Just promise you'll eat the right foods between now and then."

"I promise." She held up her hand as if taking an oath.

Lottie wanted to stay for a lengthy visit with Hannah but work beckoned. She headed back to the dining hall, relieved that one disaster had been averted.

She met Fanny and Flossie along the way.

"How's our patient?" Flossie asked.

"She's going to be fine." Lottie explained the situation, and before long the twins were all smiles.

"Well, that's a relief." Fanny shook her head. "I wasn't sure how we would manage without her."

Lottie followed Fanny to the dining hall. "Fanny, I keep forgetting to mention it, but you look like, well, like you're..." She hesitated to say the words.

"Losing weight?" Fanny smiled. "Guess I must be. My dresses are all getting bigger. Thank goodness my sewing skills are intact." She ran her hands over her stomach. "I must admit, it feels good. Life in the mountains has truly benefited my health."

"Well, you're just a shadow of your former self."

"I've been so busy I hardly think about food anymore." She gave them a little wink. "Guess I've had other things on my mind."

"I daresay you have. How's that going, anyway?"

"Oh, you know." Fanny's cheeks turned pink. She'd just opened her mouth to say more when Grace rushed into the room.

"You're not going to believe it! You're just not!"

"Believe what?" Lottie and the ladies gathered around her.

"It's Prudy."

"Oh no!" Lottie sank into a chair. "Tell me she's not ill too."

"No, she's not ill." Grace giggled and tossed a package onto the table. "She's—she's…married!"

"Married?" All the women spoke in unison.

At once the cacophony of voices overtook the room. Lottie did her best to make sense of this. "How? When?"

"I'm not sure, but I'm guessing they got hitched that day we were on the mountain. I—I guess she really did find her courage. She went straight to town that afternoon, dressed in her finest, and married Augie Miller."

"I don't believe it." Lottie shook her head, dumbfounded. "So the night the fellas did their funny little melodrama…"

"She was already married to Augie. That's why she almost tore Margaret's eyes out for wanting to untie him from the tracks."

A giggle rose up inside Lottie. "I don't believe it. I truly don't. I mean, I do…but I don't." A full-fledged laugh now caught her by surprise. "Oh, will wonders never cease! Where are they now?"

"Well, this is how I found out. I went into town to buy fabric for that last dress you asked me to make." She gestured to the package on the table. "While I was there, I overheard someone on the other side of the shelves giggling and talking about buying fabric for curtains for her new home. I felt sure I recognized the voice. Only when

I walked around behind the shelves did I realize it was Prudy." Grace's face turned red. "Oh, you should've seen the kiss he gave her. It was scandalous!" Another laugh followed.

"Not exactly scandalous if they're married," Lottie said.

"Right, but here's the funniest part of all. Several ladies from the Women's League were in the store at the time and they saw it too. Oh, were they ever riled up. That one woman—Althea?—well, she took off in a hurry."

"Oh dear." Lottie rested her head on the table. "Oh dear, oh dear."

"Did Prudy see all of this?" Fanny asked.

"Heavens, no. She was so busy kissing Augie that she didn't see any of us. Oh, it was the sweetest thing ever!" A fit of giggles began again.

Lottie glanced up, her concerns lifting. What difference did it make what Althea Baker thought, if Prudy and Augie were man and wife? Why, everyone should be celebrating right now, not worrying.

"I still can't get over it," Grace said. "Augie's running for mayor. If he wins the election, Prudy is going to be the first lady of Estes Park."

"Who would've dreamed it?" Lottie rose and paced the room. "A girl so afraid of her own shadow. Now, if things go as planned—and I'm sure they will, since God has a sense of humor—she'll be married to the mayor of the town. Can you imagine how much fun that's going to be?"

Fanny cleared her throat. "Well, folks, since this seems to be a day of confessions, I'd better get something out in the open too."

* * * * *

GILBERT APPROACHED the ladies just in time to hear Fanny say, "Would you like to know how Jeb proposed?"

He almost lost his breath. *Jeb? Engaged?*

Gilbert listened in as Fanny continued, her eyes now twinkling. "He wrote me a song."

"A song?" Gilbert could hardly believe it. "I didn't realize he was a songwriter."

The women turned to look his way, likely astounded that he'd interrupted their little meeting without notice.

"Well, it wasn't the kind of song you sing, exactly," Fanny said. "He played it on his saw. And since I've told you all this, I might as well come out and tell you something else too."

The women all leaned forward in rapt silence. Gilbert joined them, equally as curious.

"I bought Katie Sue and returned her to her rightful owner."

A gasp went up and then the ladies cheered.

"Best news I've heard all day," Gilbert said. He reached to give Fanny a warm hug then stepped back so that the women could celebrate with her. Gilbert's gaze shifted to Lottie. All this talk of weddings had him stirred up. Yes, it did. Now, if he could just figure out a way to share his heart, he might snag a wedding belle too.

* * * * *

THE REHEARSAL WENT BETTER than anyone expected. Afterward, Gilbert walked Lottie home. She practically floated through the front door of the house, blissfully happy. Everything appeared to be coming together. Well, almost everything.

She found her mother in the front parlor, dressed for bed, her eyes filled with tears. Mama gestured to the sofa, speaking with a strained voice. "Lottie, please have a seat."

"A seat?" Oh no. After such a perfect day, would Mama ruin it by lecturing? Would she forbid Lottie from participating in the show?

She reluctantly took a seat. "W–what is it, Mama? Tell me."

"I met with the attorney today."

Lottie's heart hit her toes. "O–oh?"

"Yes. And there's something I must tell you, though it pains me to do so."

Lottie felt absolutely ill. Would her mother's next words put an end to the show they'd worked so hard to put together?

Tears ran down her mother's cheeks as she whispered, "I never wanted you to know this."

"Know what?"

She reached for Lottie's hand and gave it a squeeze. "Promise you won't hold this against me?"

A shiver ran down Lottie's spine. "Of course not, Mama. Just tell me."

Her mother rose and paced the room. "You never met your grandmother...my mother."

"No. I knew she lived in Loveland and ran a boardinghouse."

"Boardinghouse. Hmm." Mama wrung her hands and continued to pace. When she finally stopped, she faced Lottie. "Perhaps you've wondered why I've been so intent on stopping these women at the lodge."

"I've never understood your passion or the way you've gone about it."

"My passion comes from my own experience, Lottie." Mama dropped onto the sofa next to her and took her hand again. "I—I never wanted you girls to know this, but I was raised in a place much like the one those Parkers are now running."

"What are you talking about, Mama? You were raised in a pretty little white house in Loveland. You showed it to me once."

"No. I wanted you to think so, but it's not true. I was raised among women who..." She shook her head. "Anyway, I left when I was fifteen and got a job working for a wonderful family. They took me in. And then, of course, I met your father." Her expression brightened. "That man turned my whole world around."

"Mama, does he...I mean, does he know?"

"He's always known." Her mother's expression shifted. "And now, I'm afraid everyone is going to know. It's really my own fault. That attorney..."

"What about him?"

"When he saw that my pie was being featured at the pie parlor, he started asking around about me. I don't know how he did it, but he discovered my secret. I guess I shouldn't be surprised. He is from Loveland, after all, and that's where..." She paused. "Anyway, he's unwilling to take our case. He says it's for my own good. Says he's afraid Augie will get hold of it and splash it across the front page of the *Mountaineer*."

"Augie would never do that, Mama, but I do understand Thad's concerns."

And will thank him later for sparing you the grief.

"After the ruckus I've made?" Her mother squeezed her eyes shut and released a slow breath. When her eyes opened, she gazed intently at Lottie. "So I've asked him to stop the petition."

"Stop the petition?" Lottie gasped. "And there's not going to be a lawsuit?"

"No. It's over, Lottie. I can't protect you from those women, but I can protect myself from the shame it would cause our family if my story went public."

"Mama, listen to me." Lottie gripped her hand and gazed into her eyes. "Once and for all, please listen. Those women are not what you've accused them of being. In fact, several of them are about to be married ladies."

"Married ladies?" Mama used her hankie to dab her eyes.

"Yes. So dry your eyes. I have a lot to tell you, and this is a story you'll want to hear. I promise, by the time it ends, you'll be cheering for the very people you once accused. Won't you give them a chance, Mama? Please?"

When her passionate plea ended, Lottie's hands shook so much that she could barely keep them still. And though Lottie could scarcely believe it, her mother responded with a nod.

Whispering up a prayer, Lottie began to share the real story of the wedding belles.

TWENTY-THREE

ALL'S FAIR IN LOVE AND WAR

Come one, come all, to Parker Lodge Theatrical Society's first-ever melodrama, which opens tonight! We've settled on a name for the show: All's Fair in Love and War, *suggested by local resident Althea Baker. Enjoy the camaraderie of your friends and neighbors as you eat a tasty meal by master chef Jeb Otis and nibble on slices of pie named after the various characters in the show. My favorite is the Justin Credible Pecan Pie. It's just incredible! Those who were fortunate enough to get tickets for tonight's show will sit alongside veteran theater critic Gerald Jefferson. Together, they will witness the talents of locals and new residents as they take to the stage to give the performance of their lives. You're sure to be thrilled with their abilities. A special thank-you to the Women's League for purchasing more than a dozen pies. Proceeds will benefit Parker Lodge and the surrounding areas. See you tonight at the show, folks. Until then...break a leg! —Your friends at Parker Lodge*

ON THE AFTERNOON of the opening show, Lottie buzzed around the dining hall in happy anticipation, putting the finishing touches on costumes, props, and set pieces. She could hardly believe how seamlessly things had come together. If she had any doubt in her mind, this morning's visit from Mama and Althea Baker laid all her concerns to rest. And how funny, in the midst of their conversation, that Althea had inadvertently given them the title for the show. Yes, all was fair in love and war, but living in peace was so much better, especially with the Lord at the center of it all.

As she rounded the corner into the hallway, Lottie bumped into someone familiar. Actually, a couple of someones—who happened to be kissing.

"Winifred?"

Lottie looked on as her older sister stood with her arms around Thad Baker's neck.

"Oops." Winifred giggled and took a step back. "Guess the cat's been caught with the cream." She gazed with intensity into Thad's eyes. "Oh, but what cream!"

He pulled Winnie close and planted a kiss on her forehead. "Why would I mind if anyone sees us kissing? I think we've already established that folks around here are accustomed to dealing with rumors." He waggled his brows. "So let's start one. Let's tell everyone we're getting married."

"Getting married?" Lottie laughed. "Now, that would be quite the story, wouldn't it? I can almost see the expressions on faces now."

"We are, Lottie." Winnie held out her left hand and revealed a lovely opal ring.

"Wait…" Lottie shook her head. "You two are getting hitched?"

"Yes, we're getting married. I've known for a couple of days but didn't tell anyone because I didn't want to disrupt the show. That's the most important thing right now."

"More important than my sister's happiness?" Lottie practically flung herself into her sister's arms. "Nonsense! You're more important than some silly melodrama, Winnie. Heaven help me if any production ever becomes more important than the people in it. If—or when—that happens, I pray someone will slap me upside my head."

"Silly Lottie-Lou. No one can ever accuse you of paying more attention to the play than the people in it. I think you made it clear that you love your cast and crew. And they love you too."

"Speaking of love…" Thad swept Winnie into his arms and gave her another kiss. Lottie took this as her cue to move on, though she could hardly believe what she'd just seen. Would wonders never cease?

She reached the pie parlor just in time to see Doc Jennings working behind the counter alongside Hannah. Lottie offered him a smile, which he returned.

"Just keeping an eye on our patient, Lottie. That's all."

Sure it is.

She looked at Hannah, who gave her a wink. "So, what's going on in here?"

"Oh, just selling pies, as always," Hannah replied. "We've done a lot of business today, but we're saving as much as we can for the show. That's why I asked William to help, because I'll be so busy on stage."

"William?"

Hannah gestured at Doc Jennings, who had ventured over to speak to Mrs. Parker on the far side of the room. "William Jennings, the doctor. You know." Hannah almost lost her grip on the blackberry cobbler in her hand. She set it on the counter and looked at Lottie. "It might sound silly, but I'm ready for things to change."

"How so?"

"My life has always been the same—day in and day out. That's not to say I don't love the theater. It's just that I'm looking for more."

"More what?"

Hannah smiled. "Not sure. Just…more. And when I'm with William, I feel more alive than I ever have."

"Well, of course you do. He's a doctor. It's those vitamins he's been giving you, along with that new high-protein diet."

Hannah giggled. "You're so funny, Lottie. But that's not it at all, though the vitamins have improved my stamina. I feel more alive when I'm with him because—because…" She giggled. "Oh, you might as well know it. I love the man."

"W–what?" Lottie could hardly believe it. Of all people for Hannah to fall in love with. Doc Jennings. Why, she couldn't have arranged this any better if she'd tried all day.

She'd just started to ask for more details when customers swarmed the pie parlor. Hannah turned her attention to waiting on them. Oh well. Lottie still had a lot to do. Better get to the kitchen to check on Jeb.

She found him there, as always, but appearing a little distracted, with Fanny in his arms. Better move on. There were a few questions she needed to ask Grace about the choreography. Lottie found her on stage, behind the closed curtain, going over dance steps with Chauncy, who—for the first time—looked perfectly natural in taking the lead. Lottie decided not to disturb them. Might be better to visit with Flossie about those last-minute changes they'd made to the script.

She couldn't seem to find her in the dining hall, so she checked backstage. Heavens to Betsy. Flossie and Phineas were located in Gil's office, amid the costumes…kissing. And giggling. And basically acting like a couple of kids.

Must be something in the water.

Something in the water. "Hmm."

She smiled as she thought about the many, many times she'd waded through the shallow rapids of Fall River, letting God minister to her heart. Oh, what blissful confidence she'd found in that place. Yes, there was certainly something in the water at Parker Lodge, and it appeared to be contagious.

* * * * *

GILBERT BARELY HAD TIME to take a few bites of his dinner before getting into costume. Even after weeks of preparation, he still felt unsure about his role as Justin Credible but would give it his best shot.

Really, the only performance on his mind was the one he'd been rehearsing for all day. He could hardly wait for *that* show to begin. With the tables now cleared and dining hall doors about to open to the public any moment now, he'd better get to it.

"Folks, I know we're in a hurry, but I need a couple of minutes of your time."

The cast grew silent. He glanced over at Lottie—beautiful, ladylike Lottie, all dolled up in the prettiest pink dress he'd ever seen. It really accentuated that lovely upswept hair. He would have to remember to tell her later that she looked prettier than any of the others in the room. Right now, though, he had something else to tell her.

Or, rather, to ask her.

He cleared his throat and called out her name. She looked at him, her brow wrinkling. "Gil, the show's about to begin."

"Yes. It is." He smiled. "So, c'mon up here before I forget my lines."

"Forget your lines?" She joined him on the stage. "What are you doing?" she whispered.

"Lottie, I have a little something I'd like to share, right here in front of our friends and neighbors."

"You haven't changed your mind about being in the show, have you? Because if you have—"

"No. I'm committed. Fully and totally committed to being Justin Credible."

This got a laugh out of the cast.

"And I'm committed to something else too." He dropped down on one knee, ready to speak the most important line of his life. Fumbling around in his pocket, he came out with a ring, one that had belonged to his grandmother.

"Oh, Gil!" Lottie clasped a hand over her mouth and several of the ladies began to cheer.

From outside the door, he heard the voices of the patrons eager to be let inside. Well, they would just have to wait. Nothing would steal this moment from him, not even a room full of paying customers.

"Lottie-Lou Sanders, I'm going to pose this question using a line from the show. As Justin Credible would say, 'I'm hankerin' fer a honeymoon.'"

A ripple of laughter went up from the crowd, and Lottie's cheeks turned as pink as her dress. "Gil, I'm not sure what you're—"

"I'm trying to propose," he said. "But I'm making a disaster of it. Wish I knew someone who was good at stringing words together."

"I'll help." Flossie stood up. "What sort of scene were you imagining, Gilbert? Deep and romantic or lighthearted and fun?"

"Guess it's a little too late to speculate about that," he said, shifting to the other knee. "Though, under the circumstances, I'd say something brief would be good. Something that cuts right to the chase. Our audience is waiting outside, you know."

"Hmm, that might be problematic." Flossie shrugged. "I only write lengthier scenes."

"I'm a newspaper writer." Augie stepped up to the edge of the stage. "I'm good with short pieces. What would you like to tell her, Gil?"

"If I knew that, I wouldn't need your help."

"Good point. Give me a minute. Maybe something will come to me."

Hannah approached with a smile. "I'm pretty good with words, Gilbert," she said. "And I'm a woman. I can tell you what I think Lottie would like to hear."

Gil nodded in their direction. "True, but I think I'd better do this one on my own." He gazed up at Lottie—his precious, beloved Lottie—and smiled. "Where was I?"

"I'm pretty sure you were proposing." She went into a fit of giggles, which gave him the courage he needed to forge ahead.

"Will you marry me, Lottie?" he said. "Will you marry me and make Parker Lodge your home? Will you bake pies alongside my mama and direct plays and raise our babies and walk in the river with me?"

"Gracious. In that order?" Lottie chuckled.

"I'll take it in any order I can get it, as long as you're beside me."

"Then the answer is yes."

He slipped the ring on her finger then rose and wrapped her in his arms, completely overcome. Their lips met for a kiss that would make the ladies blush, but he didn't care. After waiting for so long, Lottie deserved to know his feelings once and for all. And he would go on showing her...for the rest of his life.

* * * * *

For a moment, Lottie felt as if she'd somehow drifted off into a lovely scene from a play. Had Gilbert just proposed? And in front of all of their friends? And that kiss! Ooh-la-la! What a doozy! She glanced down at her left hand and took in the beautiful ring he'd slipped on her finger, and the tears started.

"There's no crying in theater, kid," Flossie hollered out.

"Only the tears caused by evil critics," Fanny added.

"Oh! The critic." Lottie started to attention. "Does anyone know what time it is?"

"Six forty-eight," Gilbert said.

"The doors were supposed to open at six forty-five." She clapped her hands together and hollered out her instructions to the group. "Backstage, everyone! I'm about to open the doors to our audience."

As everyone scrambled, she paused just long enough to give Gilbert another kiss. Well, maybe two. Or three. What did it matter, in the grand scheme of things, if the audience members sat down at six forty-eight or six forty-nine?

Or six fifty.

She finally opened the doors, a rush of emotion kicking in as she saw the crowd. The ladies were dressed to the nines, just as Augie had predicted. And, oh! She'd never seen such hats! What fun!

With the doors open, she returned to the area backstage to wait until time for the show to begin. In her mind, she rehearsed the order of events. Mrs. Parker and a couple of the local ladies would go from table to table, taking orders for food and pie. Jeb would play an opening number on his saw. She would greet the audience and fill them in on the story. And then…well, then the play would begin.

From backstage, she peeked out at the dining hall, stunned to see the chairs filling so rapidly. One unfamiliar fellow took a seat up front and straightened his coat tails with dramatic flair.

Cornelia joined Lottie and peeked out at the room. "Ooh, that must be the critic. He's sitting front and center. That's where they always sit."

"I figured as much."

"Are you worried about him?" Cornelia asked.

"No, not at all. The way I see it, we've already faced our critics head-on and won. So what can he say about us?"

"Still…" Cornelia's lips curled up in a smile. "He's nice-looking, for an older fellow. Oh! Lottie, look!" She pointed as Althea Baker landed in the seat next to the critic, with Thad and Winnie on her other side and a young man, about Cornelia's age, next to Thad. "Who is that, do you suppose?"

"I think it must be Thad's younger brother. Winnie told me he was coming, but I'd forgotten."

"What's his name?" Cornelia's lips curled up in a delightful smile.

Lottie shrugged. "Daniel, if memory serves me correctly."

"Daniel." Cornelia giggled then clasped a hand over her mouth. "Oh, sorry. It's just that he's awfully handsome. Is he…"

"Married? No. Very single and quite the businessman, from what I've been told." Lottie turned to gaze at her friend. "Why?"

"Oh, no reason." She blushed. "Just wondering."

Lottie turned her attention back to the audience and tried to get a better look at Mr. Jefferson. Unfortunately, he had turned toward Althea, who must've said something that put a smile on his face. Then he reached down to pick up her program, which had fluttered to the floor.

"Guess I'll never get a good look at him," Lottie said. "Not sure what to make of the way he's acting around Althea."

"I'll tell you what I make of it," Sharla said from behind them. "She's flirting with him."

"Flirting?" The women spoke at once.

"Sure." Sharla chuckled. "I could teach lessons in flirting, but that woman doesn't need any. She dropped her program on purpose so he would pick it up for her. And look at how she's patting her hair. Women only do that when they're flirting."

"O–oh?" Cornelia stopped fidgeting with her hair and shrugged. "I had no idea."

"Ironic, isn't it?" Gilbert slipped his arms around Lottie's waist and drew her close.

"What's that?" She nestled into his embrace, completely content.

"Althea might just make use of that honeymoon suite yet."

Lottie gasped. "Oh, Gil, I'd forgotten. She won the contest."

"Yep. We chose her title for the show." His brows wiggled playfully. "Maybe the Lord knew what He was doing all along."

"Doesn't He always?" Lottie giggled.

Before they could say anything else, Jeb took the stage and began to play his saw. "That's our cue." Lottie grinned. "Everyone ready?"

Her cast gathered around her and she gave them a little pep talk. Oh, if only she had time to tell them all what they meant to her—how she'd grown to love each and every one. Instead, she offered up a quiet prayer for the Lord's favor over their performance.

Afterward, Gil slipped next to her and gave her a confident smile. "The drama's about to begin!"

"*About* to begin?" She chuckled and then glanced back at her cast and crew. "If this is just the beginning, then how would you explain all the drama we've been through over the past couple of months?"

"Oh, that..." Gil swept her into his arms and planted kisses in her hair. "That was just the rehearsal. Trust me when I say the best is yet to come." His words were whispered in her ear, causing a delightful shiver to rush over her.

Yes, indeed. The best was yet to come. And no villain, no foe, could steal it from her this time around. With Gil's hand in hers, they could face any drama that life might send their way...on stage or off.

For years I've been enamored with Estes Park. There's just something about the snowcapped mountain peaks, the shimmering waters of Lake Estes, the winding drive up that curvy, narrow highway to get into town, the quaint Alpine-like feel of the shops, and, of course, the majestic Stanley Hotel. I love it all! When presented with the opportunity to write *Wedding Belles*, I knew I had to set the story in scenic Estes Park, for only in that familiar place could I capture both the rugged feel of the West and the necessary whimsy for this lighthearted tale.

K